*Dedicated to Gina,
the better half of
my eternal soul.*

Published by
Dreamers Unlimited Publishing
PO BOX 71036
Rochester Hills, MI 48307

Printed by
CreateSpace
1200 12th Avenue South
Suite 1200
Seattle, WA 98144

ISBN:
978-0-9796137-2-2

Printed in the United States of America

OPHAN

PRINCE
OF
THRONES

Story and cover art by
Edward L. Paciorek

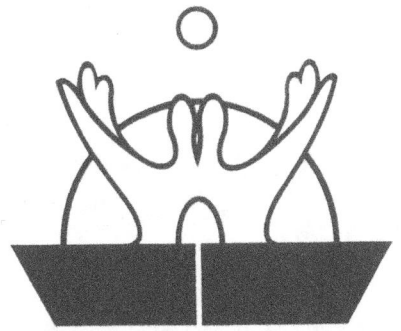

**Dreamers Unlimited
Publishing**

Table of Contents

1974

1975

Ophan, Prince of Thrones
Edward L. Paciorek

1974

CHAPTER ONE
Supernatural Chew Toy

I awoke with a start from a perfectly dreamless state, gasping frantically for air and feeling like some unseen force was trying its best to choke the very life out of my body. I twisted in my bed and tried to get a grip upon whatever was at my throat, but there was nothing there.

Desperate to take a breath, I grabbed my own neck, and I experienced the chilling sensation of feeling like I was touching flesh that wasn't my own. My neck was familiar to me, but somehow between my fingers and my own skin, there was a slick and chilly, rubbery plastic sort of sensation, almost too subtle to discern. As a young child, I had played with a neighbor's Thingmaker set, where one would squeeze a thick liquid goop into molds, and cook it into shapes like worms and bugs and little dragon parts. That dead, cold, slick, and creepy feeling crossed my mind again as I struggled for air, releasing a dozen fragments of prayers to Jehovah and Jesus in my panic. I managed to sit upright, and then, after what seemed like many minutes, but was probably only a few cosmically long seconds, the choking sensation stopped for some unknown reason.

I blinked several times and tried to adjust my eyesight to the dark. I looked over at my alarm clock, which was on my old wooden chest of drawers, just to the right of my small bunk bed, and I saw the large numbers glowing red in the darkness.

3:33.

I watched the clock change immediately to 3:34.

Again, I had been accosted by something unseen in the middle of the night. I wasn't completely clear about the spiritual significance of the hour between 3 a.m. and 4 a.m., but I did know that if something supernatural and nasty was going to pay me a visit, then it would probably be around this time.

Whatever it was, it was gone, although certainly not forgotten. There was a lingering smell in my nose, like I had been reckless enough to dive headfirst into an open septic sewer. The stench was overpowering, but thankfully, since it wasn't physical in nature, the smell was dissipating quite quickly. If I hadn't been cold sober, startled-to-alertness-because-I-feared-for- my-life awake, I might've thought that I had just struggled out of a bad dream.

Whatever it was, it was gone, but probably not for good. Whatever or whomever this entity was would be back. Of that I was certain and I had no idea how I could train myself not to sleep from three a.m. to four a.m. each night in order to avoid being attacked again, not that it would probably matter.

Whatever this thing was, it hated me for some reason, and it liked to attack me in a totally unpredictable manner, like I was its favorite chew toy that it had forgotten about for a time.

The basement was silent, except for the nervous shuffling of our German shepherd, Vicky, who slept at the foot of the basement steps. I heard a brief, deeply-throated growl, as if something or someone unpleasant had come to her notice, and then it stopped. Perhaps she had sensed that our house had been violated, once again, by something that wasn't welcome.

The only light in my tiny 6' by 11' bedroom under the stairs came from my alarm clock, and from a small window above the foot of my bed. The night sky was a deep indigo blue, and I could just barely make out the shadow of the large tree in the back yard dancing in the pale moonlight. My room was small, but that didn't matter, because I didn't have much by the way of belongings. My closet was under the stairs, and my stepfather, Nathan, had built three drawers into the wall under the stairs right next to it. I had a chest of drawers by the bed, and an old bookcase under the window with a very small 13" TV on top of it.

This was my personal world.

It was always a bit chilly and clammy in the basement. There was an old, rusty dehumidifier at the other end of the basement on the other side of the central wall, and it would occasionally rattle itself to life and try to drain some of the dank from the atmosphere, but it was always fighting a losing battle, and if I forgot to empty the water reservoir, it just stopped working altogether.

I reached down next to my bed and picked up my Bible. I always read several chapters before going to bed each night. I had read the Old Testament six times and the New Testament seven times. There was nowhere in the Bible, that I could recall, where it gave instructions on what to do if visited by something evil in the middle of the night.

When in doubt, pray, was all I could think of at that moment.

I placed the Bible in the bookcase that served as part of the headboard of my bed, and I tried to settle back down to sleep, Bible at the ready, to quote if I could, or to swat with, as needed.

If I really strained to listen, I could just barely hear my stepfather snoring in the upstairs bedroom, at the opposite end of the house. Many people would probably find sleeping in a cold, dark, heatless basement creepy, and it was, but compared to what happened quite often upstairs on a Friday or Saturday night, creepy was a healthier choice. Although I obviously didn't understand the forces at work in the basement that tormented me from time to time, I did understand the major forces at work above me, on the main floor of the house. Simply put, my domineering and belittling mother made it a hobby of hers to put my 6'1" carpenter stepfather in his place whenever possible, or convenient, or when she was in the mood, or when she was awake. Physically, he bore a striking resemblance to Dean Martin, albeit a six month pregnant Dean Martin. Having a rather limited vocabulary, except for catchy phrases like "Your a—sucks wind," he would take her needling until payday or the weekend arrived, whichever came first. Then, after hours of imbibing liquid courage at one of the local bars, he would come home and level the emotional playing field by threatening to level her face, which, so far, he hadn't done. She would spend the next day being absolutely silent until his hangover was gone, and then she'd slowly pick at him until she was back up to full needling speed by the end of the workweek. During her silent I'm-showing-my-displeasure-with-you time, she'd elect to sleep in the living room on the couch.

It was a quiet weeknight, and so the two of them were enjoying a temporary emotional ceasefire and sleeping in the same bed.

Residing in the other two, regular-sized bedrooms upstairs were my younger brother, Steven, who was two years my junior, and my half-sister, Danielle, who was four years younger. Steven resembled a barely house-broken spider monkey in appearance and actions. To say that my brother and I didn't get along would be an understatement, which was supposedly why I was relocated to under the basement stairs when I was about eight years old. I was told that the difficult, destructive, unpredictable child had to remain where he could be watched, and so my generally good behavior was rewarded by being sent down to live in the dark and dank bowels of the house.

My sister was a bit younger than Steven and I, and she seemed to spend most of her energies finding excuses to be away from the home, which I could understand, or crawling out of screened-in windows in the middle of the night, which I couldn't understand. Whether she was upstairs at that particular moment was anyone's guess. She had shoulder length, dark brown hair and resembled a china doll, if they manufactured china dolls that swore like sailors and smoked whenever they could find a suitable hiding spot. Even at her tender age, it was obvious that she was bound and determined to try everything that people considered "adult" long before she should.

To say that our family dynamic was quirky would be an understatement. To say that it was often dangerous, emotionally shredding, and surreal would probably be more accurate. I used to joke to my friends in high school that in my family, the weak were killed and eaten.

That line always got a laugh.

I wasn't really kidding. The killing was emotional, not physical, but it was there.

Most of the jokes that I made up were amusing from the listener's perspective, and barely metaphoric from my own perspective.

My books, my models, my meager and mostly coverless comic collection, my rickety art desk, and my very basic art supplies resided over in the other part of the basement, trying to stay out of everyone else's way. Usually, I had the basement to myself, except when the laundry needed doing, or ceramics needed firing, or someone wanted to dirty up or stink up the downstairs bathroom. My stepfather, Nathan, had an affinity for White Castle hamburgers, even though his body didn't seem to agree with his choice, and he would use the downstairs bathroom after feasting on a number of the little meat treats, much to my lasting nasal dismay.

The rest of the family referred to the basement as "The Dungeon."

Even though my belongings were out of the main thoroughfares of the house, often my things would end up getting lost, misplaced, or mysteriously broken. If I had been foolish enough to publicly state that I took pride in something, like a ship model that I had just completed rigging, it seemed that the fates would then target that model for injury or destruction. My money often disappeared, my possessions were often moved, and my projects were often damaged in The Dungeon that no one seemed to frequent but myself.

My mind started to wind down from the choking incident, and I tried to find a comfortable position in bed. Changing position in my tiny bed was mostly a matter of trying to defy gravity, for there was no easy rolling from one side to the other. The bed, being only three feet wide, required more of a vertical lift-off, twist in space, and land in a different position in the same physical spot, type of technique. Normally, I didn't like to sleep with my back to the dark hallway and my face to the wall, but the right side of my body was rather stiff from always facing one way. I turned over, adjusted the covers, said a prayer that I would be protected for the rest of the night, and closed my eyes.

After a moment, I opened my eyes again, straining to see into the darkness.

I knew that it was there, even though I couldn't see it.

I had developed a sort of radar sense about these things after years of sleeping in the basement. It also made a sort of sick sense that after being choked in my sleep that I'd have to deal with at least one of "them."

I slowly got out of bed and went to the bathroom down the hall and to the left. I got some toilet paper and crept back into my room. I quietly lowered myself down on the bed so that I could both turn on the light and reach the wall on the side of my bed at the same time.

I flicked on the light and lunged!

It was about three inches long, with innumerable spindly legs, and it tried to run the instant that I turned on the light, but I was too fast. I smashed the meaty centipede into the wall with my toilet paper. Though normally a peaceful person, centipedes had always bothered me on a very basic level, and any centipede stupid enough to violate my personal space, especially my personal sleeping space, deserved what it got. I mashed the paper into a small wad, trying to make sure that all life had been crushed out of the intruder; then I slowly opened up the paper to make sure that it was dead.

It wasn't there!

That meant that it was somewhere hiding in the covers of my bed.

Oh MAN! It was going to be another one of *those* nights.

CHAPTER TWO
Labor Day

It was Labor Day, September 2, 1974, and I was about to start my senior year at Silver Lake High School. The summer had been frittered away all too quickly, and somehow the start of school had come once again, bringing with it the usual restocking of school supplies, the new outfits, and the obligatory new school shoes.

Of all of the rituals relating to the start of school, I didn't like shopping with my mother for shoes at all. She always took the three of us to what we called Worthless Shoes, where we were instructed to "Pick the shoes that hurt the least." It wasn't considered appropriate to wear tennis shoes for anything other than gym or running around the neighborhood, and so a proper pair of leather dress shoes had to be purchased.

For me, this always meant blisters and pain.

It took forever for me to break in a new pair of shoes to the point where I could wear them without band-aids on my heels and little blisters across the tops of my toes. I never wanted new shoes. The silver foot-scale thingy always said that I should get such-and-such size of shoe, but those shoes were always too narrow, my feet being unusually wide, and so I'd have the choice of either compressing my feet lengthwise, or trying to lace them down so that they didn't wobble around in shoes that were too long. Although there were obviously wide feet in the world, my feet never met any shoes designed to fit them, or perhaps more accurately, the shoes that were in my mother's budget didn't allow for wide options.

I could imagine other kids getting excited when their mother said to them, "Get your shoes on, we're going shopping," but such was not the case with us. We *never* went shopping with our mother, except for shoes for the opening day of school. She refused to take us to the grocery store with her, she bought our school supplies for us at Kmart or at Woolworths, and we were *never* allowed to go shopping with her to a toy store. I couldn't remember ever shopping with her, except for the annual foot-mangler tour of Worthless Shoes. If our feet had been somehow detachable, then she probably would've bought our school shoes without us.

We were also denied the opportunity of getting an allowance. If it weren't for our grandparents, Menafay and Eugene MacDonald, the three of us probably wouldn't have seen the inside of a department store or a toy store until we were old enough to drive, and the only way we had of getting any sort of money was by doing odd jobs for them. In the spring, it was turning over the soil in the vegetable garden. In the summer, it was weeding the various flower beds, and in the fall it was raking the leaves from the four massive 50' tall maple trees lining the driveway of their house.

Being a senior, I had been driving for a couple of years now, and the freedom driving allowed me was beyond measure. As long as I complied with whatever demands my mother made of me without question or attitude of any kind, I was allowed to drive her old car, a 1963 T-bird. The T-bird was a 4,000 pound, champagne beige, streamlined, chrome-plated, rear-finned ticket to I-don't-have-to-stay-at-home, and I loved her beyond measure. The price of gas was about forty-four cents a gallon, but it hadn't been too long before that the gas wars had gotten the gas prices down to nineteen cents a gallon.

As for clothing, my mother purchased for us whatever was on sale, without consulting any of us about what we preferred to wear. This had resulted in some of the most embarrassing double and triple polyester outfits that the mid-seventies had ever produced, bought fresh off of the pile at the blue light Kmart special. After getting yelled at for refusing to be seen in some of the more garish wardrobe design malfunctions of the day, I managed to get my mother to agree to buy me nothing except solid colored anything. The preferred solid color of the day was denim, which I personally didn't gravitate to, but anything solid was preferable to anything techno-shockingly decorated with paisley. I had a pair of green and white plaid pants that skirted the thin line between fashion and self-mockery. I begged her not to buy me unnatural fibers, decorated in inexplicable colors, executed in surreal designs, and for the most part, she complied. Although, every now and then she pressured me into wearing something humiliating that she'd purchased for me to wear to school. Among the more bizarre dress-up options of the day were leisure suits, sweater vests, and dickies, which were strange little turtleneck things designed to be worn under a dress shirt. Whereas the 60s fashions had been colorful, natural, and creative, the 70s fashions were, in my decidedly unfashionable opinion, often an unappealing mix of technology applied to unbridled tastelessness.

Hence, my preference for solid colors in natural fibers.

Being the last day of summer freedom, my school supplies were neatly stacked, my new clothes were clean and hung in my closet in order of wearing likelihood, the most likely in front, and the hideously embarrassing hidden in the back, and my new "shoes" were waiting patiently to torment me the following day while walking the hallways of Silver Lake High School, searching for my new classes.

There would be plenty of time to think about new shoes, sore feet, and bulging blisters on the morrow, for this day was to be one filled with family, sun, and summer treats. If I concentrated on spending time in the immediate vicinity of my Grandma Menafay and my Grandpa Eugene, then three out of three positive events would be possible. If my immediate family took control of the day, then at least I still had the sun and the treats to enjoy.

We took two cars to get to my grandparent's house, which was about a mile away. My stepfather drove my mother and my sister in his Ford Ranchero, and I drove my brother, Steven. He parked in the long driveway along the side of the house, and when I got there, I parked on the street.

My grandparent's house had a long and elaborate history, for a house. It currently resided on the corner of Morton and Lincoln Avenue, the main road leading through town closest to the lake, although the house had not always sat there. Their house was the most mobile building that I'd ever heard of. It was originally built as a one-room schoolhouse in 1870. Then, in 1898, the school district had subdivided and the house was sold and moved a half mile north up Lincoln. In 1926, the schoolhouse was decommissioned, sold to a private citizen, and then moved one block south, to where it currently sat. Although a half mile and a block aren't terribly long distances for a person to travel, I figured that it was very rare that a building would accomplish such a feat.

My grandparents had purchased the house in 1943, and had lived there ever since. They rented out the upper floor of the house to long-term boarders. When I was born, in 1957, my mother and father and I had lived upstairs, at first. I'm told that we moved when my father, who was known for his fondness of motorcycles, welding, and beer, tried to take me to the local bar to show me off. According to family legend, my Grandma Menafay disagreed with his intentions and tried to stop him from taking me. The results were a broken finger and a tumble down the front stairs for my grandmother, and a threat of legal prosecution for my father.

Not long after, the three of us moved into my father's old family home, about two miles south.

My grandparent's lot was quite large, since it was the last lot on the block. There were many large trees on the property, in addition to the four huge maples next to the driveway. There was a tall walnut tree in the back corner of the lot, a large evergreen out front, and a burgeoning pear tree next to the garage at the back of the lot. A large portion of the side lot was taken up with a pond and a vegetable garden, with its crops of corn, beans and tomatoes. In the center of the lot was a large, circular rock garden with a cement birdbath in the center. In the spring it was a sight to see, with all of its crocus, daffodils, and tulips in bloom. After their always-too-short early spring blooming season ended, Grandma Menafay liked to remove the dead plants and put in plastic flowers to make the garden appear fresh to those passing by. At first, no one could really tell that the flowers were plastic, but after a couple of seasonal re-paintings, a brightly unnatural look was achieved. Each spring, she gave the ring of stones surrounding her favorite garden a fresh coat of white paint, although one year it had been leftover pink paint. Scattered about the yard were several other gardens, most of which were filled with roses, petunias and zinnias. They were particularly fond of roses, and they had roses of every type. Some were growing in large bushes, some were climbing up formal trellises, some had gone wild and were in the process of taking over the alley wall and fencing, and some tiny tea roses were tucked into corners. Their yard and their gardens were their pride and joy, second only to their cooking. For this picnic gathering, Grandma Menafay would be mostly inside, at least at the beginning, preparing the favorite family casserole of macaroni and cheese, and Grandpa Eugene would be standing vigil next to his evergreen-colored, hammered-metal-finish grill, keeping careful watch over the hamburgers, the hot dogs, the sausages, and the slowly rotating BBQ chicken.

Steven got out of the car quickly and ran to join in the picnic. He was always irresistibly attracted to yard games like horseshoes, or Jarts, where large lawn darts are thrown at plastic circles. Whether he particularly liked horseshoes or

Jarts, or just liked throwing heavy, dangerous things was never clear, although I preferred to stay clear of him whenever he had anything that could inflict pain in his hand. He seemed to have two predictable talents, to "find" lost money and lost wallets, and to have a serious predisposition to having accidents. If Steven decided to throw a stone straight up into the air, there was a better than even chance that someone was going to the hospital to get stitches in their scalp. As long as there was something to swing or throw, Steven was likely to remain occupied.

"Welcome, welcome. Happy Labor Day," Grandpa Eugene called out, moving to greet my mother and Nathan. "Nathan, can I get you a beer?"

"A beer would be great," Nathan replied, trying to be friendly but as obviously out of place as a cat in a room full of rocking chairs. Nathan only seemed comfortable around his own family, on the rare occasions when we had all visited them at Christmas time. Even then, things didn't always go well. One Christmas, I overheard Nathan's mother advising my mother to be careful because Nathan wasn't a very good person, which seemed a bit brutal for a mother to say. Nathan tended to be quiet and keep to himself whenever he was around my mother's family. He smiled as much as he could, but if anyone cared to pay attention to him, they'd notice that he was anything but a conversationalist.

My mother moved to Grandpa Eugene, kissing him on the cheek. Grandpa Eugene was in his mid-seventies, had the remnants of wavy red hair that started at the top of his head, and he sported a small moustache. He liked to smoke small cigars from time to time.

"Hello Daddy, where can I put these chips?"

"Your mother's got some bowls in the house. Follow me." Grandpa Eugene and my mother disappeared and I wandered into the yard, looking to find a quiet corner for myself that wouldn't intrude upon the quiet corner that Nathan was trying to find for himself. There were a number of lawn chairs set up, along with a picnic table and a hammock. There was far too much equipment for just our family, and that meant that Uncle Dominic and his family would be arriving soon.

My heart skipped a beat.

My Uncle Dominic was a unique individual, with powerful opinions and a sense of self that was second to none. He had been in the military and acted like he had been given the rank of four-star general. He was taller than Grandpa Eugene, and he had a fuller head of reddish hair. Previously, he had asked me to create a new logo for his son, Arthur's, hockey team. I had done as requested and was ready to turn the artwork over to him when he arrived. The fly in the ointment moment had come when my mother insisted that I ask him for money for the artwork. There was no doubt that this was going to lead to unpleasantness, and I had only two choices. I could refuse my mother's request, whereby she could and would make torturing me her own personal project or I could ask for money from my rich but incredibly stingy uncle and suffer the loud and immediate consequences, which would be embarrassing but relatively short-lived.

I weighed my choices.

Abused indefinitely or abused for the afternoon.

It didn't seem like a tough decision.

The screen door at the back porch burst open and my energetic grandmother strode down the steps with a pitcher of lemonade in one hand and a bowl of chips in her other hand. She had been born in the south, from mixed Cherokee descendents, and she had long legs, which she liked to talk about frequently as she reminisced about being the best girl on her high school basketball team. Small talk was made all around.

"Hello, Nathan. How are you today? Have some chips. Steven, be careful with those darts around your sister. Danielle, stay away from that picker bush or you'll be sorry.

Nicholas, come over here and give your grandmother a big kiss."

As I walked towards her to give her a kiss, as if by cosmic intervention, my Uncle Dominic and his family pulled into the driveway. My uncle watching me kiss his mother shouldn't have raised any eyebrows, but Dominic had a particular ire towards anyone that his mother showed affection to who wasn't him.

"Oh, nicely staged," I mumbled to myself as I glanced up into the sky in the general direction of what I imagined to be a chuckling God.

I was hoping to give Grandma Menafay a quick peck on the cheek and get off of Dominic's radar as quickly as possible. For as long as I could remember, Dominic and I hadn't gotten along. There seemed to be something about me that brought out the absolute crabbiest version of him, but when he was letting his crabby out, he did show a distinct family resemblance to my mother. The true mystery was how these two kids could be the children of my grandmother and grandfather. It was said that Dominic had disliked living at home so much that he had signed up to fight in Korea at the age of eighteen. Who hates living with their parents so much that they'd prefer to be in a foreign country around people intent upon killing them? My mother left home by marrying my father, but then the "leaving home" part worked out to be only as dramatic as moving upstairs. As brother and sister, it was said in secretive, hushed tones by my grandparents that they didn't really get along. Once, after a particularly dramatic argument, my mother chased Dominic out of the house brandishing a bb gun. From halfway across the yard she hit him between the eyes with a pellet.

I'm not sure which aspect of the story impressed me more, her level of raging anger, or her accuracy with the rifle. Either way, I had learned quite early never to cross my mother about anything, if at all possible. Telling her to stop buying me sale clothing had taken all of my young nerve.

"Hi, Mom," Dominic yelled, waving.

Instead of immediately diverting her attention to him, as I was praying she'd do, she made a fuss over me and gave me a big, wet kiss.

I was going to have to pay for that transgression before the day was over. My uncle had been on the property for less than two minutes and I already knew that it was going to be a day to remember, right up there with Pearl Harbor.

I scampered out of Dominic's crosshairs, surreptitiously watching his family unload themselves from their car, and a general social chaos descended upon the scene. People snacked, chatted, and interacted in preparation for the serving of the big holiday meal, which was imminent. The real giveaway that dinner was almost ready was the appearance of the dish of devilled eggs, peacefully waiting consumption under their plastic wrap tenting. Within minutes, everyone was gathered together around the picnic table or card tables, elbow to elbow.

Selecting my seat was a bit of a challenge. A part of me wanted to sit near my grandmother and my grandfather, for I dearly enjoyed their company, but if I did that, then Uncle Dominic would become irritated by my proximity to his mother. I wanted to give Nathan a wide berth because, although I didn't irritate him as intensely as I irritated Dominic, there was still a palpable tension between us, which might've been as simple a problem as I just wasn't his kid and he wasn't that fond of kids, let alone kids that weren't his kids.

Having already been noticed by Dominic once, I decided to move to the back of the group, out of all conceivable lines of verbal fire. Let someone else rack up some unwanted family attention was my plan. I would blend in with the grass and the trees. So, after heaping my plate with the bounty offered, I went to my seat to quietly enjoy my repast, with the intention of bothering no one and nothing beyond the confines of my plate.

Uncle Dominic was a walking mystery to me. According to him, he was quite wealthy, and yet he was always going on and on about how he scammed this person out of something or how he pressured someone else into lowering their price, even though the original deal was a steal. He once refused to buy a handmade quilt for sale at an outside flea market simply because he couldn't have the last word on the price. Walking away, I had heard him mutter to his wife that the quilt was a steal as offered, but that he just couldn't let the other fellow have the last word. Dominic's wife was from the south and her name was Bobby Lee, which sounded like a very strange name for anyone living in Michigan, and so we all called her Jane. I was never sure if she was hard of hearing or just audibly immune to her husband's cutting comments. When the discussion came around to food, it seemed that Bobby Lee knew better than to offer any insights, for Dominic considered himself quite the chef, and he was more than willing to educate all those within earshot about his culinary mastery. Somehow the discussion at the "big" table had gotten around to cooking in general and Uncle Dominic's chili in particular. He was in the process of explaining how he needed special, Vietnamese chili peppers that had to be handled with gloves because they could give the handler a chemical burn, when I heard him shout.

"Stop it!"

Everyone looked up from their plate to see what had offended him so.

"If I have told that son of yours once, I've told him a thousand times not to do that around me!"

"Do what?" my mother inquired, a bit irritated at the outburst.

"He's chewing ice again. D--- it, he knows how much that irritates me! Tell him to stop or by God, I'll stop him."

Sensing several sets of eyes upon me, I looked up into the seething gaze of a nearly apoplectic madman. Uncle

Dominic was doing his best to stare a hole right through my forehead.

I slowly spit the piece of ice that I had in my mouth back into my glass, and I lowered the glass to the table.

"Sorry."

As I wracked my brain, trying desperately to remember when Dominic had ever said anything to me about chewing ice, the frigid silence slowly evaporated, and people got back to their plates and their various conversations. I was sitting a good ten feet from the man and it mystified me that he could hear me chewing on an ice cube over the din that was dinner. I thought about having seconds, but in order to do that, I'd have to go to the big table to get some more food.

That wasn't going to happen anytime soon.

As much as I loved my grandmother's macaroni and cheese, and my grandfather's knockwurst, I wasn't going to risk any more verbal dismemberment by getting anywhere near Uncle Dominic again. Just as I completed that thought, I heard.

"Nicky, do you want some more of my macaroni and cheese? Bring your plate over to me and I'll serve you some, Hon."

Here was yet another unpleasant choice. I could lie and tell her that I didn't want any more of her macaroni and cheese, and then she'd probably be hurt and ask me why, or I could timidly comply and hope that Dominic didn't "accidentally" knife me in the ribs before the event was over. As I rose to bring her my plate, I thought to myself, "Why think in such dramatic exaggerations? Dominic doesn't really care that I'm having...," and then I saw him staring at me as he ripped the flesh off of some BBQ chicken, and I decided to take the long way around the table, the way that avoided coming within his reach altogether.

The rest of the party was relatively uneventful, at least for me. I decided to help clear away the mess and wash the dishes, which conveniently took me out of the yard and placed me at the kitchen sink. Although there weren't all that many things to be washed, I stalled as long as I could, listening intently at the kitchen window to hear if anything else that I was doing or had done had offended him. When I ran out of things to pretend to wash and put away, I was urged back outside by Grandpa Eugene, who insisted that I join the party and bring everyone up to speed on what I had been doing.

"So, are you looking forward to your senior year, Nicholas?" Grandpa Eugene asked.

"I suppose so," I replied, not wishing to promote a long conversation in my honor.

"What do you mean, 'I suppose so'? Your senior year is very important. I still remember my senior year as if it was yesterday. I was the most popular girl in school, and the center on the girl basketball team," Grandma Menafay reminisced. This path down memory lane was ridiculously well-used.

I noticed my mother's eyes start to roll in her head. As much as my grandmother showing me affection bothered my uncle, my grandmother talking about herself drove my mother to distraction. There was some sort of odd, competitive energy between the two of them that I never understood. I had asked my grandmother about it once, and all she would say is that, as a child, my mother refused affection to such a degree that she actually made my grandfather cry because she was so standoffish.

My grandfather crying I couldn't imagine.

My mother being cold and standoffish I definitely could imagine.

"And you left home because the boys were all getting too serious for you," my mother chimed in, as if she had been required to memorize the story.

"That's right, and that's the type of senior year that you should try to have, one that will bring you warm memories for the rest of your life. Be your best at everything you do, and do everything that you can. Be adventurous, that's my advice," Grandma Menafay pontificated.

"Life is not about watching," my mother added.

"Life is…," Grandma Menafay looked over in my mother's general direction and, realizing that she was being politely mocked with her own words, replied, "That's right, and that's sound advice for anyone."

Nathan stood up and went to get another beer.

"Well, Ma, we need to get going. Tomorrow's a big day for the kids, you know," Uncle Dominic said, giving her a hug.

"Wait, I've packed up some of dinner for you to take home for tomorrow. I'll go and get it," she said, rushing off to the house.

I thought about mentioning the artwork that I had in the car, but I reconsidered, believing it would be best just to let the moment pass. Maybe he'd remember when he got back home and I could just mail it to him.

"Did you still want that logo design that you asked Nicholas to draw?" my mother blurted out.

"Right, I can't leave without that. Arthur's team needs it in order to get the team patches made up. Where is it?"

"It's in the car. I'll get it," I said, trotting off to the T-bird. Ah well, my plan of avoidance had been a complete failure. Maybe I could "accidentally" forget to ask for money.

I handed Uncle Dominic the design.

"Not bad, not bad. It should look good on their jerseys. Thanks." My grandparents looked over the design as my mother made eye contact with me. I tried to look away but it was clear from her demeanor that if I didn't do what was expected of me, there would be hell to pay.

"Um, Uncle Dominic…" I started in.

"Yes?" he replied.

"Do you think it would be possible for me to get paid for my artwork?"

At first, I thought that his lack of immediate response meant that he was considering the question, but then I realized that he was merely deciding which words to use to pound me into the ground like a tent stake.

"Money? Is money all that matters to you, you selfish, self-centered weasel? I'll have you know that when I raised my kids, I taught them the value of family, and how important it is for family to be supportive of each other, and how family members need to be willing and able to share their God-given gifts with each other, without being selfishly concerned about getting paid for every little thing that they do. Did I charge you for dinner the last time that you ate at my house? Did I? Where did you get this idea that people owe you for every little thing that you do for them? What a shallow, hollow excuse for a human being you are..."

I was fully prepared to be steamed alive in the ire of Uncle Dominic's anger for another thirty minutes or so, but Grandma Menafay intervened, using all of her persuasive powers to diffuse Dominic's outraged soul.

"Now, now, he didn't mean to come across that way. He's young and he wasn't thinking clearly. Here, take your food and your artwork, kiss your mother and your father and have a nice drive home," she pleaded.

Uncle Dominic looked at me like he was going to have the last word, even if he had to go against his mother's wishes, and then, thinking twice, he hugged her and called his family to leave. Just when I thought that the event was over, he turned to my mother.

"You need to do something about that greedy kid of yours," Dominic snapped.

A look of anger flashed across her face, but I couldn't tell if the anger was because I hadn't gotten the twenty dollars from him that she had wanted me to, or because he had told her to do something, and no one bossed my mother around and emotionally lived to tell the tale.

From that moment until I finally got home, and hour or so later, I couldn't help but dwell upon how I preferred to be in my dark, dank basement with the centipedes, rather than struggling to understand and survive the intrigues of my immediate bio-illogical family.

CHAPTER THREE
Stinky Things

Although the drive home took very little time, my mind explored many things before I eventually pulled into the Exeter Street driveway. Steven was, as usual, quiet and aloof, which I very much preferred as opposed to his other mode with me, insulting and rude, so my thoughts were uninterrupted as I turned on to Lincoln.

Although I had always enjoyed visiting my grandparent's house, there were many times when I experienced strange occurrences there. In fact, if I really thought about it, I experienced strange occurrences fairly frequently. I never liked going into hospitals. There was something about a hospital that weighed me down, drained my energy, and made me want to get out of there as quickly as possible. I had only been in the hospital once for an ailment of my own. I had my tonsils removed. However, after joining the high school choir, I found myself in hospitals and nursing homes much more frequently because several of us had formed a caroling group of costumed singers and we performed there during the Christmas season. Nursing homes affected me more oppressively than hospitals, but funeral homes and cemeteries were the absolute worst. I felt almost violated in a cemetery, and I would always get flashes of things out of the corner of my eye. It's easy to dismiss such things as tricks of the light, until it happens with a frequency that one cannot dismiss. I don't know what it is about the corner of the eye, but it catches glimpses of many inexplicable things, at least mine do.

During the party, I had caught a glimpse of a man dressed in a blue shirt, standing on the back porch. Just as I focused my attention, the back screen door had burst open and my grandmother had come bounding out onto the porch. The man had faded from view instantaneously.

There was a spot on the driveway, near the third big maple tree that I had privately named Luke that had a stench to it that I couldn't begin to describe. I would walk past the spot and try to figure out where the smell was coming from. It smelled like a sewer leak, but there were no sewer pipes anywhere near the spot. The smell never diminished and it never shifted. I could go back to the same spot after an hour and it was still the same size, about the size of a person, and it was still as strong as ever. As interesting as the smelly spot was, the astounding part of the story is that no one else seemed able to smell it. I would watch as person after person would cross the yard and walk down the driveway right through the stinky place and their face would never change, which I knew to be improbable if they could actually smell what I smelled.

I had seen other spirits on the property over the years, especially when I'd stayed overnight with my grandparents. They had a set routine to their evenings. We'd all watch their favorite programs, like *Gunsmoke*, there would be the traditional evening bowl of ice cream, then my grandfather would stay up to catch the weather on the 11 o'clock news, and we'd all go to bed, with me sleeping on the couch in the living room. The couch was old, was upholstered with a rough, pebbly-textured fabric, and had a board under the cushions which made it uncomfortably firm, but the living room came without an endless supply of centipedes, and so I was happy.

On two specific occasions I saw spirits.

Both times, the spirits had been sitting on the front steps.

The first time, I saw a young boy, probably ten or twelve years old, dressed in overalls and a flannel shirt. He had blonde hair and reminded me a bit of Tom Sawyer or Huckleberry Finn. He looked out of place by about a hundred-and-fifty years. He just looked up and smiled at me, and then he faded away.

The other time it seemed that I had intruded upon a conversation between two spirits. They were both attractive young ladies, but each one was an improbable size. The larger of the two girls was regularly proportioned but only about three feet tall. The smaller of the two ladies was also regularly proportioned, but she was like a doll, only about fourteen or fifteen inches tall. I came around the corner, they stopped talking, although I hadn't been able to hear them before I saw them, they looked up at me, smiled, and then faded from view.

There were also many times when I was certain that I saw dark mists skittering across the ceiling when I entered a room. They seemed to be trying to get into a shadow or dark corner as quickly as possible. I often dismissed these things as tricks of the light, but some had behaved so oddly that they would occasionally come back to my mind.

As strange as these encounters might seem, I had just experienced something equally as improbable just a little while earlier, when I had come out to the T-bird to get my logo design for Uncle Dominic. As I was walking down the driveway towards the street, along the side of Nathan's Ranchero and Dominic's Cadillac, I noticed a young woman walking towards the house from the corner of the street. She was a strikingly attractive, young blonde woman, wearing a bright purple blouse, black pants and black shoes. I didn't get much time to study her face because she looked over at me and I didn't want to be seen staring, so I politely looked away. As the two of us neared the end of the driveway, my view of her was blocked by the first large maple tree on the property, Matthew. I stopped, intending to be polite and to let her walk across the driveway first. She didn't appear from behind the tree, which was curious. Assuming that she was behind the tree waiting for me to walk out, I stepped forward and scanned the sidewalk.

She was gone!

As impossible as it seemed, she had disappeared into thin air! She couldn't have run back to the corner of the street without my seeing her. I walked down the sidewalk to where she would've stood, on the opposite side of Matthew from where I had been, and I experienced a rancid stench, much like the smell of the stinky spot down the driveway near the back porch. For some strange reason, the image of her smile, a strange, Cheshire cat sort of smile, lingered in my memory, although I couldn't recall the other features of her face clearly. One minute, she had seemed as solid as any other person that I might see on the sidewalk, and the next, she was gone like a mist.

It was just another footnote to my life that I couldn't explain, like being nearly choked to death by nothing.

CHAPTER FOUR
The Ties That Blind

I used to believe that family was based upon biology. As I grew older and I realized that I had absolutely nothing in common with my mother, my father, my uncle, my brother or my half-sister, I decided that real family was based upon affection. That realization pretty much made me an instant orphan, except for my grandparents.

I had experienced affection from very few people in my family hydra – errr - tree. As I mentioned earlier, I had no idea how my grandparents could give birth to a pair of angry, judgmental people like my mother and my uncle.

I used to try to explain away my mother's situation by saying that all she needed was freedom from worry. If I had a million dollars and I gave it to her, then she'd be free from worry and, therefore, free from crabbiness. That fantasy had gotten me through junior high, but beginning in high school, when I began being exposed to other friend's home environments, I began to suspect that my mom was just angry, and for some reason, she felt comfortable that way.

The day she quipped, "Grow a moustache, you look just like your father," I knew that I was in for a bumpy ride.

My mother had made it quite clear while I was growing up that she loathed my father.

How they got together, I really have no idea.

Why they got married, I really have no idea.

How they didn't end up killing each other, I really have no idea.

From what I was able to piece together from family gossip, my father had been a motorcycle riding troubled-youth sort of kid, and the few pictures that I had seen of him before I was born seemed to bear that assumption out. Whether he was really troubled or whether my Grandma Menafay had just labeled him as troubled, I will never truly know. My mother didn't discuss her past – ever!

According to Grandma Menafay, with the quiet assent of Grandpa Eugene in the background, my mother had always been a cold, emotionally distant, difficult child. She was extremely competitive in all things, and she had enjoyed winning trophies in archery and bowling with my father before I was born. I had never seen the trophies, but I had seen pictures of her with them. Actually, I couldn't be sure that I had never seen the trophies because most of my young child memories seemed to be missing whenever I got a flashlight and started searching the dark recesses of my brain looking for them. Another thing that I learned by hanging around other people is that they could remember huge pieces of their childhood. I, on the other hand, could recollect only about ten or fifteen minutes of mostly random images from before I was in junior high.

My first memory was of me at around the age of five, listening to a violent, screaming argument in the other room. I got out of bed, slowly folded back some sort of grey accordion door sort of thing, and then I saw my father either shove or punch my mother backwards over the end of a couch. I used to crawl out of my bedroom and watch TV from behind my mother's chair at night. There's another memory of my playing across the street from our second house after moving out of my grandparent's second floor, where we were making dragon parts with a Thingmaker. The texture of the cooked goop gave me nightmares. I have a dim memory of some sort of dinner party at my grandparent's house where my mother and father were together and they were all celebrating Dominic's marriage to some woman who was not Bobby Lee. My grandmother didn't like to talk about her. It was like the family had decided to erase her from all memory. She had allegedly gotten an abortion because she didn't want to have any children, which had incensed my Uncle Dominic, who promptly bounced her bottom out of our lives with a speedy divorce.

We moved to the Exeter house when I was around six, right after my mother acquired my stepfather, and my memories of life then geometrically increase. I can recall being in Cub Scouts and having my mother as a den mother. I can recall her being angry with me because I had outgrown my Cub Scout uniform and she didn't want to transplant all of my badges from my old uniform to my new uniform.

I can remember her being angry about something pretty much always.

I have only one memory of her sincerely laughing lightheartedly and that was during the honeymoon period of her marriage to Nathan. He had completed building a bar at the far end of the basement in our new Exeter Street house and they were having a party. Their friends were calling her "BB" and she was laughing like a little girl.

It was a little chilling to me.

I found her laughter far scarier than her angry screaming.

I know that most people don't say such things about their mother, but then again, I assume that most mothers don't give their children cold sweat nightmares.

I'm not sure what my dad did, but she ejected his backside from our lives when I was around five. After moving out of her parent's house, we had moved into his parent's house, and then his parents, Grandma Zotia and Grandpa Nelek, had moved several miles up Highland Avenue, so divorce/reconciliation talks took several bizarre twists, according to rumors. Negotiations lasted over a year, and by the time they were done, my dad had moved out, gotten the secretary where he worked as a welder pregnant, and had promised to marry her. My mother had somehow held a refrigerator or freezer hostage from Grandma Zotia and Grandpa Nelek, had eventually offered to reconcile with my father after he had gotten another person pregnant, and had then declared him eternal persona non grata after he decided to take her at her original word that she loathed him and that they were eternally through.

After she decided that she loathed my dad for all eternity, she noticed how much I looked like him, much to my eternal dismay. My brother, Steven, oddly enough, looked nothing like my father at all. Whereas I was a very solid young mass of Polish genes, weighing in at an impressive seventy pounds at a mere three years of age, Steven was the tiniest toothpick of a child, with spastic and random energy to spare, like a chimp on drugs. According to my father, one of my mother's last broadsides in his direction was, "You'll never know if Steven is your son or not."

She then went trolling the local bars for a suitable replacement. She thought that she'd hooked a man with property, his own boat, and a taste for the finer things in life. What she got was Nathan, a simple carpenter, who had no real property, no real boat, a predisposition for grand exaggeration, and a seemingly unquenchable thirst for Budweiser beer.

That was the first grand splitting of the family hydra. My mother, Nathan, Steven, Danielle and I became one trunk of the hydra, and my father, my stepmother, and their eventual five children became the other trunk of the hydra, and then there was the Dominic offshoot.

A lot of people, a lot of opinions, and a lot of emotional pain could've become our collective family motto. One game that my mother liked to play with us kids was what I referred to as "Two in, one out." This was where she would confide in two of the three children about how disappointed she was in the one that was out of the circle. More often than not, I was the Out, but sometimes, Steven or Danielle would mouth off to her and I would be allowed into the inner circle for a time.

Truthfully, the outside of the circle was nicer than being on the inside.

My first transgression against her seems to have been the day that I was born. I was three weeks ahead of schedule, I had three teeth already in my head, and I had decided to arrive on her birthday, upstaging her and ruining her birthday party. Over time, she seemed to adjust to me on the whole, but then she and my father parted company and I became a living reminder of how much she didn't like him.

She used to call me Little Lord Fauntleroy and Goody Two-shoes for no reason that I could figure out.

Did I mention the nightmares?

Anyway, I never crossed my mother, as a rule, and I became a very quiet child, the kind that colors for hours alone in a corner. My Grandmother Zotia and my Grandmother Menafay seemed to sense that I could use a hug or two from a kindly heart, and I dearly appreciated their efforts. However, attention from them often brought negative reactions from my uncle and my dad, who both seemed to share a territorial quality concerning their mothers, whether they realized that quality about themselves or not.

To add yet another layer to the travesty of the family hydra, my grandfather, Nelek, had decided that he was going to loath my mother, and everything related to my mother, with at least as much vitriol as she held for my father. Grandpa Nelek was a scowling, shrunken-apple headed rock of a man, with solid Polish ditch-digger genes. His dislike of my mother made for several unbelievably cruel moments when Steven and I were with our father for the holidays and we were publicly snubbed. One Christmas, at a large family gathering, Grandpa Nelek lined up all of the children of his three sons and his daughter, and he proceeded to pass out five dollar bills, to every outstretched hand except for Steven and mine.

These slights were painful to ignore, but I was much better at it than Steven was. Steven became obsessed with these injustices and slowly became filled with barely repressed anger, towards nearly everyone, except for the author of all of these actions, my mom. Somehow, he found comfort in her outbursts. Perhaps it was because she never surprised us, whereas Grandpa Nelek had astounded us with his nastiness and public rejection.

As I was growing up, I tried to gain my mother's favor by becoming the perfect child, the "A" student, the admirable offspring, and the overachiever. Not only did this technique not work, but it forced Steven to go through the grades two years behind me as "Nicholas' younger brother." From time to time, he liked to smack me on the back of the head while we passed in the hallway, call me n-gger, and then blurt out that I had ruined his life.

My ability to offend the family hydra seemed to be almost like a superpower, although I would've preferred the ability to fly, or emotional invulnerability. I had my Batcave, otherwise known as Centipede Central, but beyond that, I barely had enough gas to fill the tank of my borrowed Batmobile.

When sober, Nathan was, for the most part benign, although he once scolded me at the breakfast table that he didn't like the look of my eyes. After that morning, I ate my cereal uncomfortably slumped down behind my box of Frosted Flakes while he sat across the table, hidden behind his paper. Nathan got along a lot better with Steven, and the two of them had built a three car garage together in the back yard. Whereas Steven absolutely craved the opportunity to scamper up a ladder and across a partially finished roof, I preferred to stay safely in my basement, drawing at my art table, where no ladder could mysteriously be knocked out from under me. If I was in the immediate vicinity of my mother or my stepfather, chances were very good that I would be found to be in the way, or standing in front of what they wanted, or sitting on something that they needed. If I made myself scarce, then there was a better than even chance that I was going to overhear how I was too snooty, or aloof, or too lazy to be counted on.

That was just the way that I was raised, and it took me a long time to realize that this type of stressful environment was different from everyone else's family experience.

Some families actually liked their children.

Whereas Steven was becoming fairly predictable in his temperament, Danielle was a walking conundrum. One minute, she would come off as wanting a big brother and wanting to be advised and protected, and the next minute she would be flipping me the bird and telling me what I could do with myself in no uncertain terms. She didn't know who she was or what she wanted to be. She knew that she wanted to be valued as a daughter, but she didn't want to receive dancing lessons from her father when he was staggering, almost-passing-out drunk.

All three of us were brought up with family memories that we'll never forget, but for most people, family memories are cherished and do not need to be erased by trained professionals, like social workers and psychiatrists, or filled in with joint compound. I can say from experience that nothing quite wakes up the senses and the reflexes quite like having a full hot skillet of goulash thrown across the kitchen at you. That happened when I was an amateur at reading body language. As I got older and wiser, I learned to read the signs of impending doom and remove myself from the field of battle long before Nathan even thought of reaching for something hot, heavy, or sharp.

My mother never resorted to physical violence, perhaps because it wasn't her strong suit, but she sure had a way in winding Nathan up until his spring broke. The most innocent victim in the house was, of course, our loyal and loving German shepherd. It took a few times of being kicked down the stair by a drunken Nathan for Vicky to realize that he was not to be trusted on the weekends.

This was my family. This was the family dynamic, and until the powers of the universe saw clear to grant me money and freedom, this was the world that I had to survive and thrive within, for at least one more year. After I graduated from high school, perhaps I could get a scholarship and get out of my Dungeon.

There didn't seem to be a war on the horizon, so there was always the choice of signing up with Uncle Sam. Much as I didn't like being an emotional target, I really didn't see myself wanting to become a physical target, like Uncle Dominic had.

Hopefully, God had something wonderful in mind.

CHAPTER FIVE
The Temple of Ba'al

I find that the strangest thoughts that I have while sleeping are some combination of, "What's going on here? I know that I'm in bed and I know that I'm asleep," and "How come I can see everything so clearly and everything seems so real?"

Whatever happens after I have these thoughts I tend to call a vision.

As for my dreams and nightmares, I don't remember them for more than a few minutes past waking up, so there's no real confusing the two situations.

I found myself standing before a great cathedral, of sorts, but this building was so old and decayed that most of the front of the edifice had collapsed and rotted away. The proportions of every aspect of the building were skewed, as if mice were expected to come and pay homage to a giant. The steps may have been made for tiny legs, but no normal person or group working in tandem could've possible opened the two great entrance doors had the master of the place wished them to stay closed. The front doors were barely hanging upon their unbelievably massive hinges, and each door itself was large enough to easily crush most of the houses that I'd ever seen in my life. I stood for a while, trying to mentally adjust to what I was looking at. It's one thing to see a picture of a skyscraper and then to mentally relate to the building being made up of many human-sized floors, stacked one upon the other. It is quite another think completely to reevaluate one's position of significance in the universe by contemplating intruding upon the domain of something that would consider a human to be about as significant as a bipedal dust bunny.

If the steps were in keeping with the proportions of the doors, then entering would've been impossible, without securing the assistance of huge ladders or scaffolding.

Little people like me were obviously allowed into this structure.

A shiver ran down my spine when I asked myself if little people were also let out.

I listened intently, and other than the sounds of creaking and dripping coming from somewhere deep in the bowels of the building, all was quiet.

With great apprehension, I stepped inside, careful not to disturb any of the rubble, or to make any noise.

Although designed to hold untold thousands, this place was obviously not built to convey a sense of peace or to provide anything resembling comfort. There were railings, of a manner, arranged in row upon row, all facing the dark center of the space. Whether all of the worshippers faced one way or were arranged all around the huge central altar was hard to say. The immense size of the building could accommodate worshippers radiating out from all sides, but the dimness and the chaotic piles of debris made it difficult to discern the actual layout. Perhaps there was no definite layout, for there was something about the disconcertingly grotesque statuary and the architectural details that seemed to protest against symmetry, balance, and order. The railings came in two heights. One height seemed too tall to comfortably lean against, and the other seemed too short to comfortably sit upon. I inspected one of the taller railings closest to me. It was grimy and covered with stains that looked vaguely like dried blood. Could part of the ritual in this macabre place be the pounding of one's forehead upon this railing? Was it some form of religious ecstasy, or some form of religious self abuse, intending to please the unholy deacons of this place?

In my mind's eye flashed a glimpse of thousands upon thousands of writhing souls, abusing themselves vigorously in order to avoid the attention of dark shapes that patrolled every isle and physically hauled away any whose worship seemed less than enthusiastic. Hauled away for what purpose, I wondered, and then I saw it.

In the center of this dim, surreal, purposefully constructed monstrosity I saw the altar clearly for the first time. Sitting atop the altar was an enormous throne, and at the base of this altar was a series of chained in ramps, which resembled the types of labyrinthine passages one might see in a stockyard, where cattle are forced into a passage that they cannot escape from, and they are forced to the end, and to their ultimate doom. Upon closer inspection, it became clear that all of these ramps converged upon huge fire pit areas placed around the central altar. This was not only a place of sacrifice, but a place of immense, unspeakable sacrifice. How long did the services here last, and during those services, how many were brutalized and burnt alive to appease the giant who watched and bellowed from his throne.

Above each fire pit, so blackened with soot that it could only be clearly read by those who were about to be thrown into its raging bonfire, it was inscribed:

I am Ba'al
Tremble at the mention of my name.
I am empowered by the spilling of blood.
I am the singer of the many songs of revenge.
I am the God of Anger, and all nations belong to me.
Render unto oblivion all of your vain hopes,
As you render unto me all that you possess.

And there, deep inside this dung heap which had been cobbled together with the mortar of despair, up upon the immense altar of dust and filth, I saw the spirit of Ba'al, a giant dozing upon its massive throne. It was dozing upon the throne that it had built to itself, resting from a recent worship service, I imagined, where untold numbers were sacrificed in order to feed its never ending appetite for blood. Looking just over the edge of a smoldering fire pit, I caught sight of the glowing embers, the innumerable blackened skeletons, and the terrible smell of burnt flesh.

If this vision had anything else to teach me, I was no longer interested in learning whatever it was. I was seized with an immediate desire to leave, as quickly as possible. It was at this moment when I turned that I realized that the Ba'al giant didn't see its surroundings with the same eyes that I did. To Ba'al, the sanctuary was ablaze with wonder and magnificence, a place to inspire and awe. The spirits of the darkness lived within churches of their own creation to themselves and their dark masters, and they lacked all ability to see the wretchedness of what they had created. Being energies of decay and death, they didn't recognize the repulsive aspects of decay and death as viewed by the spiritually alive.

Thinking my lessons over, I quickened my pace for the door, but there were still a couple of things that the darkness had to teach me before I left.

There was some sort of movement over to the side, amidst the rubble.

For some unknown reason, Ba'al began to stir from its gluttonous slumber.

I looked at my feet, and I realized that I was standing on top of something, something glistening, which was just beginning to bubble and slither up slowly from under the decayed carpeting. I faced the door and began to run, for there was no more time to take a more meandering circuitous route. Something was awake in addition to Ba'al, and I was absolutely certain that I didn't wish to make its acquaintance in this dreary place. Realizing that I had been foolish in allowing myself to be so curious, I began to pray for assistance in escaping this place of torture and death.

A viscous fluid began flowing towards me from every side. In many aspects it was like mucous, although mucous doesn't normally have the ability to move by itself. It began trying to block my way, intent upon trapping me within the crumbling sanctuary. Whether it was doing its master's bidding and would feed me to the giant, or if it was intent upon torturing and eating me itself was not clear. What was clear was that every time I rolled, dodged, and evaded one of its traps, it would strike again with renewed ferocity and increasing speed. Tendrils reached out for me as I kept scrambling and spinning towards the gaping hole through which I'd entered. For a moment, I became trapped by one of its smaller tendrils, and the mucus-like substance tried to pry my mouth open, in order to enter me.

Some of it began invading my nostrils, but I managed to grab a piece of rubble and beat the thing off of me.

Ba'al was on its feet and staggering forward, like some surreal moment from a cheap Japanese monster movie. Ba'al didn't seem to pose any immediate threat to me, due to its slow shuffling and unfocused gaze, but I knew that if I were caught up in the mucus tendrils again, I'd probably never make it out of that ruin alive.

With a litany of prayers running through my mind, I sprinted for the safety of the dim light outside. Twisting and thrashing, I fought my way out, barely escaping becoming engulfed in the sentient wave of goo that had pursued me right up to the threshold of the building.

For some reason, the mucous seemed to be afraid of venturing out into the open, and it recoiled back into the rubble and the shadows, slowly seeping back into the cracks and the debris.

Panting on the ground, my body was wracked with convulsions, and after several seconds, some of the evil fluid began oozing out of my mouth and nostrils. Pulling with all of my might, I dislodged the material, which was like trying to remove a determined octopus arm, and I threw it far from me.

I scampered a bit farther from the hole in the wall, and I watched as the mucus slowly slithered back, to rejoin its greater self, which returned to lurking just out of sight in the darkness.

"And what have you learned?" a voice behind me asked.

I spun around and saw a beautiful woman. She was clothed in a flowing, sky blue garment. She was thin and attractive, but her face didn't seem to match her body. Her face was full and round and extremely cheerful. She wore a sky blue kerchief on her head, which covered most of her hair. Her hair not held by the kerchief flowed down over her shoulders in golden waves, like the rays of the sun. Her face reminded me of a smiling sun.

"Excuse me?" I replied.

"What did you learn, my boy? Certainly you can't believe that I brought you here merely to have your existence threatened by a big wad of evil snot."

"You brought me here?" I asked, as I collected myself up out of the dirt.

"Well, you certainly didn't bring yourself, although you do have the ability to be a Lightwalker. If your soul had decided to go for a stroll, of all of the dimensions and all of the places and all of the times that you would have to pick from, why in Heaven would you choose to come here?"

"I never would choose to come to a place like this," I blurted out.

"So, we both agree. You didn't bring you here, which must mean that there's some credibility to my claim of having brought you here. Now that that's settled, what did you learn?"

"I was supposed to learn something?"

"I should hope so, otherwise your near future, particularly your senior year, is going to be full of much more pain and dismay than is absolutely necessary."

"It's necessary for my life to have pain and dismay?"

"All life has pain and dismay, and there's always a purpose for it."

"What I've experienced has a purpose?" I quipped.

"Oh yes," the beautiful lady replied.

"Can I know what that purpose is?" I pleaded.

"Not quite yet; it would just overwhelm you."

"Did I ask for this life? I can't imagine that I'd be ignorant enough to ask for a life where I would be disliked by almost everyone that I meet. Did I ask for this?"

"Not exactly," she said.

"Oh, you've got to be kidding me. Who, exactly, are you?"

"I can't tell you that just yet."

"Can't or won't?"

"If I answer your questions, you're going to be unable to cope with the information. All I can tell you is that everything will be made clear to you in time, but right now, you haven't got enough of the puzzle pieces figured out to make any sense of my answers, if I were to give them to you."

"Telling me your name would be overwhelming?"

"Oh, you can be certain of that. It's important that you not waste time on your journey misunderstanding things, and the first step to misunderstanding something is to limit it and name it."

"So, the only thing I can really be certain of here is my own name," I sighed.

"You can believe that, if it gives you comfort."

"Are you saying that I don't even know my own name?"

"I'm saying that I know you as well as I know my own son, and you've just proven my point. You think that you're one name. Someone named you, and you believe that you know all about you."

"I do think that I know all about me. Well, I might have some gaps in my early memories, but for the most part, I believe I know about me."

"I orchestrated those gaps in your early memories, and you're welcome."

"You're responsible for the gaps?! What if you removed something that I wanted to keep?"

"Trust me when I tell you, there was nothing that I took that you wanted to keep."

"And I'm supposed to trust you because…?"

"Because I'm cute, and I'm an enigma, and because there's a little part of you that realizes that you and I go back a very long way, even though you can't for the life of you, figure out how."

"You're funny."

"No, actually, you're the funny one, and we dearly miss your jokes, but now, back to your assignment."

"My assignment, you say?"

"Your assignment would be a more accurate description than your life."

"I don't have a life, I have an assignment?!"

"Now see, one little tiny puzzle piece provided to you and already your brow is starting to furrow."

"My assignment, you say?"

"You're going to get wrinkles. Can we get back to my original question, please? What did you learn by coming here?"

I started to blurt out another of the thousand questions bumping together in my head, jostling for position, trying desperately to get to my mouth, but the pretty lady just reached up and covered my mouth with her hand.

"Focus," she said, ever so quietly.

Her touch caused a peace to come over me, a peace unlike any that I'd ever experienced. Actually, her touch made me wonder if I'd ever known a moment of peace in my life, for certainly I'd never felt like this moment before.

"Answer my question and I'll give you one more puzzle piece before I go."

As she removed her hand, I asked, "Do I get to pick which question?"

"No, it will be better for you if I pick. Now, focus. What did you learn from coming here?"

"What I learned from coming here is that everyone, even the devil's princes, live in a cathedral of their own construction, where they see everything that they've built and everything that they believe in as right and perfect and just. Ba'al thinks that his shrine to himself is magnificent, and yet it is obvious to all that are not caught up in his self-worship and delusions that it is a sad, putrid, and crumbling structure."

"And what could this delusion be called?"

"Idolatry," I responded.

"You must be aware that the greatest barrier to bringing Light and Love and Truth to others is this delusion that is idolatry. Many good-natured people believe that the term only applies to those outside of their faith. They do not suspect that they themselves are caught up within its snares. You must try to bring Light into their darkness, without falling prey to that darkness."

"Right, I'm supposed to try to convince people who have been spiritually prerecorded by millennia of traditions that they need to rethink everything that they understand to be truth. No problem. Is there any chance that I'm just going to forget this dream and quietly return to my life of predictable abuse, without the mandate to seek out an additional level of rejection above and beyond my normal fare?"

"We do miss your humor," she smiled, giving my cheek a fond pinch.

"Will I be coming home soon?"

"That's classified."

"And my puzzle piece?"

"Oh yes, let's see. What would be uplifting and intriguing, without being overwhelming or causing you to experience spiritual conundrums at this stage of your spiritual understanding?"

"I vote for no conundrums and not being overwhelmed."

"How's this, I know you by 4,935 other names above and beyond the one you're using now."

"Brain starting to explode…"

"Good-night, my darling, sleep tight, and I'll take care of the centipedes from now on.

CHAPTER SIX
The First Day of School

Just like remembering how to ride a bike, the first day of school began with the usual morning ritual, which allowed for the lingering of a certain mental fuzziness until full consciousness was required at school. The alarm did its thing, which set my series of things into motion. Having barely opened both eyes fully, I found myself safely entrenched behind my cereal box, trying to be three-and-a-half feet tall in order to stay off of Nathan's radar. Steven didn't usually show up at the breakfast table. He seemed to have a manic amount of energy generated without the intake of solid food.

There was one time in elementary school when the office had called me down to ask me if my mother ever fed him, because he never seemed to eat lunch, and they couldn't get a coherent answer from him when they asked. Steven had made an art form out of two things, above and beyond pestering me, and they were finding reasons to dislike various foods (like coffee cake has coffee in it), and making the food disappear from his plate as if he'd eaten it, only to be discovered later, hidden away. Under his bed was a favorite food cemetery, as was the little metal dish between the legs of my grandparent's 1950s kitchen table. He used to feed Vicky when he could get away with it, but at home his special storage place was under the cushion of his chair. When my mother was contacted by the school counselor and then discovered the remnants of meals gone by, petrified, squished, and fused to Steven's cushion and wooden chair, she was not impressed. I'm not certain what his punishment entailed. He had brought her parenting skills into question by people outside of our home, and that was a very bad thing. When I realized where that discussion between them was going, I made myself scarce. I didn't wish to become collateral damage once her ire was in full, lethal bloom. He was grounded, certainly, but I sensed that there were other, less obvious addendums to his punishment. I wasn't insane enough to ask what they were and get a taste of them for myself, so I let the subject die.

Danielle was on a different schedule for the junior high, so my only obligation beyond getting my own bottom to Silver Lake High School, was to make sure that Steven was in the car with me before I left. He had assured me that he would find his own way home with his friends. This relieved me greatly, because I planned to be involved in several after-school activities: choir, Junior Achievement, Boy Scouts, the Silver Lake Drama Club, or the local young people's theatre group. All that mattered to me was that I would be unavailable for family abuse on Friday nights, so whichever group was meeting then, I was committed to serving faithfully.

I muttered my good-bye to my stepfather and he grunted something Neanderthal-ish in my general direction, but there was no "We're going to talk about your attitude later" aftertaste to his comment, so I was safe.

The Don's ring had been metaphorically kissed just enough to buy me another day of peaceful coexistence.

Steven was, in many respects, like a human super ball. He started off slow, but seemed to pick up speed throughout the day. In the morning, he was as physically and mentally alert as chilled maple syrup, but heaven help his last hour teacher if he managed to consume sugar for lunch. I smiled at the fact that his end-of-the-day state was not going to be my concern, and backed out of the drive-way.

Silver Lake High School was in the middle of a housing and enrollment boom that showed no immediate signs of tapering off. There were so many students now crowded into the building that the seniors had two different options of schedules. The seniors on schedule "A" would arrive at 7:00 a.m. and be finished at noon. Those seniors with a "B" schedule would begin at 8:00 a.m. and be finished at 2:40 p.m. Because of my interest in the many after school opportunities, I had signed up for schedule "B" along with most of my friends. Only those rabid to get out into the work force had signed up for schedule "A", and rabid to work, I was not. It was not that I was against working. I was just against tedium. I was quite prepared to work throughout the night on a theatre set, but I was not quite ready to ask, "Would you like fries with your third-pounder?" at the local Burger Chef.

The school itself was shaped, more or less, like a giant 8 if viewed from overhead. The lower half of the 8 had a second floor, and the upper right corner of the 8 had a huge wart on it, the auditorium wing. That was where I spent most of my spare time. At the other end of the school was the Kingdom of Jock-itude, along with the required baseball field, football field, and track.

Like many schools in the area at that time, the building had expanded more or less willy-nilly from a core school structure that might have originally included a cafeteria or gym, or these things might've been bolted on at a later date. Everything seemed to be packed to the seams and flirting with exploding at that time, which included the large-but-nowhere-near-large-enough parking lot at the west end of the school, outside of the auditorium.

Steven bolted from the car as soon as I had slowed down sufficiently to park, and I eased into a space in the back forty acres.

"So far, so good," I thought to myself, as I began walking to the auditorium entrances, and then my shoes started to hurt my feet and I realized that, in my pre-waking stupor, I had neglected to put on or bring band-aids.

I knew that I would regret that mistake before the day was through.

I blended in with the crowd entering the school. My hair was a little long and over my ears, but it was relatively short considering the styles of the day, and my clothing was color-coordinated without the use of paisleys or sweater vests or corduroy elephant-bottoms, so I felt fairly good about how I looked. God had even allowed be to lose some weight and appear mostly normal, having been quite solidly overweight for almost all of my life. The only part of me that still seemed a bit disproportionate were my upper thighs, which bulged a bit like a weightlifter's thighs, or a frog's thighs, depending upon the viewer's desire to be impressed or to mock.

I proceeded to my homeroom, to discover whether the schedule that I thought I had made for my senior year, was indeed the schedule that I had for my senior year. Like a blast of a tank from the past, Mrs. Sherman's voice resounded throughout the building, reminding us of where we were all expected to be. I recalled fondly a joke announcement that she had made last year on April Fool's Day, where she had come over the PA system and announced that all students at the east end of the building should immediately report to the west end, and that the west end students should immediately go to the east end. She had ended by instructing the students caught in the middle to direct traffic.

A flash went off in my face and I nearly walked into a door frame in the breezeway connecting the auditorium wing to the older parts of the school.

"First day of school pictures for the yearbook. You're famous," yelled Darryl Sandusky as he attempted to swim upstream, probably to get pictures of the congestion in the parking lot. I had known Darryl for a long time, although our friendship was a strange thing. When I was in third grade I used to go to his house after school and assemble fishing lures for a couple of pennies per lure. His family had a shop on Lincoln near Decadia where they sold fishing supplies. I used to love reading his comic collection when I was at his house because he actually had comics in order, and I could read a whole story. My comic collection was mostly made up of random and coverless discount comics that I'd purchased with my yard work money at the little market near my grandparent's house.

"There's my buddy! How was your summer, or at least the last few weeks of it?" yelled Moriah Weinstein, as she bumped several people out of the way in order to give me a big hug. Moriah was a cute, long-haired, spirited girl, and a good friend of mine from choir class. I'd dropped by her house to visit several times throughout the summer, that is, until my bike was stolen from in front of her house.

"How'd your mom take your bike getting stolen?" she asked.

"How does she take good news?" I quipped.

"With chilly indifference," Moriah replied.

"Then you can imagine how unimpressed she was with me over my losing my bike."

"You didn't lose it, it was stolen."

"My dear, you don't understand the world that I live in. My bike having been stolen would imply that I am innocent of aiding and abetting the act. My losing my bike puts the blame squarely where my family believes it always should be, right upon my shoulders."

"Remind me not to drop by your house unannounced. We'll talk later, during lunch. I've got to go. See you in choir, Bud."

To say that the halls were crowded and difficult to maneuver through would be an understatement. I wasn't sure how many students the building was designed to hold, but my guess was that there were at least five hundred more in the place than they built it for. The last people into any classroom might well have to sit on the floor from lack of desks, and so I hurried on my way. My homeroom was on the second floor of the east end, down by the gym and cafeteria, where I seldom had any classes. If I had planned things better, I would've walked around outside of the building instead of trying an internal route.

I finally arrived and found a place in the back to call my own. My homeroom teacher was Mr. Olsen, a charming man with a tendency to need three to four times the time required for most people to accomplish simple tasks, like taking attendance or passing out schedules. I enjoyed being in his class because it gave me the opportunity to complete my homework before leaving school each day, but I doubted that I'd have him this year. They tended to give him the underclassmen, because the newbies were less likely to make trouble for him, and he was easily flustered. As I had predicted in my head, the passing bell rang and several of us were still without our schedules, so I had to wait for him to finish sorting us out.

I grabbed my schedule and bounded through the door on my way to first hour, which was – my heart dropped. I had drafting first hour with "The Voice." A first hour class with The Voice! I now had to get myself halfway across the school, to a back hallway room located under a staircase, and I had to do it in less than five minutes. It was not an impossible task, but with everyone searching for their classrooms, it would be an improbable task, and to get there by going outside would require my circumnavigating about two-thirds of the building. I plowed on.

I had been a student of Mr. Maymo before, and as I dashed around the corner and entered his room I could hear his voice like déjà vu saying, "Next time, Mr. Freeman, you should plan your route a little better and be here on time. Thank you. Have a seat."

It wasn't the snippet of embarrassing attention that I had dreaded as I approached his room, but rather his completely monotone voice! His voice had the power to suck the very life out of me. I was going to have to sit there every morning first hour and listen to him explain to us how drafting had created the modern world, with a voice that never changed a tone or a beat! The only thing even remotely interesting about being in Maymo's class was watching what happened with his coffee. Mr. Maymo had an obsession about his coffee and he brought an enormous thermos to class every day. On the rare occasions when he would use the bathroom during class, some of the more disrespectful or mentally underdeveloped students would put things in his coffee cup, like eraser shavings, etc. So, as a natural response, when he returned to class he would automatically dump his cup out of the window and refill it from his thermos, never batting an eye about having his personal space and property violated.

One day, a particularly clever Moriarty of a social failure decided to pour the contents of the pencil sharpener into his thermos.

Mr. Maymo returned to class, dumped his cup, refilled it from the thermos, and proceeded to emotionally explode in a manner that had never been seen before in the history of Silver Lake. It wasn't the language and it wasn't the rage that caused everyone in the room to fear, it was when his voice shifted to something that sounded like it belonged in the soundtrack of a horror movie that stopped every heart for a beat.

No one ever trifled with his thermos again, although the tradition of dumping nasty things into his cup continued unabated.

I found a seat in the back and I tried to listen to his first day expectations speech. As he droned on I got a mental picture of his voice acting like an audio tranquilizer, slowly erasing all of my conscious thoughts until my mind was a pattern of late night TV snow.

"Don't pass out yet, the class is just starting," I heard from the seat to the left of me. I turned and saw Shirley Kowalski, who used to be friends with me when we were in junior high. At some point along the road of our physical development, she had become cool and I had been left behind with the masses, the common, less-pretty folk. Being one of the non-cools, I was part of a group that greatly outnumbered the cools, but the cools didn't seem to care. All of the cool kids had older siblings, and so they always developed earlier than the rest of us. They tried things that we wouldn't think of, and they had their own secret rituals and lifestyle. If someone was going to get caught smoking or drinking, it was going to be either a cool kid or a burn-out. If anyone was going to be "caught" in an altered state, it would most likely be a cool kid because the burn-outs were almost always a little off, so catching them clear and alert would be the rarity. The cool kids were the ones most likely to have had sex when they were in sixth grade, when I was barely sure of how to spell the word and was much too embarrassed to use it properly in a sentence.

The Saturday after my bike had been stolen from Moriah's house, I had gone for a walk. Shirley lived near the corner at the other end of my street. As I had been walking by, she noticed me and she invited me into her garage to watch some of her older brother's stop motion animation movies. It was odd to be included in Shirley's cool group, even if it only lasted for the afternoon. We laughed at the movies, ate popcorn and drank soda, and then the cools were looking for something more exciting to do. They decided that it would be way fun to fill old plastic model cars up with lighter fluid and fireworks, light them on fire, and then run them off the roof of the house, to explode into fireballs in midair.

I tried to look unconcerned, like I did this sort of thing all of the time, but the thought of being near flaming, exploding things caused me great concern. After a handful of impressive explosions which rained flaming and melted debris all across the front lawn, I decided that I should best be on my way back home. I thanked Shirley for the lovely afternoon and got out of there as quickly as a polite exit would allow.

The fact that she was deigning to speak to me in class seemed to indicate that I had not totally embarrassed myself at her home those few weeks before.

"This is my friend, Lynnette Frazho. Do you know Lynnette?" she asked.

"No, I can't say that I do. How do you..."

"Mr. Freeman, if I could interrupt your social life for a moment, I'd like to direct your attention to the handout that the rest of us are going over, please. Thank you," Mr. Maymo announced.

It was cosmically ironic that the cool girl who had initiated the disturbance was not noticed or embarrassed at that time. The cool kids seemed to have some sort of indescribable force field that prevented them from being publicly injured, as we common people often were. The class settled back down into its quiet, collective breathing, staring at the clock on the wall that seemed to be moving excruciatingly slowly.

Any slower, and we would all be traveling backwards in time.

"You've dropped a little weight in the last few weeks. You're looking good," Shirley whispered.

I was shocked on several levels. First, a cute girl had paid me a compliment, second, the compliment wasn't really an insult hidden within the fake shell of a compliment, and third...my mind just lost all focus and I replied...

"Thanks."

She smiled, and my mind came back to reality quickly. Her smile reminded me of a toothy cat, and cats like to toy with their food. I decided then and there that it's difficult to tell the difference between a cool kid on a recruiting drive, and a cool kid on a minion drive, or a cool kid on a new emotional plaything drive.

I had enough trouble trying to seem like a harmless minion to my family, without emotionally becoming one.

I hadn't thought about this aspect of my senior year. Lynnette glanced my way, but never said a word. Shirley looked my way a couple of times, but I pretended not to notice, and I spent all of my time drawing a caricature of Mr. Maymo on the back of his handout of class rules and expectations.

I could barely make out Rod Serling's voice in the back of my consciousness, saying, "There is a fifth dimension beyond that which is known to man. It is a dimension as vast as space and as timeless as infinity. It is the middle ground between light and shadow, between science and superstition, and it lies between the pit of man's fears and the summit of his knowledge. This is the dimension of imagination. It is an area which we call 'The Twilight Zone'."

I would swear that the clock hand hadn't moved in five minutes!

Second hour was English class, and my teacher was Mrs. Rowling. She had a pleasant, relatively quiet demeanor, but when someone offered her an impertinent remark, her face shifted to a smile that seemed to say, "I've been here since before they poured the foundations for this place. Cross me again and they'll never find your body." Classroom control was obviously not going to be a problem for her. I had been fortunate enough to have been assigned to a teacher who actually had a desire to teach us something. She was in charge of the school newspaper and the yearbook.

There were several other "old hands" in the building that had made an art form out of collecting their paycheck without actually having committed a single identifiable act of teaching anyone anything. The fellow who had won the "Teacher of the Year" award the year before had been the instructor for my Myths and Legends class as a junior. He came in the first day, passed out a syllabus that covered the entire semester, gave us our books, and then settled in for his daily ritual of reading the sports pages, while we filled in worksheets that he hadn't altered since his first year of teaching. If we made marks on the worksheets that resembled English, we got an "A" in the class.

Sad as he was, he hadn't been the worst teacher that I'd ever had. I had an art teacher who was supposed to teach us about using acrylic paints. The first day of class, we received our paints, which we had to pay him for, and then he pointed us to the criminally uninspired still life set up on a table in the middle of the room that we took a whole semester to "paint."

Third hour was Advanced Algebra and Trigonometry, taught by Mr. Scobas. Although, as a person, he was as quirky as the day was long, his former students said that after you got used to him, he was quite effective. Rumor had it that he always dressed the same way, every day. He wore a grey two-piece suit, with polished black shoes, a white shirt, and a black bowtie. His hair was always slicked straight back on his head, and he had a mild facial tick, where he'd scrunch up the right side of his face.

The favored story shared amongst the student body was of his giving a lesson on teaching base ten to a Martian. He pantomimed having a Martian enter the room and sitting at his desk at the front. He then engaged the Martian in a lengthy, if one-sided, conversation about how the Martian's base eight system of counting differed from our commonly-used base ten system of counting. The difference, he explained, was that the Martian's system had evolved from counting upon his fingers, and the Martian only had three fingers and a thumb on each hand, whereas we had four fingers and a thumb. After the lesson was complete, Mr. Scobas had suggested that the class get started on their homework, and he sat down at his desk. One of the more verbose students in the room had shouted out, "Mr. Scobas, you sat on the Martian!" Ever desiring the last laugh, Mr. Scobas had jumped up, pulled the back of his suit coat around to the front, and then asked the class "Is my coat green?"

His humor might be old and punny and corn-doggy, but at least it engaged the brain, as opposed to The Voice, which anesthetized the brain through the ears.

Fourth hour was choir, with Mr. Chase. Mr. Chase was a wonderful, caring man, but some of the more unkind souls in the school referred to him as "Popeye." When he was younger, he used to drive a bus. One day, he had driven his bus up an unusually steep driveway and the two tow hooks under the back bumper had dug into the blacktop of the driveway and had brought the bus to an immediate halt. His head had slammed down into the steering wheel, cutting the top of his right eyelid. The wound had healed, but his eyelid could no longer completely retract, which gave him the appearance of having one half-closed eye, hence the cruel nickname "Popeye."

The choir room was one of my favorite places in the school. I was impressed by its tiered seats. As one entered the door from the main hallway, you would be at the same level as the main floor of the school, but if you walked down the tiers to the bottom area, you would then be as the same level as the stage of the auditorium complex next door. The walls were covered with sound absorbing panels and there was a baby grand piano down at the front of the room for the accompanist. On the main level, to the right of the main entrance door, was the choir director's office. At the bottom of the room on the right side were the double metal doors to the music storage room, where I had spent many an hour sorting file cabinet after file cabinet of old music. I enjoyed bringing order to chaos.

Why did that passing comment seem so profound?

About half of my closest friends would be in choir with me this year. The other half, the decidedly unmusical half, I would see when the Drama Club met. Most people that I knew tended to have a set group of people that they gravitated to. I just floated around to whatever group would have me, making me a man without a definite country, but a ship accepted at nearly every port. I say nearly because there were groups of people who specialized in having no friends and making no friends. They tended to grow their hair long, often over their eyes, and hang out in the same general vicinity during lunch or between classes, but they acted more like the bumpers in a pinball game than interactive, sentient souls. They were almost like ghosts, and that was the way that they liked it. From time to time they'd show up in the back of one of my classes, but as long as no one bothered them, they just came in, took up space, did whatever they could to get a "D-" and then they peacefully drifted away. There wouldn't be any of that group in the choir class.

Choir was full of energy and had a healthy dynamic. Even those who sang relatively quietly found the energy to let their personalities off of the leash in choir. We had fun. We were a family, of sorts, and that was all because of the personality of Mr. Chase. He had a way of teaching that was more of an "I know that *we* can get this right" approach, as opposed to a "Why do *you people* keep getting this wrong?" approach. We choir members were very protective of our leader, and anyone making a crass comment about his eye ran the risk of acquiring a black one for themselves.

"So, are you going to run for choir president this year?" Moriah asked, giving me a healthy hip check as I walked through the door.

"No, I take great pride in my human wallpaper status, if you don't mind," I replied, as I peeled my upper shirt from the sound panel on the wall, which made an odd sound as it released me.

"Do you know what musical we're doing this year?" she continued.

"Not being as well-connected as you, I've only heard rumors. Do you know for sure?"

"I've heard that it's between…"

"Hi, Nick, how was your summer?"

I was a little surprised that Juliet had been so bold. She was usually a quiet type of person. Juliet and I had been friends ever since first grade, when my family had moved to this side of town. Never having been given an allowance, she had been my sole source of income throughout elementary school. She paid me a nickel a drawing to make large copies of Peanuts characters. She was a very quiet girl and seemed just as content to be sitting near a group as to be in the middle of a group. She had a generous nature, which is hard to find in school kids.

We heard, "Choir boys are fags" from the hallway and the sound of someone running away.

Moriah shouted back, "Those are pretty big words for such a small mind to use," and we all laughed.

"I doubt that he could spell all of his insults correctly, which is exactly why we're here, isn't it? We're here to stamp out stupidity, and bigotry, and..."

"And let's all take a seat, please," said Mr. Chase, entering from his office.

"That guy's lucky he ran away. If he'd stayed around, I would've crippled him with my rapier wit."

"Or at least confused him with words like 'rapier'," Juliet added.

"Let's all sit in our proper sections. Mike, unless you've undergone surgery over the summer that I'm not aware of, you're in the wrong section. You know where the tenors are, and Diane can last a few minutes all by herself without your attention," Mr. Chase announced.

The class laughed good-naturedly at Mike's mild flush of embarrassment, but everyone knew that Mr. Chase was just using a little humor to bring order to the class.

"Make some room, Nicki. I have to wade through the losers to get to the winners," Mike stated, attempting to get a laugh that was not at his expense.

Once he was seated, I leaned over and whispered to him.

"I don't swing at the easy pitches, my boy. If your wits are aching for a breakin', see me later." He laughed and gave me an affectionate slap on the shoulder.

"Welcome back, I hope each of you had a refreshing summer, because we've got a lot planned for the choir this year, not the least of which will be marching in the Thanksgiving Day Parade in front of Santa Claus."

The room got quieter and eyes got bigger. The Detroit Thanksgiving Day Parade down Woodward Avenue was a huge deal, and it was televised!

"Yes, let that thought sink in. You're all going to be on TV, and that means that your singing talents are also going to be on TV, which means that we all have some serious work to do. Another important item of business is electing new choir officers. Do I hear any nominations?"

The hand of a girl that I had never seen before shot up. She had reacted with an intensity that made me wonder if she hadn't just injured her wrist.

"And that reminds me, we have a new foreign exchange student with us this year. May I present Miss Gloria De la Vega."

The girl with the impressive enthusiasm jumped to her feet and turned to face the class. She smiled, waved, and then sat back down with the sopranos.

"And now, back to our nominations. Do I have any nominations for choir president?" Mr. Chase asked, as he grabbed a piece of chalk and walked to the blackboard.

"I nominate Nick Freeman," Moriah blurted out. She smiled at me and I pantomimed wringing her neck.

"That's one, anyone else?"

Miss Gloria De la Vega was waving her hand like her pants were on fire.

"Yes, Miss De la Vega? And who would you like to nominate?" Mr. Chase asked, patiently.

"I would like to nominate myself," she said, jumping up again and facing the class.

"Thank you for your enthusiasm. We have several positions to fill, folks: president, vice president, treasurer, secretary. Can we have some more nominations, please?"

After what seemed like an unusually long time, people were found to fill each position and it was tacitly agreed by the group that Gloria should be elected president, for certainly there was no one else in the room so rabidly obsessed about being elected to the job. Whether she actually spoke English fluently or not, we weren't sure yet, but we knew that it would all work out in the end. Traditionally, the choir officers were mostly honorary positions anyway.

"Vice president?" Moriah asked, as we were getting ready to have lunch.

"A secondary title, designed to appease a runner-up and to bestow upon them an honor that comes with minimal, if any, obligations. If someone decides to assassinate Gloria de la-enthusiasm, then I move up. Otherwise, I serve as her mindless puppet. Oh, the fickleness of politics," I said, smiling, "I've got most of the glory with almost none of the responsibility. I'll take it."

"I know you too well. Like you're going to sit back and let her drive the bus," Moriah replied, with a dubious look upon her face.

"Well, at least for the time being, I'm content to sit at the back. Once she bounces us off the roof once or twice, then maybe I'll rethink my position."

"Do you think that she's going to know how to design and build a float for Homecoming?"

"Time will tell," I shrugged.

We all settled down to our bag lunches and small talk. Most of us ate in the choir room because the cafeteria was just too crowded and too far away. Mr. Chase would allow us to go and get food, but by the time we had traveled the quarter mile to the other end of the building, gotten at the end of a five-hundred person line, purchased our food, battled hall monitors and returned, we'd have had about five minutes to scarf our lunch down.

Mr. Chase always had his lunch at his desk. He was on some sort of special diet and his wife made his lunch for him. Each day, he would carefully arrange his sandwich, his soup, his small salad, his juice, his fruit, and his cookie in a neat array before beginning. It was a ritual, and it felt a bit like sitting down to a family dinner.

Everyone settled back into their traditional lunch practices: Mike was chatting up Diane, Juliet was reading one of her Peanuts books off sort of by herself, only surrounded by a gaggle of chattering girls, and Moriah was getting me up to speed on the latest choir, drama, and general school gossip.

"She told the entire class that she got married over the summer, and that she had divorced him after only three days!"

Everyone seemed to be in their own world, except for a junior by the name of Marci Eston. I thought that I caught her looking at me several times during lunch, but she never came over. I had danced with her in last year's musical, *No, No, Nanette*. She was nice and she laughed at my feeble attempts at jokes, but there seemed to be something going on with her, just behind her smile. As Moriah slugged me to make sure that I was paying attention, and then returned to chatting away, I found myself wondering if Marci would've come over to say hello if Moriah hadn't been so close to me.

Fourth hour, the best hour of the day, inevitably segued into fifth hour and I had to leave my little family to go out into the cold, cruel school to Chemistry class with Miss Heinkel. I really wasn't sure why I had allowed myself to be talked into taking Chemistry. I certainly didn't need the science credit, and I had no idea what I would do with what I learned in that class in real life. Of course, I had the same general situation with math. I was good at both math and science, but I wasn't going to pursue careers in either field. I had taken Biology "B" earlier, which was the simpler of the two intro science classes offered at Silver Lake. I was a bit bored silly, but again, I wasn't looking for a career in science. The teacher, Mr. Rudd, who wondered what I was doing in that class on several different occasions, used to grab my test from the class pile and use it as the answer key.

Whereas I had many friends in choir class, I found that I had none in Chemistry. The classroom was full of bones and skeletons and taxidermy exhibits of small animals, but the worst part of it all was the large terrarium at the back of the room, filled with live snakes. Even if I was looking at the front of the room and copying notes off of the board, there was a part of me intently listening for any type of sound coming from behind, from the slithery things. The rumor had been that she used to keep tarantulas too, but that they had died. All that was left of them was their discarded husks stored in a glass case. I quickly discovered that the rumors were wrong, for a large and perfectly healthy specimen of a tarantula was sitting squarely in the middle of Miss Heinkel's front desk. I wasn't interested in the anatomy, the social habits, or the history of things that slithered or crept silently upon eight legs, but trapped in Miss Heinkel's room, there was no way to ignore her preoccupation with such things.

Miss Heinkel herself was different, to say the least. She looked each student up and down when they entered the room, as if making some sort of mental note about something. When I walked in she muttered to herself, "Interesting. I've never seen an aura that color before." It was unnerving that she was muttering to herself, and in passing, I noticed that I probably shouldn't have been able to hear what she said about me, but somehow, I had. I wondered what an aura was, and why mine wasn't like everyone else's.

There was also a disturbing smell. I couldn't tell if it was coming from her, or if it was coming from the preserved dead things that the room was full of, and by day-long association, stuck to her. There was nothing about her room, her things, her person or her teaching style that made me feel comfortable, so I made a promise to myself to try to blend in with the scenery to the point of near-invisibility. When in doubt, disappear, had always been a motto that had worked for me in the past. As I looked over at the other faces in the class, I got the impression that they were nowhere near as on-edge as I was myself. I was about to introduce myself to a fellow sitting next to me when I saw the notes that he had taken in his binder pertaining to Miss Heinkel's class rules and expectations.

A chill ran up my spine.

The notes were executed in a tiny, precise hand that only went halfway across the page, like the scribe was used to being restricted to a certain column width in order to write.

Images flashed immediately through my mind that threw me back into my chair. Fortunately for me, this didn't make enough noise to attract the attention of Miss Heinkel, or of the boy that I had leaned over to introduce myself to.

I saw columns, columned books, book on top of book on top of book. He wore a grey uniform, and he was filling in seemingly endless columns with names, hundreds and thousands of names. The records must be precise. Every name needed to be spelled correctly and each entry date and each death date recorded. Treblinka, what on earth is a Treblinka? It was a place, a place where they killed almost 1,700 people a day! Where was this information coming from? Who was this creepy kid next to me, meticulously noting everything that Miss Heinkel said to the class in a hand that made the hairs on the back of my head stand up?

I felt that I had just been paroled from prison when the class change bell went off. I couldn't get away from that class fast enough. Thoughts of requesting an immediate schedule change filled my head, as I was bumped and elbowed down the hallway.

My last class of the day was Independent Study in Drama, which was actually my taking Drama 2 for the second time as independent study because there wasn't such a thing as Drama 3. The class was in the auditorium, and the teacher was Mr. DeVries. Mr. DeVries and I got along fairly well, at least in the beginning. I had gotten a couple of small parts in his earlier shows and I had done quite well. I had also taken upon myself to learn everything that I could about theatre set design, theatre make-up, costumes, and special effects. The more that I delved into theatre, the more Mr. DeVries seemed to look at me with an air of "Are you bucking for my job?" The year before, to assist him in casting for the fall play, I had written down the number of lines each character had on each page of the script, as an aid in figuring out what sections should be copied and used as audition scenes for what characters.

He took it from me, looked it over and said, "Who taught you this?"

"No one, it just seemed like a logical way to figure the audition scenes out," I replied, innocently.

"Really, we never used anything like this at Central," he muttered, as he walked away.

"Glad I could be of use," I whispered after him, "A thank-you for the effort would've been great, but you're welcome anyway."

The more I learned, the more he seemed to suspect that I knew, and the more uneasy he seemed to get around me. When I had told him my junior year that I didn't need his assistance with my make-up, he was a bit taken aback. When I showed him that I had mastered the application of theatre make-up, he seemed impressed, for a fleeting moment, and then he happily assigned me the task of supervising everyone else's make-up, which is what he had been doing. From that point on I had endless opportunities to show off my abilities. It was a compliment, of sorts, I tried to assure myself. Anyway, over the last two years we had established a working relationship, which often meant that he had an idea and I did the working, but hey, I was there to learn anyway.

The only part of Mr. DeVries that I really didn't care for was stored in the locked bottom of a file cabinet in the first stage left storeroom. He, like my stepfather, liked to drink. He, unlike my stepfather, preferred hard liquor, and I had a feeling that before my time with him was over, that little bottle hiding in the shadows was going to rock all of our worlds, in one way or another.

Since I was on independent study, I got the honor of doing the more mundane tasks, like taking attendance and filling out forms. Whenever Mr. DeVries needed something demonstrated I was to be his marionette. Considering how much I loved the theatre and loved being in the auditorium, I really didn't mind. My theatre friends weren't in the Drama 2 class for one of two reasons, either they had already had the class, or they weren't actors, they were techies, and they would show up to build and paints sets, avoiding the drama classes where they were required to do pantomime, perform monologues, and act out scenes.

The big hams had already come and gone, and the little hams only came out on stage when the conditions were just right. I guess that made me the super-ham of the analogy, because I had found a way to extend my drama experience and still get class time credit for it.

As the first day of class was ending, I saw Mr. DeVries watching a red-headed senior girl leave, and I heard him mutter, "If only I was twenty years younger."

Not knowing if he had intended me to hear his comment or not, I grabbed my supplies and left. I did not wish to establish a dynamic with Mr. DeVries that would potentially include listening to more of this same type of comment in the future. I just pretended not to hear.

"See you tomorrow, Mr. DeVries," I said, as vacuously as I could. Being around this man was definitely going to help me with my acting skills, I decided.

CHAPTER SEVEN
Zotia

Other than knowing that my grandparents had come to America directly from Poland, had endured having their family name butchered at Ellis Island, and that my Grandpa Nelek had spent a time working the coal mines of Pennsylvania, I didn't know much about the history of my family. I didn't even know what our real name was, Grandpa Nelek having officially changed it to a generic and American-sounding Freeman after the painful Ellis Island incident. I didn't get to see my Dad's family very often. We usually saw them around various holidays, when my Dad would pick Steven and myself up, often without warning. Getting home from school on a Friday or on the last day of school before a break and finding a suitcase waiting for us at the front door was a sure sign that we were leaving.

There was a fairly regular pattern to our time spent with my father. He would pull into the driveway, my mother would say good-bye, we'd load into his car, and then we'd drive away. If we were going to his home, north of Gaylord, then the long drive would begin with a sort of "So, what have you done lately?" inquiry, to bring him up to speed on any bragging points that there might be. After having parts in plays for two years, I realized that he had never made the time to see me in a single performance.

Our time together was never about him acting like a father; it was always about our acting like obedient and respectful children. We may not have been all that important to him, but I was thankful that at least he didn't seem to dislike us.

After an hour or two, we'd stop for dinner, and the conversation would drop away dramatically. My Dad didn't like engaging in "fatherly" talks and avoided delicate subjects altogether, so it wasn't long before we were riding in silence in the dark.

After a drive of over four hours, we would arrive at his house, set on a piece of property thirty-three acres large. My Dad, my stepmother, and their five kids lived in a metamorphic sort of house. What had initially been a fifty-foot trailer anchored on the edge of the woods, had grown into a large two-story house that was still under construction after several years. Instead of a house with a kitchen addition on the side, the trailer, which included the kitchen, had a full grown house that had grown out of it.

My Dad was known for his big ideas.

With the second floor of the house incomplete and the main floor of the house barely livable, he had decided that he eventually wanted to live in a house where he could drive his car down a ramp and park in the basement, and so, near the north edge of the property stood a foundation with a long, sloping driveway to the bottom of it. He had mostly lost interest in the foundation, just as he had mostly lost interest in the main house. The only thing on the property that had been completed was a large welding shop, located at the end of the circle driveway and just south of the big house.

My father had been a successful welder and had originally set up his shop near the Hazelnut Racetrack on Decadia. He and his men used to frequent the racetrack during their lunch hour, betting on the horses. Eventually, he got the idea into his head of moving his entire family to the great north woods and setting up shop there. Normally, finding enough welding to do in that area of Michigan would've been somewhat of a challenge, but he had hit upon a money-making scheme with his new brother-in-law, Chester. Through Chester, he would be awarded a contract with General Motors to weld the open ends of seatbelt links closed, for a few pennies each piece. With this major job lined up and believing that the money would be flowing indefinitely, he erected a large welding shop on his property and began transporting the seatbelt pieces north.

It looked like everything was going to go fine with his new business, but then his brother-in-law Chester got greedy and wanted an increase in his kickback for securing the job. It seemed that General Motors had a policy expressly prohibiting close relatives of employees from being granted company contracts, which was an attempt to eliminate just the sort of greed and graft that my Dad found himself unexpectedly embroiled in. My Dad had acted like the king of the hill at the beginning of the previous summer, when we'd come to stay with him, because the money was flowing and there was no end in sight. By the time the school year had started, all that had become a bitter memory.

Because of the immense debt incurred setting up the welding shop, Chester concluded that my Dad had no choice but to agree to funnel more of his profits back into the brother-in-law's pockets. My Dad, prideful and stubborn as he was, refused to agree to the additional blackmail. Then Chester cancelled the contract, threatened my Dad not to try and make trouble for him with General Motors or our family would have "accidents," and then found another welder who was willing to kick back the percentage of the profits that he was looking for.

This left my Dad in a terrible situation. He had an expensive welding shop located in a charmingly woodsy corner of upper Michigan that didn't have the local work necessary to support it, and he was in debt over the whole situation right up to his nose, on top of the incomplete main house and the purely decorative open basement foundation nestled in the tall weeds. My Dad's family, I was told, was mostly oblivious to his dire financial situation, and they continued to ride their bikes and motorcycles around the back woods trails, while financial clouds of ruin collected around them, just out of sight. There was no telling when the bank would decide that enough was enough and take possession of the property.

The truly sad aspect of the story, at least as related to me by my Dad, was that Chester got off Scott free, having blackmailed what he could out of my father and then moving on to suck someone else financially dry.

When we were to be staying locally, my Dad would pick us up and usually take us to his parent's new home at Trinity Corner and Highland, about twenty miles north. I could see why my grandfather would want more property than he had when he lived locally, but I couldn't understand why he had bought the house that he had. It wasn't really a house at all. It was a large cinderblock garage that had been subdivided into a living space and a garage space. It was surrounded by a few acres of farmable land, where my Grandfather Nelek planted corn, beans, and tomatoes. Behind the cinderblock house/garage the previous owner had built an additional garage for the tractor and the field tools. On the property at the back, my grandparents had sold the land to my Aunt Carmen, and she and her husband Billy had built a new house there, complete with a pool table in the basement, making them the envy of the immediate family.

My family, and particularly my father, thrived on competition. My Dad told tales of having supported himself through high school by hustling pool. He didn't talk so much about bowling and archery because it seemed that my mother had been better at both endeavors than he, which he found a bit embarrassing. I took his stories as the truth for I knew what lengths he would go to in order to crush me in a chess game or a pool match, which was why I almost never played any games with him. From time to time I'd agree to play chess, and then I play without rhyme or reason and drive him crazy with my irrational tactics, right up to the moment that he would win.

Although I liked my Aunt Carmen as a person, I never found her to be the brightest bulb in the box. One time when I was there visiting, I overheard her tell my stepmother, Vivian, that she never washed the bottoms of the dishes because it was a waste of time and no one ever eats off of the bottoms anyway. Then I watched her stack the plate that she had in her hand on top of another stack of plates.

Oi!

Back to my grandparent's "house," it was always chilly and damp, much like my dungeon basement, because it was built on a concrete slab and was never intended to be a home. Water to the house was provided by a well pump house located up the driveway, closer to the main street. It was an odd-looking but thoroughly robust little construct, having been made completely of cinderblock and only about the size of an outhouse. No one ever went there, but it brought attention to itself every once in a while by the clicking and the pumping sound that it made drawing up the well water. The water in the house had a metallic taste that was quite unlike anything that Steven and I were used to, so we never drank it if we could avoid it. It left iron stains on the sinks and the toilet. On the main floor of the house there was the kitchen sink, the stove, and the refrigerator in the kitchen "area," one small bathroom, a back room and a stairway leading up to the second floor. There was a single space heater located centrally in the living room, but it was all functionally one room. All the space heater accomplished was keeping the ice from forming on the inside of the walls, and anyone who used the bathroom in the dead of winter and closed the door endured an event much like using a real outhouse, for the water would start to freeze in the toilet. There wasn't even the psychological illusion of heat in the back room or on the second floor. Sleeping upstairs meant lying under several blankets or quilts with only your nose and forehead exposed to the frost. It felt a lot like having been baked into a pie crust, with all of the weight of the blankets bearing down. These were the primitive, third-world types of conditions Steven and I would endure when my Dad brought his family for a visit.

Grandpa Nelek would be sitting on the couch, watching TV, while Grandma Zotia was busy on her side of the room, cooking. Her livelihood of spirit and the wonderful smells emanating from the food that she was preparing were the only uplifting things in the place.

I could say that she was a handsome woman, but that would probably be misleading. She was plump, and had a manly look about her, even with her longer, salt and pepper hair. My father and I bore a striking resemblance to her, and since we looked like mildly handsome men, she was not a person of particularly dainty features. That said, it didn't matter, because the sound of her voice, the sparkle in her eye, and the love in her cooking were valued by me beyond measure, and more or less diametrically opposed to the impression that Grandpa Nelek conveyed.

Other than having worked in the coal mines of Pennsylvania as a younger man, and being able to weld and farm a little, I knew essentially nothing about Grandpa Nelek, other than he could scowl with great effectiveness.

Steven and I were related to my mother, and the law forbade Grandpa Nelek from strangling us on the spot to get back at her, so he didn't really speak to us except long distance through his scowl.

Before arriving at the house to hook up with the rest of the family, my Dad had a tradition of stopping at the corner hardware store in town. There we would be given the opportunity to select whatever it took to keep us quietly occupied for the rest of our visit there. I would often select a plastic Aurora model to build, and my younger brother would select balsa airplanes, balls, and such to occupy his time. The visit would often start with me on the inside, trying to put my model together with no tools, cheap glue, and no paints, and Steven would start outside, flying his plane and generally running all over the yard. Before long, Nelek would decide that I should clean up my model mess and go outside in the fresh air, probably because he didn't want to look at me anymore, and Steven would be brought inside for punishment because he almost invariably would snap the branches off of the big willow tree in the front yard and whip the other kids raw with them.

Just before crossing Steven's path at the front door, Grandma Zotia would often give me something to eat on my way out, as a preview of dinner which would be served soon. This gesture of affection was always appreciated by myself, but not always appreciated by the other related men in the room, as I have touched upon before.

Over the years, I had brought to this house several items that Grandma Menafay and Grandpa Eugene had considered getting rid of from their house. Sometimes the items were little things, like decorative knickknacks or candy dishes, and sometimes the items were actually worth something, like the time I was allowed to bring them a pair of silver candelabra because Grandma Menafay had grown tired of cleaning all of their little blackened grooves. Grandma Zotia had been overwhelmed by the generous gesture, and Grandpa Nelek had deigned to look in the direction of the candelabra, which was a big thing for him to do. Although they couldn't have possibly looked more out of place in that dingy, chilly, almost room, Grandma Zotia placed them on a shelf for all to see, and she asked me to thank my other grandparents energetically.

Grandma Zotia spent almost all of the time that we were together making food. She made perogies from scratch, gwumpkies, and pan-fried pork chops, the very mention of which would make my father's mouth involuntarily water. She never had any spare time, and I didn't have any recollections of her where she wasn't cooking or cleaning in the kitchen, although my Dad did mention that at the end of the day she did enjoy a stiff drink. We never went out as a family to a restaurant, or to a park, or shopping, and I don't have a single memory of her being outside of her kitchen, except for after she died.

Because Steven and I were outsiders when it came to family matters, I had no warning that my grandmother was ill. When my father called, a couple of weeks after school had begun, it was just to say that Grandma Zotia was dead and that he'd pick us up for the funeral.

Amidst my tears, I prayed for her soul and I drew a picture of her, with the wings of a bluebird, flying up to Heaven. The picture made my father cry, and he promised to put it into the coffin with her.

At her funeral was the last time that he saw her, but it was not the last time that I saw her.

As a rule, I almost never invited anyone over to see our house, and more specifically, my dungeon. After we heard that the fall play was going to be *Arsenic and Old Lace*, I invited several people over to read lines the weekend before auditions, so that we would have a better idea about what parts we wanted. The girl parts were never really in question because Crystal and Hayley had the two main roles sewed up, as far as the rest of us were concerned. Crystal was the female ingénue of the Silver Lake Players and this was her senior year, so that didn't take a lot of heavy thinking to prognosticate. Hayley was a junior, and she and Crystal had become fast friends, bosom buddies, and Siamese twins of sorts, not that this was always a good thing. I had known Crystal for a couple of years now, and I had always thought of her as being quite talented and determined. She was the captain of the school's dance troop, which was sarcastically called "The Flying Flab," but that label was misleading. They were actually quite good. She had performed major roles ever since stepping on stage in tenth grade. The year before, she had starred in the school musical *No, No, Nanette*, but that had pretty much ended her singing career, because she came to realize that she really wasn't confident in the area of singing. In the areas of dancing and acting, she was virtually unmatched. When it came to singing, she was a little bit of a fish out of water, and so she had reconciled herself to a senior year focusing upon her strengths and avoiding her weaknesses.

There had been a time, at the end of my junior year, when I had contemplated riding my bike over to her house and seeing if we could be better friends. I drove by several times, but I never got up the nerve to knock on her door. I thought that she was a sweet girl who occasionally had a catty side that cropped up without warning.

Then she hooked up with Hayley and the proportion of sweet to catty seemed to shift overnight. Hayley had older siblings and so she gravitated towards the cool kids, the ones who already knew all about the world because they had either heard about their older siblings doing practically everything, been exposed to the friends of their older siblings doing practically everything, or they had done practically everything themselves

Crystal seemed to have lost her kinder, gentler side somewhere along the way, which made her amazingly like Hayley.

Hayley had a way of covering her mouth with her hand and laughing at you from across the room that made you feel absolutely worthless. When Crystal started to develop her own sort of "Let's mock the lesser people together" laugh, the play people group got to be significantly less fun to be around. I still had hopes that it was just a silly adolescent phase and that both girls would grow out of it, but with the two of them playing the murderous female leads in the play, Martha and Abby Brewster, growing out of it seemed unlikely. If anything, a perfection of their cool and superior techniques seemed assured.

The real question was who was going to play the male roles. There was the male ingénue, Mortimer Brewster, and everyone thought that this would be a good part for me, but I looked over the lines and found them boring and predictable. The part I really yearned to play was the crazy guy, Teddy Brewster, who thought that he was Teddy Roosevelt, charging up San Juan Hill. The funny part was coveted by an almost-friend of mine who lived on my grandparent's street by the name of Victor Carnevale. He had glasses and longish hair that seemed to predictably drape across his forehead and face like some sort of scar. He also liked to stand with his shoulders forward, reminiscent of a Frankenstein monster at rest. Like a bulldog with a new chew toy, he wasn't going to let go of the role willingly, and who was I to say, "Hey, the male lead doesn't really interest me. Do you mind if I try to take your smaller, funny role from you?" My old Boy Scout buddy Kevin was there and it seemed that he was gravitating towards trying out for the Boris Karloff part, which was fine by me. He was a very easy-going person and would be just as happy if he was given the part of designated dead body in the window seat. Before I was granted access to a car, I used to walk to school each day, joining up with Kevin at the end of his street for the almost two-mile trek. Kevin was always fighting inside of himself between his acting side and his techie side. More often than not, the techie side won. He had helped me wire a six foot chandelier that I had assembled out of plywood arms, butter bowls, and coffee cans for last year's play. Strung with plastic baubles, the chandelier had been quite impressive and had cost basically nothing to make.

Our pre-audition meeting wound down and everyone started leaving, until only Kevin and I were left in the basement. I had promised to give Kevin a ride back home and I went into my bedroom to get my windbreaker from my closet. The instant that I stepped into my bedroom, I knew that something was wrong. I sensed something standing at the foot of my bed, between myself and my closet. The room was dark, but there was enough ambient light coming in from the hallway and the other side of the basement to see fairly well.

Before my gaping eyes, a shape coalesced just past the footboard of my bed.

There was a negative shape of a person, and it seemed to be growing closer, getting larger. I was frozen in place. I was being approached by a shadow, and then I recognized the shape of the shadow. It was the shape of my Grandmother Zotia. This realization washed over me just as the shadow form reached me. An electrical current began running wildly up and down my spine, like my back had been plugged into an electric socket.

From the other room, I heard Kevin yell out. I rushed to the other side of the basement to find him staggering.

"What was THAT!?" he yelled.

"What was what?" I asked.

"I just had some sort of electricity run up and down my back," Kevin stammered.

"I don't know. It just happened to me too, while I was in my bedroom."

"That was seriously WEIRD," he exclaimed.

"I'll get my coat and be right back."

"Yes, sir, I'm definitely ready to go home now."

I entered the bedroom with more than a little trepidation, but there was no sign of the shadow of my grandmother. The more that I thought about what had happened, the more a sense of calm began to wash over me, which seemed to be the opposite effect to what was happening with Kevin, and he continued muttering loudly to himself in the other room. I grabbed my jacket and we left the basement.

"Next time, let's do this at my house," Kevin exclaimed, as we pulled out of the driveway.

I was quite certain that there wasn't going to be a next time. Whatever had happened had been a unique, once-in-a-lifetime occurrence.

"Close, but not exactly," my grandmother's voice seemed to say in the back of my mind, "You'll get used to it after a while."

I pondered for a moment how one would self-tighten a mental screw, for one in my head seemed to be coming loose.

Grandma Zotia laughed loudly in my mind, which was both comforting and disconcerting at the same time.

CHAPTER EIGHT
Homecoming

Every year, the high school made a big deal about Homecoming, which occurred in the middle of October. For those of us still attending Silver Lake, it was a busy time, and for us who were seniors and involved in several groups, it was insane. To begin with, there was going to be a school parade, and all of the classes and all of the various clubs and groups were expected to build floats. So, somehow, a person like me was expected to be involved with the design and creation of the senior float, the choir float, and the Drama Club float, all being constructed at different private residences scattered around town.

I decided to focus my attentions on the choir float, mostly because I was the vice-president and Gloria was causing some confusion about how the choir should react with the rest of the world this year. She had several noble intentions of using the choir to increase the world's awareness of various social outrages, like the plight of the migrant farm workers, or the work of Amnesty International. However, turning the choir into a political action group was far from Mr. Chase's dream for us for that year. And so, with each attempt by Gloria to get the choir to make signs of outrage concerning this or that, or to stage a rally or a sit-down protest, it became my unofficial job to reel her back in to the boundaries of traditional expectations. She wanted the choir on the front page of the local newspapers each week, shouting outrage and changing the world, and the school preferred that the choir be featured on page five or ten, every month or so, photographed entertaining the world. Although she tried her best, the wishes of the school administrators were quietly conveyed to Mr. Chase, and then to the rest of us, and active social reform became the main focus of someone else.

The theme for the parade was nursery rhymes, and the middle of September school announcements were filled with requests for trailers and large, convertible cars for the Homecoming Court and various local school dignitaries to ride in. Once a driveway and a trailer had been secured, then it was time to design the float to fit the trailer and to begin the process of manufacturing tissue pom-poms to decorate the float with. Although color selection was far from infinite, there were several basic tissue colors to choose from, and if the group wanted to take on the additional effort of cutting up colored plastic bags into strips to be made into shiny pom-poms, then even more effects became possible. Dates and times would be set up and people would drop by over a two or three week period, for the most part to make pom-poms, what we usually referred to as "flowers." A small group of students, those who were more adept with screws, nails, and power tools, were given the task of creating the wooden forms needed to affix the flowers to. The floats were being made in every size. Some floats were constructed on tiny, six foot long trailers, while others were built on car-hauling trailers. The difference in effort required between these extremes in size was incredible.

The choir decided to do Jack jumped over the candlestick. Considering my artistic background, I was given the task of designing the float and guiding the building of the framework. Jack was to be halfway in his leap above a very large candle with a particularly malicious face on it. The candle was about four feet tall, and Jack, if he were straightened up from his leaping posture, would've been nine or ten feet tall. Coming out of Jack's mouth at the moment of his leap was a musical note, broken in the middle because of his closeness to the candle's flame. It was quite a large undertaking. Every week, the call went out for volunteers, and every week a few new faces would trickle in. The float-building process slowly built up momentum towards the evening before the parade, which would traditionally be a full-out frenzy of assembly, lasting long into the night.

I had decided that I should ask a girl to go to the dance with me that year. For other, more confident, cooler kids, that thought would've been the merest of footnotes in the evolution of their social life, but I didn't really have a social life outside of the group activities that I was involved in. I had been out for pizza dozens of times, for instance, but I'd never really been out for pizza on a date, alone with a girl before. The last dance that I had attended was the ninth grade graduation dance, held in the gymnasium of the junior high, which had originally been the high school building constructed to replace my grandparent's one-room schoolhouse, back in the twenties. By the time I attended school there, it had grown from its original four room brick structure to a sprawling two-story complex with multiple gymnasiums and several architectural oddities, the kind found only in buildings that evolved over a long period of time through the efforts of people solving classroom problems, as opposed to adding on to original structures with architectural style. Odd nooks and crannies abounded, like the strange second floor classroom across from the library that had originally served as balcony seating for the old gym, the very long ramp stuffed in between the cafeteria and the old gym that led down to the mechanical bowels of the building, and the basement of the original structure, where the AV department worked without the benefit of natural light or air because there were no windows.

I had been on the newspaper and yearbook staff my last year in Kickapoo Junior High, and so I became familiar with most of what was happening in the school, not that I could be a part of it. I was expected to be home after school during those years, and so I wasn't a part of any extracurricular group. The only activity that I got permission to attend was the graduation dance. I thought about asking someone to go to the dance with me, but I chickened out.

Actually, it was less a matter of my chickening out and more a matter of losing interest in the girl involved.

My infatuation with Zephyr had begun almost the minute that I transferred into Beechnut Elementary School, halfway through first grade. I have no idea why we moved then, but it probably had something to do with my mom and dad's divorce becoming final and my dad's parents wanting my mother out of their old house so that they could sell it. At any rate, I found myself plucked from my previous school and plopped down into a room full of people who all knew each other, and it was a bit daunting. Slowly, over time, I made new friends, mostly through my artistic abilities. My first friend was Juliet Norris, who became the first member of my artistic fan club. It was refreshing to have Juliet blurt out how marvelous my drawing ability was, and I was often taken aback that someone would be so complimentary to me. My Grandpa Eugene and Grandma Menafay were always praising me, but I just assumed that it was part of their official code of being proper grandparents. My mother never complimented me about anything because she thought that I'd get a swelled head if everyone raved about my talents. She said that she was bound and determined to make sure that I never got a big head. She seemed to take that oath to heart.

I guess that one could say that I have a quality of sticking to a project, either to its completion or to its destruction. For some reason that even now I can't explain, I found myself oddly fascinated by this very quiet girl in my class, with her very big hair, and her very big eyes that reminded me of Bambi. To say that she was shy wouldn't begin to describe her. Unless called upon directly, she never talked, and I got it into my mind that I wanted to be her friend. And so, I tried to connect to her, with classroom Christmas cards and Valentine's Day cards, and even fleeting moments of attempted conversation. She would just smile, blush, and look away, and I'd get embarrassed and walk on, feeling that I'd made my gesture for the day and that maybe tomorrow, she'd respond with something more substantial than a change in her cheek coloring.

This went on, pretty much unchanged, for about seven years. In the intervening time I had discovered, not from her, of course, that she was the oldest of three daughters of a local marina owner, which explained her rather unique name, Zephyr. She was adopted at some point by some of the cool kids, although I have no idea why. She certainly didn't have the dynamic required to be a cool kid, so she must've been regarded as a minion, or maybe a cute pet. The cool kids sometimes adopted pets for a time, and then discarded them, but Zephyr being a part of their group continued through elementary school and into junior high, inexplicably. Perhaps it was because of her family's access to the marina and family boats.

As I said, I tend to stick with things, often disregarding logic.

She became the mystery that I was determined to solve, and as long as she didn't tell me to take a long hike off of a short pier, I convinced myself that anything was possible, and so I quietly pressed on.

Trying to get a real conversation out of Zephyr wasn't the only thing on my to-do list.

While attending Kickapoo Junior High, I did several notable things, at least notable in the life of a person who hadn't really done anything.

In my three years there, I had the pleasure of having the same English teacher for two-and-a-half-years straight, which became a sort of private joke between Mrs. Quarn and me. By the time I was in ninth grade, she considered me a sort of official classroom assistant, merely because of mathematical improbability of my having had her semester after semester when there were eight other English teachers in the building. To cap off my extended time with her, I decided to give an oral report on Mark Twain, dressed in costume and make-up, minus the almost obligatory cigar.

What had prompted this major endeavor had been my stumbling over a photo essay of Hal Holbrook putting on his Mark Twain make-up for his one-man show, *Mark Twain Tonight!* Although I didn't have any access to a real theatrical wig, or a bald cap, or stage pancake, I decided I'd give it a try using an old Santa beard that I'd found, and whatever leftover make-up Grandma Menafay would give me. And so, armed with a pile of supplies that were not exactly what I needed, I tried to recreate Hal Holbrook's Mark Twain face. To complete the illusion, I borrowed Grandpa Eugene's light grey suit. Fortunately for me, he'd kept all of his old suits from the time that he was a purchaser for the Ford Products Company. My early acting career starred his old clothing as much as it starred me.

I used the Santa beard sort of upside down and backwards to make Mark Twain's hair and I held it in shape with bobby pins and a heavy dosing of Aqua Net hairspray. A careful trimming of the beard gave me enough extra hair to make the moustache, and a little rubber cement held the moustache in place, although the rubber cement was a bit rough on my young skin and it gave me a little rash. The base that my Grandma Menafay used was quite pink, but with a bit of careful blending and the use of a black and brown eyebrow pencil, the end result was fairly impressive for someone who had no idea what he was doing. I applied the make-up in the boy's bathroom by the main office during English class, and when I walked to Mrs. Quarn's outside portable room past the office, I turned quite a few heads.

Mrs. Quarn was both surprised and amazed at the effort that I had gone through to present my speech because I was getting a solid "A" from her anyway, so additional effort on this scale was not required. I found that I liked overachieving in this fashion, especially when the people involved didn't see it coming. I had found the looks from the office secretaries quite refreshing when I had walked by. Their expressions had shown that they hadn't known whether to ask me if I needed directions, or to let me continue on my way out of the building without bothering me. They seemed to think I really was an old man.

I had spent a year learning how to type while having the rather tedious job of typing three different copies of index cards for each new book acquired by the library. I enjoyed working in the library, but there were several times when I regretted having taken on the job of typist before having taken a typing class. I became much more proficient than a typical hunt-and-peck two-fingered typist, but I never learned to use all ten of my fingers. As long as I knew what I was going to type, or I was able to look in the general direction of the keyboard, I was a fairly impressive six-fingered typist, although I did get an eraser with an attached brush as a Christmas gift from Mrs. Kugan because of my predisposition to strike-over, rather than erase my mistakes.

I also came to the attention of one of the counselors there, a Mr. Wilson. Mr. Wilson asked me to paint his caricature on the side of his file cabinet in his office. I painted him putting a key into a student's ear and opening up the top of the student's head. He was immensely pleased with the results, and it was the first thing that a person saw when they entered his office. The summer before entering Silver Lake High School, Mr. Wilson paid me to paint a large mural on the wall of his condominium basement. It was a Bible passage about the lion lying down with the lamb. After extensive research of the Bible, I discovered that a specific verse saying that didn't exist. The saying was a synthesis of two adjoining verses. He picked me up over the course of several Saturdays and he paid me to paint the 8'x10' black and white mural on the basement wall, at the bottom of the stairs. After I finished the mural, I gave him the original sketch. He had the sketch professionally framed, and then he presented it to the Kickapoo Junior High librarians to be placed on permanent display.

My most obvious and lasting contribution was designing the logo for the school and painting it on the center of the gym floor.

My most obvious and lasting memory had to do with the ever-mysterious girl by the name of Zephyr and the ninth grade graduation dance.

The ninth grade graduation dance was going to be the biggest event of our three years at Kickapoo, and everyone was abuzz about it. All of my friends seemed to be going, although who they would be going with wasn't very clear because most people in ninth grade didn't have a dating life or a person that they were officially connected to. There were quite a few couples by association in school, but that wasn't the same as being officially declared off limits to the flirtations of classmates of the opposite sex. The dance was having an odd way of prodding casual relationships up to the next level. I didn't have to worry about any next-level stuff because I had never had a relationship with any girl, other than maybe eliciting a chuckle at a joke from time to time from a girl. As the end of the year crept forward, conversations turned to, "Who are you going with?" and "What are you wearing?" In my art class, we were busy making signs promoting the graduation dance, and it seemed that every ninth grader was emotionally required to be involved with the process, or risk being labeled as a disinterested loser.

As I scratched my hasty illustrations into the last edition of the school newspaper with my stylist, trying my best to score the mimeo film without tearing it, I decided to ask Zephyr to go to the dance with me. After all, what had I to lose? I'd always been nice to her, and I couldn't think of anyone else who'd ask her. If I didn't ask her, she probably wouldn't go, I deduced. Although she was a cool kid pet, that didn't make her the date of a cool kid, and so she'd probably be left out, and that was sad.

I finished my work and set about making her a card, asking her to the dance. I was much more confident in my artwork speaking for me than in my voice speaking for me. Since she was almost never alone, if I wanted to ask her out verbally, I'd have to do it in front of other people. With a card, she could open it at her leisure, without prying eyes around, and decide whether she wanted to go with me without being pressured.

That was the plan, I decided.

I finished the card, which asked if she'd like to attend the graduation dance with me in a fashion that was both respectful and affectionate without seeming stupid or mushy, and I began looking for an opportunity to give it to her.

Well, things didn't go as I'd hoped, and every time that I found her for the next couple of days she was surrounded by a gaggle. There was no way that I could've swooped in undetected, said hello, given her the card and disengaged without drawing major attention to myself, which was the last thing that I wanted to do. I was not a cool kid, and so my swooping into the personal space of a group of cool kids would've been considered almost an act of enemy aggression from a foreign country, and I had no desire to be shot down in that manner. Finally, I saw Zephyr sitting in the library, right after school. She was probably waiting for one of her friends to go to the bathroom or to get something from their locker, so I knew that I had a small window of opportunity to act. Rushing down the length of the library in a manner that would get me there quickly but wouldn't bring unwanted attention to myself, I got the card out of my notebook.

"Hello Zephyr, how's it going? I said, and before she had time to respond, I put the card on the table in front of her. "This is for you. I hope that you'll consider going," I stammered.

Just then, her friend Shirley came into the library. Shirley had seen me giving Zephyr the card and she shot

Zephyr a, "Why are you talking to him?" sort of look. Zephyr looked flustered for a moment, and then she stood up, picked up the card, looked at it, and then handed it back to me.

"No thank-you," she said, and then she gathered up her belongings and went to stand with Shirley to wait for some other member of their "in" crowd.

I wasn't sure what to make out of what had just happened, other than I had been shot down in what I considered a particularly cruel manner. She hadn't even looked at the card. In a daze, I exited the library at the other end of the room, but God wasn't quite done having His fun with me yet. After I stopped to talk briefly with Mrs. Kugan, I exited the building and found myself walking home right in front of Zephyr and Shirley and Lance, one of the founding fathers of the cool kids. Although my heart was racing, I couldn't think of how to get out from in front of them without stopping and watching them go by. Usually, I noticed that Zephyr walked towards the back of the cool kid group and didn't seem to be involved with the discussions. Today was obviously a different kind of day. Zephyr was leading the discussion and I wasn't sure exactly how I could hear her so clearly because her voice was low and they were a good ten or twelve feet behind me.

I heard her say, "Can you believe his nerve? I'm sure that he was trying to ask me to the dance, like I'd go with him and his pig nose and his big pig butt."

Shirley and Lance laughed along with her and I found myself dying a bit inside. My grandparents lived at the end of the next block from the school, and so I decided to pretend that I was going to their house for a quick visit. I swerved to the right and walked across the yard. I waited in the shadow of one of the large maples until I was sure that they were far ahead, and then I continued walking home.

That had been my first experience with asking a girl to a dance.

About two-and-a-half years later, I decided that I'd try my luck again. I didn't want to ask one of the girls that I was friends with in choir or the drama club, because if things didn't go well and they found me tiresome or a bore, I didn't want my reputation to be ruined, not that I had that much of a reputation to ruin. I think my entire reputation could be summed up in one sentence, "He's artistic, polite, and a nice guy who can be funny, from time to time." I didn't want to risk losing my funny footnote if I got unusually nervous during the event.

I had been getting along quite well with Shirley and her friend Lynnette in Mr. Maymo's class, and I decided to ask Lynnette. How to ask her became problematic. I was never going to try the let-the-card-ask-for-me method again, and there was no way that I was going to ask her directly, with Shirley listening on. Knowing that she was there for the ridicule that came from my Zephyr attempt made my desire to keep her out of the loop intense, so there was no way that I would ask Shirley for Lynnette's phone number. That would be about the same as asking her in front of Shirley.

How could I get Lynnette's number without getting anyone else involved, in case I couldn't find the nerve to follow through?

I decided to ask Juliet Norris for a favor. She worked in the school library and I knew that the library had all of the names of the students and their vital information on file. Juliet could get me Lynnette's number, but then I'd have another problem. Where would I call Lynnette from? I couldn't use the phone at home because it was centrally located on the kitchen wall and everyone would know my business. I couldn't ask my grandparents to use their phone, because they had a party line, so even if I got them to let me make the call privately, I had no guarantee that someone in their neighbor's house wouldn't be listening in to everything that I said. I couldn't use a phone at school, because Lynnette would be at school with me, and if Lynnette was home, then the school would be locked and I wouldn't have access to the phones.

Finally, I decided to call her from the phone booth located in front of the little store near my grandparent's house, where I bought my coverless bargain comic books. Although someone might see me in the phone booth and wonder why I wasn't making a phone call from my grandparent's house, a couple of hundred feet away, at least there was no chance that anyone would hear what I was saying.

A viable plan had been born.

I decided that girls were a lot of work, as I sought out Juliet in the choir room to solicit her help.

The Saturday before Homecoming arrived and, armed with my illegally-obtained personal information about Lynnette, I drove the T-Bird to the store and parked it on the side street where it couldn't be seen from anywhere on my grandparent's property. I waited until there was an obvious lull in traffic, and then I entered the phone booth. Nervously, I put in the required coin and dialed the number.

After two rings, a man's voice answered.

"Is Lynnette there?" I asked.

The male on the other end of the line yelled for Lynnette, and it became obvious that it had been her older brother. After a pause, I heard her come to the phone and pick it up.

"Hello? She said.

"Hello, Lynnette?"

"Yes?"

"This is Nick, from Maymo's first hour class."

"Yes?"

"I was wondering if you'd like to go to the Homecoming Dance with me."

There was a long pause on the other end of the line.

"How did you get this number? No, I'm not interested in going to Homecoming with you. Good-bye."

Click.

I'm not sure how I had done it, but I felt like I had insulted her by asking her out to a dance. My feelings were hurt and I wasn't sure exactly what it was about me that made my company so undesirable, but I was glad that I hadn't just been rejected by someone that I knew well. I tried to put on a happy face and go on with my day. I went to work on the choir float.

When Homecoming finally arrived, the choir float looked great, but with barely any time left and almost no supplies, we decided to trim the edge of the trailer in flowers but not make a big skirt for it.

Darryl Sandusky gave me the high sign as he took several pictures of the choir float lined up to be in the Homecoming Parade. After the float winners were announced, Darryl passed me and said, "Well, I guess I won't need those shots that I took. It's too bad. I really thought that you guys were going to win."

We found out afterwards that the judges had disqualified our float because it lacked a formal skirt.

We didn't win the float contest and I didn't attend the dance.

Ironies heaped upon ironies. Such was my life.

CHAPTER NINE
Walking on Water

The Bible tells us of miracles, but there is no amount of reading that can prepare a person for experiencing one firsthand.

It was a Friday after school and I had decided to drop by my grandparent's house to spend some time before going home for dinner. As I turned the corner, I noticed my grandfather's Bel Air parked near the garage and my Uncle Dominic's Cadillac parked in the driveway by the street. For a moment, I pondered driving by and heading down to Ferry Avenue to go home, but then I saw my Grandpa Eugene and Uncle Dominic in the yard. Grandpa Eugene was waving hello, so driving away would've hurt his feelings, which I certainly didn't want to do.

Being easily identified was one of the drawbacks of driving a 1963 T-bird in 1975.

I parked in the street and came up the driveway.

Uncle Dominic was dressed in some sort of camouflage outfit and he was showing Grandpa Eugene his new bow and razor-tip arrows. It was obviously hunting season in Michigan again. I wasn't one of those kids who looked forward to hunting with their father with rabid anticipation. My Dad had taken me hunting once, and it wasn't for me. I didn't mind the scenery and tromping around in the cold, but the killing part bothered me. We had gone to some cabin that my Dad had rented in the woods, located in the north country of Lower Michigan somewhere, and the group of us had slept without heating, in rather ramshackle bunk beds. It was one of the few times in my life where I had slept with a roof over my head and it had been even colder than staying overnight at my Grandpa Nelek's house. We had frost on our noses the next morning, and putting our feet on the floor was almost a traumatic experience. I couldn't remember who was with us. There was my Dad, and Grandpa Nelek, my uncles Paul and Gordon, whom I didn't see very often, and a couple of other men that I didn't know.

The climax of the hunting weekend came when my Dad and I circled around a long stand of evergreens while the rest of the group went to the far end of the grouping of trees. A deer was flushed out and was running along the back of the string of trees, probably thinking that it had outsmarted my grandfather and his companions, when my Dad stepped out right in front of it. Its eyes went wide and it tried to stop and change direction, but my Dad let loose with a blast that got it right in the chest.

My grandfather felt cheated.

My Dad felt elated.

I felt sick.

I vowed to myself not to agree to willingly witness killing like that again, and I never went hunting with my Dad after that one event.

As I walked up the driveway, I could see that my Uncle Dominic was just beaming, showing off his new toys of death. After pondering my hunting experience for a long time, I had decided that it was alright for some people to hunt, those who were actually going to use the meat. On the other hand, those who were jazzed about the killing aspect I found creepy.

My uncle had fought in Korea. I wasn't sure if he fought because he wanted to protect America and save the world from Communism, or if he was merely looking for a socially acceptable way to end another man's life.

Seeing him standing there with his fascination for the razor-tipped arrows shifted my impression from the former possibility to the latter.

"Hello, Nicky. How was school and play practice today?" Grandpa Eugene asked, cheerfully.

"They were fine," I replied.

"Is there anything new or unusual happening at school?" Grandpa Eugene continued.

I wanted to reply in detail, but I had no intention of being around Uncle Dominic any longer than absolutely necessary, so I became unusually unresponsive. "Nope, just the same old same old," I said.

"How's it going, sport?" Uncle Dominic chimed in.

"It's all going great. Is it deer season again?"

"You got that right. I was just showing your grandfather the latest technology. I'll do my best to bring you all back some nice fresh venison," he said, smiling proudly at the thought, "You do like venison, don't you?"

I had two choices, to answer truthfully or to answer acceptably. When my Dad or Uncle Dominic had provided us with venison in the past, it had turned into a seemingly endless parade of venison hamburgers, venison goulash, and venison spaghetti, and I wasn't particularly fond of the strange taste of the meat. It definitely didn't taste like the meat that I was used to, but that might've been because my mother always bought whatever bulk item was on sale at the supermarket. I had begun to notice when eating at my grandparent's house that their hamburgers started off as mostly pink with little streaks of white, as opposed to the kind that we got at home, which were definitely a different color and seemed to shrink right before our eyes when being fried. My mother didn't like to cook, but somehow my stepfather had made it clear to her that cooking was part of her womanly responsibilities, and so she begrudgingly did it. Often, she wouldn't even eat what she cooked, preferring to go without, or making herself a chicken TV dinner and eating alone in the living room.

"Venison would be great, Uncle Dominic. Good luck. I'm going to feed the fish," I replied, although in order to be completely truthful, I would've had to have said, "Telling you that venison would be great will keep the peace, and so that's the reply that I'm going with."

I left them to chat about the fine art of stalking and killing while I traveled to the corner of the side yard to the pond. Over next to the flower garden, which was north of the vegetable garden and east of the rock garden, was a pond. For a backyard pond, it was quite large, being thirty feet long, about twelve feet wide and four feet deep at the deep end. Fall was upon us and so I had put the leaf net in place over the pond the weekend before. With the four giant maple trees in the yard, if the leaf net hadn't been there to catch them, the maple leaves would've filled in the pond and choked out the aquatic plants and killed the fish. With the net in place, every few days someone needed to scoop off the wet mass of leaves to keep the pond healthy. There was a path going around the pond and at the center of the kidney shape was an apple tree. The apple tree provided movable shade for the fish, so that no matter how hot the day got, there would always be a shady spot for the fish to escape the sun. I sat on the two-person wooden swing and began tossing fish pellets to the anxious fish.

Just as I got comfortable, Uncle Dominic's pit bull dog, Goliath, came bounding across the yard from investigating for rabbits in the raspberry bushes behind the garage, and raced over to see what I was doing over at the pond. Goliath wasn't a bad dog, but he was big and he belonged to my Uncle, which meant that I wasn't going to risk life and limb trying to become friends with him. He ran up to the edge of the pond on the opposite side from me.

In an instant, several things happened.

I saw Goliath stepping out onto the green leaf netting with both front feet, plunging straight down to the bottom of the deep end of the pond, thrashing and twisting with the net wrapping around him, and him drowning before I could get to him.

This vision played out in my mind's eye as I jumped up from the swing and watched Goliath step a full eight inches out onto the leaf net with both front feet.

A tingling began to run up and down my spine.

I didn't want to make any more quick movements for fear that my actions would somehow break the impossibility of what I was seeing. Goliath was standing with both front legs being supported over a four foot drop-off of water by nothing more than a few strands of leaf netting that couldn't find the strength to hold six damp leaves up over the surface of the pond.

I slowly shooed Goliath back from the edge of the pond.

Reacting as if nothing was unusual in any way, Goliath backed up, gave me a strange look, and then he ran to Uncle Dominic when Dominic called to leave. I'm not sure if Dominic said anything to me before getting into his car and driving away, because I just sat back down of the swing, astounded.

What I had just witnessed was not possible. There was no shifting of weight that would allow an eighty pound dog to have its two front legs supported by nothing and not have it pitch forward into the pond head first. One leg unsupported, ok, then it might possibly be able to adjust its balance and not fall forward, but certainly not both legs.

I was in shock.

Grandpa Eugene came over and sat on the swing with me. He grabbed my thigh and gave it a squeeze. I involuntarily jumped up in response.

"So, what's new?" he asked again.

There was no reason to share what I'd seen. No one would believe me.

CHAPTER TEN
Arsenic and Old Lace

Like I was able to see into the future, the casting for *Arsenic and Old Lace* ended up being exactly what I thought it would be. I ended up with the lead part of Mortimer Brewster, with hundreds of dry lines to memorize, and everyone else looked like they were going to have a fun time, both with their parts and in the group dynamic. Victor ended up with the Teddy part, and I knew that the audiences would roar when he did his bit running up the stairs to San Juan Hill.

It was just another of God's ironies that for the short time that I was at a weight where I could play any part, the lead part was going to be dry and dull, and the bit part was going to be wild and fun. As predicted, Hayley and Crystal got the two Brewster sisters, and Kevin got the Boris Karloff part of Jonathon Brewster, which was hardly innovative casting since Kevin had the posture of Snoopy pretending to be a vulture, and so was a natural choice. That's not to say that Kevin was lugubriously preoccupied as a person, it was just that he had posture problems, and homework problems, but that was another story. Kevin had a personal philosophy against doing homework of any kind, under any circumstance, and he was frequently seen waging a losing battle with one teacher or another over his grades. He maintained that since he aced all of his tests, that he should get an "A" in all of his classes. His teachers maintained that since he never did any homework, he had a serious character flaw relating to laziness and should probably fail all of his classes. Following his academic career was an interesting hobby that several in the Drama Club enjoyed.

Cast as the Igor-type sidekick to the Boris Karloff role was Tyler, who was a Drama Club electron. He desperately wished to be treated as a Drama Club nucleus member, but relatively short stature and his need for attention relegated him to being an electron, circling endlessly, hoping for an opening of welcome. Tyler and I got along reasonably well, but not everyone had the patience to sit through a long dissertation of Tyler's concerning the finer points of WWII and Nazi Germany. For myself, my historical interests had been more focused upon the medieval period up through the Civil War. I would sometimes listen to Tyler share, but after a while it would all seem too real and bloody for me. With the Vietnam War still in full swing, I didn't really find the discussion of modern weapons and tactics that inviting. Reading about knights on horseback or lines of redcoats with flintlocks seemed more nostalgic and less like butchery than what I saw in the news of the day. There were several other people involved with the play, and even a guest walk-on role by one of the teachers. Mr. Resser had agreed to come onstage long enough to be poisoned by the two charming old ladies.

As the rehearsals began to pick up speed and bits and pieces of the set began appearing onstage, and very unique and strange set piece began receiving a lot of attention. The script requires the use of a window seat, which functions, for all intents and purpose, like a coffin, to hide a body. Mr. DeVries didn't want to build a regular window seat out of pine boards. For reasons that were beyond my understanding, he had the producer, Miss Heinkel, whose class I had quickly dropped at the beginning of the semester, track down a real coffin to use! It was picked up by one of the custodians from Detroit Metro Airport and we were told that it was a shipping coffin. It was a grey, coffin-shaped box that had angled sides with cheap aluminum handles and it was made out of wide pine boards.

What made it distinctive was that the outside had been covered with a grey felt.

What made it absolutely creepy was that when we got it on stage and opened it, it was filled with crumpled papers that had been tightly packed around a real dead body, preventing it from moving during shipping. The impression of the dead body was quite clear, and some people backed away from the coffin, whereas others were bizarrely drawn to it because of its icky nature.

As soon as the shock wore off, Victor wanted to get his picture taken lying in the coffin. This began a frenzy of "Me next" reactions from many of the group, but I wanted no part of such "fun." Kevin did his best dead body impression for the camera, and then Victor wanted back into the coffin with his girlfriend, Monica. Face to face, it was a tight fit and a very disconcerting sight to see the two of them squished into the box, and then, of course, they insisted upon some privacy and closed the lid.

There had always been a quality to Victor that unsettled me. There was something about me that he felt needed taking down a peg, from time to time, and there was something about him that I felt needed bathing, shampooing and exorcising. During one late night technical rehearsal, Victor brought in an Ouija board to play around with. Although invited to join in, I declined. It wasn't that I thought that it was all hogwash. I explained that, to my reasoning, angels had better things to do with their spare time than to push a pointer around a board, and I didn't want to spend my time with dark spirits in the name of "entertainment." Victor had smiled at me, like I was some superstitious child, and then he and Monica found a couple of other people to "play" with them. When I stumbled in upon them in the boy's dressing room, playing with the Ouija board had been discarded and replaced with Victor in a trance, supposedly reliving a past life as an American Indian. Denny, my frizzy-haired choir friend seemed particularly receptive to Victor's trance state and he was seriously freaked out.

As Victor droned on and on, I began to slip into some sort of vision. It wasn't a single, clear picture, like watching a movie, but more like a collage of jumbled pictures and impressions. Something about me being left behind with the women and the children of my tribe while the other manly Indian men went off to ambush and kill white men, women, and children. I objected to the killing of women and children, and so I had been left behind as a woman or a child, to keep watch over the other women and children.

Victor had led a raiding party that attacked my village. I tried to defend everyone as best I could, but I was captured and many others were killed. The reason for my being left behind was made known to my captors, and my bravery came into question. To the simple-minded, bravery is the product of actions and needs no explanation, and so I was considered a coward for not being willing to kill as needed for my tribe. To prove that I was a coward, they tied me securely to a wooden frame, and slowly lowered me face-first into a bonfire. They had expected to break my will, to make me whimper and plead for my life.

They did not succeed, although proving my personal bravery had resulted in a painful death, being dropped face-first into the flames.

This explained the strange dynamic that Victor and I had shared in this lifetime. I had proven my worth as a warrior in a manner that made him wonder if he would've been able to endure the same. His fleeting self-doubt had been the thought that made him wish to correct or belittle me from time to time, and his past life as an Indian was cropping up into his present life. He was a member of the archery club, and he had acquired a notable reputation for making high quality arrows, crafted by hand.

"Can't you show me some happy past-life memories, instead of instances of torture and painful death?" I asked in my head.

I felt an internal shrug and I heard, "We desire happiness, but happiness is not always an effective teacher."

"I vote that you try to find a way to change that."

Performance week of the play approached. Crystal had learned her lines like the consummate professional actress that she was. Hayley had also learned her lines, but she had a rather disconcerting way of correcting other people about their lines. Instead of a quick hint to get another person back on track, she would recite the fumbled line word perfectly, and then shoot the embarrassed actor or actress a "Get it together, you're wasting our time" sort of look. Sometimes Crystal seemed to get into this hobby of playing with the "little people" and sometimes she seemed like she was tiring of hanging around so closely with Hayley. I wondered if she realized just how much Hayley's view of life and other people was affecting her own. Over the last couple of years, Crystal and I had shared a handful of quiet, personal moments, where she talked about what was going right or wrong in her life, and what kind of a future she was hoping for. She had been vulnerable during those talks and I missed that Crystal of old, not really trusting this new Crystal, who often came across as a puppet at the end of Hayley's arm.

Another level of strangeness came from the producer, Miss Heinkel. She seemed quite good at her job of acquiring things for the show, especially a coffin, but she also had an odd quality about her when it came to interacting with the cast members. During notes at the end of a rehearsal, Mr. DeVries would give his suggestions, and then she'd start in. Often her comments were related to things like costume details, being able to hear lines clearly, and when special rehearsals were to be scheduled, but sometimes she seemed to take a cruel sort of pleasure in correcting the ladies and praising the gentlemen. There were times when a cutting comment to Hayley about her underwear showing seemed to take Hayley down a notch, but I still felt that there was something innately unfair about Miss Heinkel making that comment in front of the collective consciousness, as opposed to mentioning it to Hayley in private.

The play appeared to have too many individual chefs, squeezed into a kitchen that was often too small.

Because of his desire to fit in and please, from time to time Crystal and Hayley would play a little game that I called "Come here, come here, go away, go away" with the Drama Club electrons. They would interact with people like Tyler as if they wanted him to be their friend, making small talk or sitting by him during rehearsals. Then, after he began to feel welcome and he let his guard down, they'd ask him questions about himself and seem to be opening up to him in return. After they'd acquired enough information to entertain themselves, they'd give him the cold shoulder. Although Tyler wasn't initially aware of these tactics, since my family had put the "dis" in dysfunctional, I could see the pattern quite clearly.

Sometimes Crystal and Hayley reminded me of the *Star Trek* episode where people somehow achieve demigod-like status, and then they de-evolve into twisted emotional brutes. Other than exchanging lines onstage, I tried to stay off of their radar. They had no real sense of how they were making other people feel, and that is one of the fundamental pillars of being a cool kid, your own perception about what is going on is all that matters. If other people don't "get you" then the defect is theirs, or so they believe.

Being the male lead meant that I was allowed to have a well-blocked onstage romance. Playing my love interest was a cute sophomore by the name of Anne. I enjoyed playing opposite her, and she, like many others that I had met along the way, aspired someday to be a professional actress. Unlike the ladies in the plays, I had no aspirations of becoming a professional actor, or perhaps I should say that it was made clear to me that I would receive no financial assistance from my family to go to college if I chose to pursue a career in the theatre. My family considered the theatre to be an interesting hobby, but nothing more, certainly nothing to risk a financial future on. The family had decided that I was destined to be an artist, and that was the only road that they would assist me with. Anne was fun and pleasant but there wasn't any dramatic romantic spark between us. Certainly I could pretend in front of an audience with the best of us, but there wasn't any fire kindled that lasted past the apron lights. We were even complimented on a scene where she takes the initiative and kisses me, bending me unexpectedly backwards. It was a great comic moment, but I felt like I was kissing my sister.

I always believed that true love required an element of the irresistible, of the inexplicable. Certainly my fascination with Zephyr had been inexplicable, but her meanness had taken care of the irresistible part.

The walls began springing up and the set got painted, trimmed, and wallpapered. With the passing of each day, nicer and more fragile set pieces and props began appearing, like crystal decanters and various antiques, begged or borrowed from the cast's relatives.

There is something naturally romantic about being involved in a school play, and several people in the cast became couples before the show was over. Crystal spoke often of her baseball player boyfriend, Jim, and it was clear that she had great hopes of someday becoming a major league baseball player's wife. He was being scouted by several major universities to play ball. Hayley showed no interest in getting romantically entangled with anyone. As I already mentioned, Victor had Monica. Kevin flirted with two of the sophomore prop girls, who blushed and flirted back. Frank, our Drama Club technician and auditorium AV crew member, was attracted to a tall girl with shorter dark hair by the name of Doreen.

Of all of the couples involved with their courting rituals, Frank and Doreen were the most interesting to observe, once one had adjusted to Victor and Monica and their odd coffin fascination. What made Frank and Doreen so unique is that there seemed to be a third element to their budding duet. Doreen was, to say the least, a girl of intense emotions, and when she was certain that the only woman in Frank's gaze was herself then roses sprang into bloom from every metaphoric corner of the room. However, when Frank's attentions seemed distant and his affections withdrawn, then the world became a very dark place for her, and for everyone close to her.

It was rumored that Miss Heinkel had made some inappropriate comments to Frank, and that they were involved somehow. I didn't pay much attention to the gossip myself, but I could tell that Doreen was paying attention to every girl in the cast because Frank had stopped paying attention to her. Doreen was a prompter and so she was needed backstage during the performances, whereas Frank's station was up in the projection booth, running the light panel. Much to everyone's surprise, at the technical rehearsal all day Sunday before we opened the show, Miss Heinkel volunteered to monitor the sound board and run the follow spot when required. That would place her alone with Frank in the projection booth for the run of the show.

I saw Frank talking privately with Doreen backstage on several occasions, and by his body language, he seemed to be trying to assuage her fears. Frank and I were friends, but I didn't feel that it was my place to pry into his personal business. He and I had walked the twenty mile March of Dimes Walk-a-thon together for the past two years, and we had been involved with the plays and musicals together throughout high school. When it came to theatre talk, we could chat for hours, but I had no idea what to say about high school romance. In that area, he was far more advanced than I, and so I watched his little private melodrama play out before me, observing from out of blast range in case anything went wrong.

After dropping her science class because of how odd the first day had made me feel, I had little opportunity to interact with Miss Heinkel other than at the play, and so I had no idea if she was trying to have a relationship with Frank, or if everything was just an ugly rumor high school that had taken on a life of its own.

It was strange to observe how other people viewed Frank and Doreen's one day hot, and the next day cold relationship. Doreen's main job was to prompt from the stage right wing, but she was also to set out and manage the prop table stage right. As we got closer to opening night, I noticed that Hayley seemed to be trying to get Crystal over near the prop table quite frequently. I wondered what that was all about, and so I listened in on one of their discussions, hidden behind the tormentor curtain. Hayley was gossiping about Miss Heinkel with Crystal in such a way that Doreen could easily overhear. I noticed that after each of these gossiping sessions Doreen would become enraged and discretely smash something from the prop table, usually an old coffee mug. There was no denying her passion, either for romance or possibly for revenge, and I caught her on several occasions listening in on the headphones to the tech discussion upstairs. She had no need to listen to stage cues for lighting, sound, and spotlight, but obviously she felt that the gauntlet had been thrown. Doreen was determined to get to the bottom of the situation, no matter what that digging cost her.

Compared to the gossip generated by the Miss Heinkel, Frank, and Doreen triangle, Mr. DeVries's drinking wasn't even a close second. It was old news, to the point of being a Drama Club tradition. Somehow, by the end of an after school rehearsal, Mr. DeVries had found the opportunity to relieve some of the day's stress by briefly "organizing" the small prop room off stage left. On weekend rehearsals, there was less need for subterfuge and he showed up to open the auditorium for us already de-stressed. Often the weekend rehearsal ended with Miss Heinkel giving copious, if seemingly trivial notes to us, while Mr. DeVries slept in the auditorium, his hands clasped before him and his head oddly pointed up at the ceiling in a manner certain to generate a crick in his neck when he eventually woke up. Unlike Nathan, who was a loud and potentially violent drunkard, Mr. DeVries was a sleepy drunkard.

I decided that the sleepy drunk was greatly preferred of the two.

I wondered if there was such a thing as a jovial, energetic, and emotionally-supportive drunkard.

Zotia laughed in my mind and I realized that the chances were slim.

When the play posters and the programs finally arrived from our high school print shop, I was greatly disappointed. The illustration that I had created of a potential victim and the two old ladies surrounding him looked like it had been drawn over with a blunt marker by someone with a shaky hand. I was oddly thankful that they'd chopped off my name from the artwork. At least I wouldn't have to explain the shakiness of the drawing to anyone outside of the play.

At last, the play came to an end, as all things do.

The show opened with great fanfare and expectation. The auditorium was huge, seating around 1,600, and we had audiences of from 500-600 people per night, which, we were told, were very good. During the show, I seldom, if ever, tried to see out past the apron lights into the audience. While looking forward, I always looked over their heads, up at the projection booth. Because of this habit, I couldn't help noticing a large flower arrangement on the sound board, right next to Miss Heinkel, during my first scene on opening night. That realization almost made me throw an important cue line, but I regained my focus and stumbled on. During the next scene, I noticed that the flowers were gone. I wondered if Miss Heinkel would be bringing the flowers out of the projection booth, for all to see, after the show. As I anticipated, she was never seen emerging from the booth with a large flower bouquet, and I wondered how she'd pulled that off. Perhaps she'd return after we were all gone to retrieve them.

I listened intently to the after show talk, and amongst all of the "Great job, you were wonderful" comments, I didn't hear a single, "Did you notice...?" and so I deduced that I had been the only one outside of the projection booth to see.

There were no obvious ceramic casualties next to the prop table, and so it appeared that Doreen suspected nothing. Opening night was on a Thursday, so everyone cleaned up quickly and went home, as we were all expected to be in school for classes the next day.

By the closing night curtain, certain things had become predictable. Victor was going to get huge laughs for his onstage Teddy antics, Crystal and Hayley were going to get seemingly endless flowers and accolades from friends and family, and I was going to get minimal and tepid applause for having known all of my relatively boring and tedious lines and holding the show together like human Elmer's glue. Everyone covets the lead part, until they get one and realize that sometimes, less is more, more fun, more stimulating, and more rewarding.

None of my family came to see the show and I got no flowers or cards from admirers, although I did get a couple of pats on the back and a "Good job" or two from other cast members, and Mo.

Crystal gave me a hug and said that I had made the show enjoyable for her. Whether it was truth or hogwash, I didn't really care. The moment reminded me of when we used to be closer and I thought that we would be close friends forever.

After the performance was over and everyone had changed, we all went out to eat at a local pizza establishment, a place called Peppi's Pizza. The room had been reserved for our group and I noticed as we filed in that we naturally broke down into our established subgroups as we picked our seats.

Hayley sat down at the center of one side of the table and Crystal sat next to her. Before I decided where to sit, Crystal shooed Tyler from sitting next to her and had me sit there instead. Now the question would be, would Crystal spend the rest of the evening leaning in to laugh at Hayley's comments, or did she actually want to reconnect with me?

For closing night, Mr. DeVries was alert and awake, and he went on and on about how wonderful the experience of directing the show had been for him.

Zotia's voice popped in, "How much of the experience does he even remember?" and then I heard the Blue Lady shush her.

I looked around the room and wondered how many of the relationships created through the play would really last. Many here would be involved in the last theatrical production of our senior year yet to come, the spring musical. The musical would be much of the same thing, only on a grander scale, involving over a hundred people, as opposed to a couple dozen people. The closing night of a play always made me wonder what the future held, since it represented an obvious ending. It was now time to dismantle the set, put the props away, and give my Grandpa Eugene back my costumes, which were really his old daily wardrobe.

I wondered, by the end of the year, what would my relationship be with Crystal, or Kevin, or Frank? Only God knew for sure, and He wasn't saying.

With everyone in such close proximity, there wasn't really any room for gossip or hard feelings that night. Everyone seemed on top of the world as the pizza and the pop arrived. Would we remember all that was the play, or would we selectively remember only the happy parts.

Had the common play experience made us all friends, or had it only put us into a situation where we appeared to be friends for a short time? Were the smiles genuine or for show? Would they last a week, or a lifetime?

Time would eventually tell the tale.

CHAPTER ELEVEN
Sammael

The strange situation with the disappearing blonde woman at my grandparent's Labor Day gathering continued to cause me much mental frustration. I just couldn't get over the fact that she had vanished, almost right before my eyes. There was definitely something strange about that girl that I couldn't exactly put my finger on.

"She's here to do you great harm. Be careful," wafted quietly in from the back of my mind.

"Fabulous, a supernatural woman who can disappear at will has dropped into my life to do me great harm. Who is she?"

It wasn't long afterwards that my question was answered, and the answer came in the form of a vision.

The same blonde woman appeared to me in the front yard of our Exeter house, standing next to an immense hole. Inside the hole was a large, stinking sewer pipe. I walked over to the woman. She looked directly at me and started speaking in a language that I didn't understand, but one that I felt that I had heard before. Just then, two horribly misshapen figures crossed the yard and greeted each other, passing gas with an enthusiasm and viciousness that I had never seen before.

They were demons.

Immediately, I knew what the vision meant, as electric tingles started to race up and down my spine. She had been speaking the language of the Abyss.

I turned to the blonde woman and said, "You can't fool me any longer by manifesting as a woman. I know who you are. You're Sammael, the Angel of Death, Lucifer's only archangel!"

She looked me straight in the eye and said, "Hic incipio pestis!"

With that utterance, the vision began to dissipate, her twisted smile being the last thing that I saw clearly.

"It's Latin. She said, 'Here begins the plague,'" I heard the Blue Lady whisper.

I woke in my little bunk bed, drenched in a cold, clammy sweat.

What had I stumbled upon? Lucifer's Angel of Death was stalking me? That couldn't possibly be good.

I began to be plagued by phantom pains, unexplained spasms, and rashes. In addition, specific areas of stench began popping up on our property. At the same time, Zotia and the Blue Lady seemed to be slowly and patiently feeding me information to help me deal with these spiritual beings. Eventually, I learned the prayers that would control them, and the circumstances whereby they could be removed by Archangel Michael and taken to The Throne of Jehovah.

I was taught the hierarchy of the Abyss, and the ranking of Lucifer's demons. I discovered that demons were tiny pieces of Lucifer's soul energy, just as human and angel souls were tiny pieces of God's soul energy.

Demons come in six levels of malignant potency, with one additional category of spiritual beings called indigo satans, which roughly translates into "new adversaries." These beings are so twisted and demented, that Lucifer had to remove their spiritual memories before incarnating them. Otherwise, they'll be institutionalized as infants for trying to eat their siblings or the family pets alive.

Through the efforts of Grandma Zotia and the Blue Lady, I discovered the laws of engagement for spiritual beings, much to the chagrin of the many nasty creatures that had been sent to harass me, for incarnated souls are not supposed to know the secrets rules of spiritual battle and karmic imbalance.

It is a question of force vs. power, as in once force has been applied by a being of the dark to a being of the Light, the victim of that force then gains power and authority over the transgressing spirit. I was taught about tiger-eye demons that look like a tiger's claw with an eye at the opposite end of the sharpened claw, and how they're sent to torment. I was taught how to pray the biting pain spirits and the stinky smell spirits away to The Throne, and soon, the base of The Throne of God began to fill up with the nasty spiritual beings that had been forcibly transported there.

Souls in the body, regular people of flesh and blood, were supposed to be easy prey to spiritual torture. We were not supposed to have the knowledge or the power to interfere with the dark's plans, or so the demons had believed, right up to the moment they had been snatched up by Archangel Michael and transported to the Light.

Day after day, they kept coming, and day after day, I kept praying them away.

Once caught and taken to the Light, their only choices were to stand there in the brilliance of Jehovah's divine Light, to allow themselves to be reborn through the Christ energy of God's Love, or for them to wish themselves out of existence in a final act of defiance to His authority, vanishing forever from all of the physical and spiritual realms.

If the evil spirit attacking me was strong enough, then I was not given the authority to have the offensive being removed until it had committed an appropriately aggressive act against me. Such an act occurred one Saturday when I was in our garage, working on a prop for the fall play. A board that I was cutting caught in the saw blade, bizarrely twisting in such a way as to knock the tip of my left thumb down into the spinning blade. I knew that the wound was serious, for when I put my thumb in my mouth I felt the bone at the tip of my thumb with my tongue.

Sammael had hoped to cause much greater physical injury to me, but she was limited by my own team of a dozen guardian angels, lead by Catherine and Conrad. They had allowed her to wound me just enough to create the karmic imbalance necessary to have her removed to The Throne. I prayed, and Sammael, the devil's Angel of Death, was removed to The Throne of Jehovah, where it would stand in the Light of God's Presence, possibly forever.

As for the wound, shortly after I got back from my long wait in the local emergency room at St. John, I had to snip the stitches that I'd just received, because the wound was healing at a rapid rate. The stitches were already causing me discomfort. The next day, I found that all of the infection from the cut had collected into a solid, smelly mass at the center of the wound, which I promptly removed. Soon, only a slight indention remained in my left thumb tip to remind me of Sammael's attack. The missing flesh eventually filled in, even to the point of having the nerve sensations return. This seemed like a mini-miracle, considering the chunk of flesh that had been removed by the saw blade.

Sammael's attack had brought about positive results.

"Although you have emerged triumphant and with only a tiny scar, be forewarned, for we have not seen the last of that one," Zotia's voice whispered.

That was a chilling thought.

CHAPTER TWELVE
The Thanksgiving Day Parade

Before we knew it, Thanksgiving Day was close at hand, and we were scrambling to get our new white choir sweaters properly adorned with our new blue choir letters and pins, our song completely memorized, and our mini-megaphone techniques perfected. Although singing "Santa Claus is Comin' to Town" initially sounded like a great idea, in actuality, a relatively modest choir of eighty or so people trying to generate enough sound to be heard over the nearby bands in the parade would prove to be a daunting challenge.

The parade turned out to be an incredible example of "Hurry up and wait." Before the sun had even pondered getting out of bed, we had to meet at school, load onto busses, and get ourselves downtown to our designated staging area before traffic became an issue. Then we had to wait there until the end of the parade to step off. We had ample time to become nervous while watching all of the other groups, floats, and balloons show up and then begin their march down Woodward Avenue.

There was quite a bit of small talk, but in essence, it was only really a toccata and fugue on the idea of "I can't believe we're here." It was as if we had been plunked down in the first few moments of the movie *Miracle on 34th Street*, only our few moments lasted several hours. We had been instructed to try to keep warm and dry, which ended up being two things almost impossible to do. The day was cold, and there was a drizzling sort of rain that seemed insignificant at first, but after a while we started to get soaked, which brought with it a chill. Many of us had scarves, but we knew that we had to leave them behind when we marched. We could sit on the bus, if we chose too, but most of the members of the group were much too wound up to do that. In addition, the temperature inside of the non-running busses was only slightly warmer than outside. The main difference for climbing into the bus was for getting out of the wind and the drizzle, and after a couple of hours outside, I was getting a bit tired of the wind and the drizzle.

After finding a seat on the bus and being there only long enough to consider wringing the water out of my stocking cap, Moriah bounded in.

"There you are, party poop, come on, there are things to see outside," she demanded, grabbing me by the arm.

"But I..." Realizing that I'd be unable to break her enthusiasm or her grip, I allowed her to drag me to the door.

"I did some research on the parade for just this moment. Did you know that the Detroit Mounted Police have led the parade since 1958, riding their trained Morgan Quarter Horses?"

"I was not aware of that fact. Hold up, Mo, before you drag me to the end of the parade and back, let me get rid of some of this excess moisture I'm carrying." I wrung out my stocking cap as best I could and put it back on, not wishing anyone to see what must've been the serious case of wet cap-hair that I was sporting.

"Did you know that the largest float in the parade is the Doodlebug? The float is an amazing 125' long and 12' wide. The main helpers along the parade route are Santa's elves. They have oversized paper mache' heads imported from Italy, I think, or maybe it was... Actually, I'm not sure where they're from, but I'm sure that they're imported."

Moriah took me by the arm and shared with me every minute secret and tradition that she'd learned about the parade, and it was a pleasant way to pass the time. After a while, I noticed Denny behind us. I signaled for him to join us but he just looked at me and changed direction. I could tell that he had a crush developing on Moriah, but it wasn't really my place to butt in and tell her my thoughts on the matter. I assumed that eventually he'd get up the nerve to say something to her. My similar experience of getting up the nerve to talk to a girl flashed through my head, and I hoped that Denny would end up with sweeter memories of his moment than I had.

Mo chatted on, and I was amazed at how much minutia she had accumulated in such a short period of time. She could've announced the whole parade.

After what seemed like forever, we were gathered together and lined up behind the floats carrying Christmas Carol and Mrs. Claus. Christmas Carol was supposedly Santa's number-one helper, and she had her own float, which was a giant gift box. In front of her was a float called Carol's Angels, where 10' tall angels rode 12' long swans around a central Christmas tree. Behind us was the Santa float, with its eight reindeer and giant sleigh in the back. The float was a mass of tubing bent to represent the winter winds, with huge snowflakes sprinkled about. It was built by General Motors and had an open structure that allowed people to see the space within, including the support framework and the large truck wheels. Behind Santa was his traditional police escort, indicating the end of the parade.

We stepped off with high spirits and a desire to do our very best. Singing as loudly as we could with our mini-megaphones up to our mouths, it was hard to tell just how we sounded, since most of our sound went out ahead of us. Because of the general din of the parade, with band in front of band in front of band ahead of us, it was likely that only those who were right next to us could make out that we were singing, but that was fine. As long as we walked uniformly and smiled pleasantly to the cameras, we felt like we were the stars of the show. Not being able to hear every note amplified a hundred times over also meant that every note that wasn't quite A440 wouldn't be amplified a hundred times over.

We looked good, we felt good, and so we believed that we were good, and there was no one there disputing that attitude. About halfway through the parade I felt my stocking cap dripping on my shoulder, but that was alright. Nothing was going to dampen my Thanksgiving Day Parade experience.

Since Santa, Mrs. Claus, and Christmas Carol represented the end of the parade, many of the spectators took to the streets behind the police cars trailing Santa's sleigh, and followed him the length of the parade route down Woodward.

The end of the parade was in front of the J.L. Hudson Department Store building, where a thirty-five foot gold and white turreted castle representing Santa's North Pole home stood. Mayor Roman S. Gribbs and his wife Katherine welcomed Santa to Detroit, officially opening the Christmas season for all when he gave Santa the key to the city. Santa's next job was to travel to Toyland, located on the 12th floor of the J.L. Hudson building, sit on his throne, and listen to the Christmas wishes of untold hundreds of Detroit children, whereas our next job was to drag our exhausted, dripping, and droopy selves back to the bus and travel the fifteen or so miles back to Silver Lake High School.

I said good-bye to Moriah and Denny, who were on the other bus, and I got in line to get on my bus, with the front half of the choir alphabet. When it came time for me to take a seat, I decided to sit down next to Marci. I wasn't sure how that move was going to work out, but I was feeling particularly brave at that moment. I figured that we could talk about last year's musical or our plans to be in this year's musical. I thought that there was little chance that she'd mention my pig-like nose or my pig-like butt in the conversation, so I would probably be OK. We could talk about how long the day had been, how we were all soaked down to our underwear, and how much fun we had. The bus lurched into motion as I tried to lurch into a casual conversation.

When I finally got home to Thanksgiving dinner around four o'clock, everything seemed normal as I pulled up to the house and parked in the street. My grandfather's yellow Bel Air was in the driveway, right where I expected it to be. The family was holding off serving dinner until I got home. I smiled as I recalled the pleasant chat that I'd had with Marci. She seemed interested in me, without coming across with a superior or creepy vibe, and she'd laughed at my jokes. Whether they were very funny or not, I couldn't say, but she seemed to have a sense of when to chuckle without anyone nearby holding up a cue card, so the ride went great.

I grabbed up all of my soggy self and my soggy belongings and headed for the front door, listening to the bubbling and squeaking from my shoes as I went. I didn't usually use the front door, preferring, instead, to sneak in quietly down the back stairs when I got home, but today was a holiday and we had company, so it was probably safe to enter normally.

In the living room, I discovered my Grandpa Eugene and my Grandma Menafay, decked out in their finest out-of-date fashions and smelling quite festive with their aftershave and perfumes. They looked a little out of place in the room. For reasons bewildering to my interior design sense, my mother and stepfather had decided to decorate the living room in a sort or Inquisition-Gothic style. The paneling on the wall was very dark, and my stepfather had put large, but fake, Styrofoam beams across the ceiling, much in the style of an eighteenth century building. There was a sectional, yellow ochre velveteen couch that looked quite minimal and modern, with the table-like corner section sporting a large musketeer figural lamp with a big yellow ochre lampshade. There was a large brown recliner by the picture window, and next to that, by the front door, was a rather small, hexagonal enclosed table where my mother kept her magazines and the Christmas Wish Book that we got from Sears every year. Directly in front of the door and across from the couch on the opposing two walls was a large console TV. My grandmother sat in the recliner, my grandfather sat across the room on the couch, and my stepfather was nowhere to be seen.

Either he was in the bathroom, or something unpleasant had already happened.

I looked closer at my grandmother's face as she turned to look from the TV to me and her look of "I wish I were anywhere but here" changed quickly to happiness.

Something had happened, something that would be talked about later, no doubt.

"There's our TV star," Grandma Menafay said, jumping up from her chair and giving me a big hug.

"Did you see me?"

"Of course we did. They had a good shot of you as you marched by. You looked very professional," Grandma Menafay replied.

"But how did we sound? We really couldn't tell. The acoustics were horrible and by the end, we were all just short of frozen stiff," I shared.

"It was great, Nicki. We were all very proud," Grandpa Eugene added.

The thought of asking, "All of us?" crossed my mind, looking at the recliner occupied by Grandma Menafay, which would normally be occupied by Nathan, but I decided not to say anything.

"I need to get out of these wet clothes, if you'll excuse me."

I went into the kitchen to find my mother preparing dinner and Danielle setting the table. Actually, Danielle was busy playing with the relish dish, making "alien fingers" by putting the pitted black olives on the ends of her fingers.

"Danielle, stop playing with the food and set out the silverware," my mother said, under her breath.

"Can I help with anything in there?" my grandmother asked from the other room.

"No, mom, I've got everything under control." She gave Danielle a quick slap on the backside of her head and

Danielle ducked, just in case another one was coming. "Behave yourself or you'll be having dinner alone in your room, young lady," she whispered to Danielle, in a very serious tone. It was obvious that the light-hearted holiday chit chat was going to be reserved for her mother and father, and that we, her children, were going to get the quiet and between-the-teeth-with-glaring-eyes type of interaction today.

Nathan had done something to set her off.

"Did you see us perform, Mom?" I asked.

"I caught a glimpse of you. I had a lot of work to do to get dinner ready, you know."

"How'd we sound?"

"Not bad, for a group of drowned rats."

Trying to focus on the joke-like part of the comment, I said, "It's true, we were quite drippy by the time we got to the end, where almost all of the big cameras were, but we had fun."

"That's nice. Go and change your clothes for dinner. The biscuits, the turkey, and the macaroni and cheese are ready and we're all waiting for you."

I changed as quickly as possible and joined the family unit at the kitchen table. We fit quite nicely with Nathan absent, and it was obvious from my mother's demeanor that not even his memory was invited to dinner. We settled down to eat with just a frosting of casual conversation provided by my grandparents and, for the most part, directed at me concerning my parade experience. My mother took her turkey drumstick and served the other on the platter for anyone to eat, but I was much too smart to take the bait. She absolutely loved the drumstick, which I was informed of years ago when I was younger and I had made the faux pas of grabbing the remaining one from the turkey platter for myself. When no one was around, she had educated me concerning my bad manners. Ever since that day, I had spent my time developing a fondness for the meat of the turkey that no one else particularly cared for, which became the thigh.

Steven loathed turkey, and he reminded us of his loathing each and every Thanksgiving dinner. If he was being rewarded for good behavior, he was given a steak. If he was being punished for unacceptable behavior, he was given a hamburger. Today, he was having steak, but that could change at any moment. Danielle was being Danielle, playing with her food and dreaming of being somewhere, probably anywhere else. The only thing on her plate that she was absolutely going to eat was the olives. The rest of the food put on her plate by my mother, maybe yes, and maybe no. Vicky would be fed the remains of the day, at least the plate scrapings. The rest would be made into turkey sandwiches, or turkey soup, and the macaroni and cheese's days were definitely numbered. The devilled eggs and the fresh biscuits wouldn't see the end of the meal. I ate like I'd been walking in the rain for three hours.

When everyone was finished, my mother started in on the dishes. In a little while, before my grandparents left, we'd have dessert. I was the last one up from the table. When I sat down next to Grandpa Eugene in the living room, he grabbed my knee and gave it a squeeze, which was one of his favorite attention-getting tricks.

"You did a fine job, my boy, a fine job," he said.

"You did a fine job on my macaroni and cheese, too," Grandma Menafay added.

"And I'm quite proud of that accomplishment also," I jibed. I leaned close to my grandfather to make sure that my mother couldn't hear me from the other room. "What happened with Nathan?" I asked.

He looked over in the direction of the kitchen doorway and then, hearing my mother at the sink, he whispered, "I'm not sure. Nathan was here when we arrived, but after a few minutes of small talk, he gave your mother an angry look, stormed out the back door and drove away.

"How'd he get his Ranchero down the driveway? Your car was in the way."

"He squealed his tires and drove onto your neighbor's driveway to get out. I'm not sure what set him off, but he was quite angry. Whatever it was, it didn't happen while your grandmother or I were here."

"I live here and I'm not always sure what they're fighting about," I added.

My mother popped her head into the room and said, "We'll have dessert in about a half an hour. Nicholas, get in here and help me with these dishes."

As much as I wanted to stay and socialize with my grandparents, there was no turning down a command performance from my mother, so I complied. She finished putting the leftovers away and then went into the living room to make small talk. That left me to take care of the dishes alone, which was the way that I preferred to work.

Apple pie with ice cream was served soon after, and our guests left. We all retired to our respective corners and wondered if there was a boxing match in store for us before the day was out.

It was around two o'clock in the morning when I awoke to Vicky being kicked down the stairs from a sound sleep, and her yelping in response to the unexpected attack. I listened intently to discern whether Nathan was going to come downstairs and use the bathroom, or go straight to his bed upstairs.

Stomp.

Stomp.

Thud.

Two stomps and a thud meant that he'd gone up the two stairs from the back landing and had entered the kitchen. I was, at least for the moment, safe. I listened to Nathan rustle around in the refrigerator for food. I could picture my mother in the living room, her back to the hallway and pretending that she was asleep, but no one in the house would be asleep after his loud and dramatic entrance. He took whatever he had found in the fridge to the back bedroom and slammed the door. This was a universally understood gesture of not wishing to be disturbed under any circumstances the next day. I, for one, was not going to go against his wishes. If my mother had planned properly, then everything she needed for the next day would be out of that bedroom. Dirty clothes under the bathroom clothes chute could be washed and worn, if needed.

To violate the mandate of the slammed door might lead to violence, and as I fell back asleep, I prayed that my mother would have the sense to leave him alone to sober back up.

Steven's birthday would be in a couple of days.

Maybe he'd have one, maybe he wouldn't. Only God knew what would be coming next and Zotia and the Blue Lady weren't giving me any insight into coming attractions.

CHAPTER THIRTEEN
The Trickster

Sometimes, after reading in my Bible and just before falling asleep, I'd be able to have a mental conversation with Grandma Zotia and the Blue Lady. I was always tempted to refer to her as The Blue Fairy, like in Pinocchio, but somehow that seemed disrespectful, so I didn't. These interactions were few and far between, and they were usually quite brief. Slowly, I began thinking in terms of viewing things from God's spiritual world looking in to the physical world, instead of the other way around, which was the "normal" view of things.

How does one go about explaining a creature that predates Jehovah, is made up of pure evil, and who can stand in The Presence of Jehovah Himself and not be detected?

The Blue Lady began my education concerning what she called The Trickster.

At first, I couldn't understand what she was whispering and I thought that I must be insane. When I was thinking thoughts that weren't mine, full of information that I didn't personally know then it all felt like some sort of miracle. However, when the information stopped making any sense, then I began to suspect that I might have a serious mental flaw.

Maybe it was a tumor.

"You don't have a tumor, now be quiet and pay attention. You need to be aware of The Trickster energy and how it can twist and use pretty much anyone that you meet as a pawn."

"How can that be possible?" I thought, "Don't religious people have spiritual defenses against being used by the dark?"

"The Trickster uses the selfish and dark reasoning of its victim in order to make it seem to that person that their behavior is a totally logical response to the given situation.

The Trickster alters the perceptions of the intended puppet, so they will react to create anger or fear, which serve as fuel for the darkness."

"Like when I meet people and they don't seem to like me at first sight?"

"Exactly like that."

"So my mother is being used by The Trickster energy?"

"Your 'mother' is a unique case and she doesn't need any help from The Trickster.

"What about Uncle Dominic?"

"He is also a unique case."

"And you're not going to give me any clue as to why they're unique, are you."

"When the time is right, I'll tell you everything, but you're not ready yet. Do you remember when Nathan blurted out that he disliked the look of your eyes? The Trickster convinced him that you were exuding attitude."

"But I never..."

"I know that you didn't, but he doesn't realize that you didn't. Can't you recall other instances where someone disliked or attacked you for no reason?"

"There was that time Mr. Mako hid my bike because he was mad that I had parked it in front of his house."

"Trickster."

"Mrs. Weis told me to get out of her yard and never come back the first time I ever stepped into it to play with her son."

"Trickster."

"I got yelled at for getting a three-pronged hook stuck in my foot at Darryl Sandusky's house."

"Trickster, they're all The Trickster energy. You need to be aware when someone else is being used as a puppet so that you don't respond inappropriately to whatever they do or accuse you of. Anger, frustration, and thoughts of retaliation all fuel the dark side. You have no idea how your energies, turned dark, would aid the dark side, which is why they have made you a target since before you were even born."

"And my grandparents?"

"They are not normally aligned with the darkness, but that doesn't make them immune to being used. Their connection to the Light is there, but it is imperfect, and imperfect connections can be strained or broken. Pray for them, but stay aware that they can be used against you, especially when they are motivated by other dark souls that you know."

"But how can The Trickster energy not be detectible by Jehovah? How can anything be beyond the abilities of God?"

"The Trickster energy has the ability to steal bits and pieces of the pure energy of others, and to use those energy pieces like a costume, a costume that seems shiny, even to God."

"But I thought that Jehovah was All-knowing."

"He is All-knowing, but The Trickster has spent a long time disguising its actions, working through others, and leaving tiny pieces of its energy hidden, believing in that way that it can never be completely discovered or destroyed. Jehovah is All-knowing, but He does not think like the darkness or like a mind full of evil."

"And why do I need to know all of this?"

"You have agreed to help us draw The Trickster energy out into the Light, so that it can be dealt with fully, once and for all. If it is not removed from the shadows, it will continue to grow and threaten the continued existence of all good things."

"Are you *sure* that I agreed to do that? It sounds potentially dangerous."

"You agreed."

"Was I happy about my choice?"

After a long silence, I heard, "You agreed."

"Did I argue?"

"You agreed."

"It sounds to me like you have more confidence in me than I do."

"I have more confidence in you than you could possibly imagine, or else I wouldn't be speaking to you now."

"Am I going to survive this?"

"If you do not, then all that has been gained will be lost."

"Thanks, no pressure."

"Don't worry about this discussion; it was all just a dream."

"I thought that I was the funny guy."

"Funny – haha, or funny – hmmm?" I heard Zotia ask.

"No fair teaming up on me, you two."

"Go to sleep. You have nothing to worry about."

"Except failing in an assignment that I don't understand and causing the destruction of pretty much everything that I value as a person."

"OK, worry a little."

"Thanks for the permission."

CHAPTER FOURTEEN
Plop!

The Thanksgiving turkey was barely cold when – whammo!

To say that nobody saw it coming would be an understatement, for on Sunday, December 1st, the Metropolitan Detroit area was pummeled by almost twenty inches of snow, which brought everything that moved to a complete standstill. On the calendar, it wasn't even officially winter yet. It was the second biggest snowstorm ever recorded in Detroit's history, the largest snowstorm having occurred way back in 1886, in April, and having brought with it almost twenty-five inches of snow.

It pummeled the metro area for a day, and then it continued to snow for two more days, several times so intensely that nothing could be seen outside the living room picture window.

Initially, the storm was welcomed because it shut down the schools and extended the weekend, but as the groceries started wearing thin and the driveway started to become nothing but a memory under an enormous pile of white, the welcome became short-lived. It was one thing to be bundled up all cozy inside watching TV, and it was quite another to realize that at some point all of the snow that was blocking the street would have to be cleared away. Once the snowplows pushed everything in the street to the sides, in addition to finding one's own driveway again, one would have to move away the compressed mini-mountains provided by the department of public works' trucks.

Adding to the mess was the fact that the temperatures rose to 40 degrees during the day on Monday, melting some of the snow, which was then turned into ice underneath everything when it got back to freezing temperatures that night.

After spending two full days safely ensconced in my dungeon, I decided to make a preemptive strike at the driveway, knowing full well that I would get a mandate soon enough to shovel it. I started on the driveway on Tuesday, knowing that my mother had an interview for a job that she needed to get to in the afternoon on Wednesday. I shoveled off a lot of the top layer of snow, making the depth about six or seven inches thick. Her new Continental could barrel through six inches if it needed to, but unless the city trucks came and plowed the streets during the night, there would be nowhere for her to go on Wednesday except to the end of the driveway. When we woke up on Wednesday, the street had been plowed, and as anticipated, the end of our driveway was a huge mess. I tackled the entranceway and had it worked down enough so that my mother could get her car out into the street and be off to her job interview when the time arrived.

I worked all through the rest of the afternoon, and when my mother finally got home, I had the approach cleared away and the snow gone all the way down the driveway to the back door of the house. The snow piles on each side of the driveway were an impressive five to six feet tall, and in some spots, it was impossible to pile on any more snow without it falling back down into the driveway.

She pulled up the driveway and got out of her car.

I asked her how her interview went.

She watched me chop away at the ice layer at the bottom of the snow accumulation for a moment and then she said, "You're doing it wrong. Bring in the groceries."

With that, she turned and walked inside.

I stood there looking down the driveway at the huge piles that I'd moved, took an inventory of my aching muscles, reflected upon how difficult it had been to actually chop the ice away down to the level of the driveway cement, and then I asked myself what I had expected her to say.

I thought that she *had* to acknowledge my efforts in a positive way. There wasn't any other logical response.

I had been mistaken.

Chilled to the bone, I decided that I liked it a little better outside, where at least I understood the nature of the chilliness.

CHAPTER FIFTEEN
Stalked

It is one thing to think that you're being stalked by nasty, unseen things, and it is quite another when you begin to feel them and see them.

I was standing in the checkout line of the local hardware store when I felt it. It felt like a ten inch spider-like creature, slowly climbing up my left leg, under my pants. It was obviously in no hurry, probably thinking, if indeed it was capable of independent thought, that there was no way that I would suspect that it was there.

The Blue Lady had a surprise or two in store for it, for when I closed my eyes and started praying about its removal, I felt it pause, tremble uncontrollably, and then disappear. I was certain that it wasn't going to like its new home, at the foot of The Throne, in The Presence of Jehovah, but it had tried to bite the wrong person.

I only saw it for the briefest of seconds and I only caught the end of it as it skittered past me when I entered my bedroom. The part that I saw resembled the tail end of a centipede, but it had relatively few legs and it was over three feet tall! My impression was that the front end of the creature looked more ant-like or demon-like.

"What was that??!!" I asked in my mind.

"That was an indigo satan," the Blue Lady replied, "the nastiest type of creature that Lucifer ever gave life to."

"Can we have it removed?"

"It came here to violate you and your space, and so, by the laws of karma, its debt to you is enough for you to take control of it. You have the spiritual authority to pray it to Jehovah's Throne," she replied.

"And I thank Jehovah for that," I said, organizing my thoughts for the prayer. "Another bug bites the dust," I quipped.

"Never doubt that spiritual awareness combined with free will is a powerful force, as this indigo satan is about to learn."

"You don't have to tell me twice."

CHAPTER SIXTEEN
The Ghosts of Christmas Presents

The pile looked pathetically small upon my bed.

It was Christmas Eve and the potential presents that I had collected together to give to my friends seemed somewhat lost, laying there on the old, tattered quilt. I sat for a moment and reflected upon these few treasures that I had decided to pass on to others in my life.

Somehow, money for Christmas presents wasn't that easy to come by this year. In retrospect, money for many things hadn't been easy to come by, but lately the financial lack was felt just a little more acutely than usual.

I had spent what money I had on my family, and even then I knew that reactions were going to be mixed. For Grandma Menafay and Grandpa Eugene I had a pencil drawing that I had done in art class at the end of my junior year. That drawing, although seeming like a simple thing, actually represented an unheard of amount of work. It was a drawing of an old man sitting on a park bench in downtown Detroit, happily soaking up the sun. It was made from a black and white picture that had been taken by someone from school in the Photography Club. I had brought the drawing home to work on it, and I had made the mistake of showing it to my mother. She decided that she wanted to give her friends a copy of the drawing, so she had ten copies made. The problem was that she had copied the drawing when it was only half completed, and then she insisted that I finish all of the ten copies of the drawing by hand! That had been a major effort to complete, but her wish had been my command, for who was I to say, "Duh, make copies of the finished drawing!" With all eleven copies of the drawing completed, I decided to give the original to my grandparents.

My grandparents would take whatever I gave them and treat it like it was gold, which is what they were to me, but I knew my younger brother wasn't going to be impressed with his Christmas gift. Instead of spending $5 each on my mother, stepfather, brother, and half-sister, I had decided to get them a group gift. It was a beautifully sculptured, multicolored candle. The wax had been molded in different colored layers and then it had been skillfully sliced and twisted and twirled.

I liked it, but then it flitted through my head that not everyone I knew thought that pretty was a measure of value. I had a feeling that Steven's reaction was going to be something along the lines of, "Nice going, cheapskate, can I burn *my* part now?"

He and I weren't cut out of the same bolt of cloth.

To be truthful, there had been times when I have privately wondered if we had indeed come from the same cloth factory.

The core family presents had been acquired and wrapped, and now I was dealing with presents for friends. It was Christmas and I felt that it was important, perhaps only to me, to give all of the people in the caroling group that I was in something to show that they were special to me.

The caroling group had been created when I mentioned to my friend Mike that I thought it would be neat to get our friends from the choir and the drama club at school together and create a group to sing around town. We had been new sophomores at the time. We decided to dress up in period Dickens costumes and carol at nursing homes during the holiday season. It sounds like a simple idea but it took a lot of time, researching costumes, finding where to buy top hats and tail coats, getting patterns for the girls' outfits, getting the music, rehearsing and setting up the performances. We all had the hang of it by this Christmas, though. This would be our second official year in costume. We were quite proud of how far we had come. In addition to singing in nursing homes, we had been asked to sing downtown this year for Noel Night, and we had appeared on a local TV program.

So there I was, an integral part of a fairly successful group of a dozen singers, and I was scrambling to find gifts for each one of them.

After much deliberation, I made a decision.

I would give to my friends my most precious belongings. I would find presents for them from what I had, but it had to be something that had special meaning to me. If I didn't want to keep it, it wasn't considered worthy of being a present. Now I was looking down at my little pile, realizing that I didn't have a lot of cool stuff to pick from. There were a few drawings and some knickknacks, but nothing of obvious value. Ah well, it was the thought that counted, I reminded myself, and I grabbed some wrapping paper. Time was wasting and there was much to do, so I started to wrap. The last thing that I wrapped, the thing that I wanted to keep the most, was a little HO scale 4-4-0 steam train. I had pestered my mother for a long time to get that train, but those moments seemed long ago and far away. Now I know it doesn't sound like much of a sacrifice, but I had waited a long time to get that train. For me it was filled with nostalgia and action-filled stories of the Old West and the Civil War. It was going to be the beginning of a huge track layout that I was going to build some day. My layout was going to have mountains and streams and bridges and buildings and...you get the idea.

My friend Mike had a huge train set-up in his parent's basement. It had multiple tracks and mountains and buildings. His dad and his brothers had spent years building it. All I had was my one locomotive and enough track to get it to run in a three foot circle. I decided that my 4-4-0 (four leading wheels, four driving wheels, no trailing wheels) would live a long and happy life with Mike's other trains, and I found a box that it would fit into.

Five o'clock was approaching fast. I gathered up my presents, my Christmas cards, and my costume, got my overcoat on and headed over to my grandparent's house for our traditional Christmas Eve meal.

It was dark and windy that night. There was snow on the ground, but it wasn't very deep. It was the kind of night where everything seemed quiet and crisp. The flakes were fine and hard and skittered across the low snow mounds, driven by the wind. The stars seemed particularly bright. I parked my T-bird at the side of the house, carefully navigating the driveway and avoiding the driveway guardians – four massive maple trees that I had named Mathew, Mark, Luke and John.

I grabbed my bundles and crunched up the wooden stairs of the back porch. The rest of my family was already there, and I could hear their muffled voices through the thick walls. The windows glowed with the amber light of the electric candles placed there. I entered the rear sun porch and stomped the snow off of my shoes.

It smelled like Christmas Eve.

There was the sound of sizzling steaks in the broiler. My grandfather was the master chef of the outdoor cooking, but tonight the master chef of the indoor cooking was on duty, and the aroma of baked macaroni and cheese was coming from the oven. My immediate family was milling around in the front living room, Steven and Danielle spending most of their time seemingly admiring the tree, but in reality, they were taking note of the names on the presents beneath the tree. Most of presents were for my grandparents, but there were always a couple more presents for the kids to open – like me! Even at the age of seventeen, I was still one of the kids.

I added my package to the pile.

The snacks were being attacked with enthusiasm. Grandma Menafay always put out special treats for the holidays - chocolates and old fashioned hard candies.

I stopped a moment to take a good look at Grandpa Eugene and the smile that was spread across his face.

Grandpa Eugene was in his seventies and he had a small moustache and curly red hair that started quite high on his forehead. This didn't bother him because most of the men he knew had white hair and foreheads that extended all the way to the back of their heads. He always wore glasses and liked to smoke cigars, not large ones but smaller, more discreet ones. Thankfully, he didn't do it all the time because I hate the smell of cigarettes and cigars. Early in his life, he had been a successful purchaser for the Ford Products Company. Unfortunately, that company was absorbed into Ford and he was let go at the age of 50. He had eventually found a job as the head custodian at our local junior high school.

Grandma Menafay was an energetic and strong-willed woman, who was for the most part generous and supportive. I say for the most part because one of the traits that she picked up from being a nurse was to be honest, and brutal is sometimes a word that can be linked with being honest. If she believed you were right, then heaven help the person who crossed her and told her that you were wrong. She had broken her back while lifting a patient several years before and had made a complete recovery. It takes a special person with a special spouse to recover from such a life-altering event. She did it, and if you had ever met her you wouldn't have been surprised. The nursing home where she broke her back had tried to deny that she had done it at work.

Well, they had made a mistake.

They had tried to cheat the wrong person.

At that moment she was celebrating Christmas, and the nursing home that couldn't be trusted was long out of business, with a little legal help on my grandparent's part. They lived a simple, pleasant life, and their main pleasures seemed to be each other, their flowerbeds and their holiday gatherings.

The moment of culinary truth had come at last.

We were invited to the dinner table, but not to the large walnut dining room set in the dining room. We all gathered around the kitchen table, a red plastic and chrome masterpiece from the 1950's. Its most distinguishing feature was a metal tray located under the table where the legs came together. This was a fabulous place to hide unwanted food items until they could be disposed of later, which was Steven's favorite trick. We didn't use the formal dining table in the dining room. We preferred to cuddle knee to knee around the breakfast table in the kitchen. You would think that it would be crowded with my grandparents, my mother, my stepfather, my brother, my half-sister and me, but it really wasn't.

My stepfather, Nathan, had decided to stay home this year. I wasn't exactly sure what the initiating incident had been, but he and my mother hadn't been speaking for weeks. It may have had something to do with my mother going out and trying to get a job of her own, but I couldn't be sure because they disagreed about so many things. Nathan liked to mix his holidays with a stiff shot of anger and alcohol, which always kept things interesting, but it seemed that he'd started his holiday "festivities" a little earlier than normal this year. By trade, he was a carpenter, so you would think that he enjoyed putting things together. Sometimes, he seemed to be better at busting stuff up.

He would be sitting alone in the living room, with the Christmas tree lit up and bedecked with tinsel and homemade ornaments, the creation of which had been my mother's latest crafty project. His only companion would be a Budweiser and its lineup of brothers. If I was lucky, he'd be passed out and snoring in bed before I got home.

The meal was fabulous.

It wasn't the type of meal that everyone had for Christmas, but that was OK with us. We feasted on thick T-bone steaks, which had been purchased at the only place in the neighborhood that was anywhere near as old as my grandparent's house, Bennett's Family Market. It was a small store complete with a butcher and his block in the back. He was very helpful and cheerful, but old, and he looked it, with his veins showing in his thin hands and a couple of missing teeth.

After dinner, it was our tradition to retire to the living room and await the opening of the presents. My grandfather would always sit on the floor near the tree and pass out the gifts. He used his pocketknife to cut the ribbons, tapes, and strings, all the while smiling from ear to ear. My grandmother would be supervising the event from her rocking chair located near the furnace grid. Most people probably don't know what a furnace grid is. This old house was heated by what they called a gravity furnace. The furnace didn't have any ductwork to speak of, and it was located in the basement, between the living room and the dining room. Above the furnace was a thirty-inch square metal grating. This meant that when the furnace kicked in, a blast of hot air shot up into the main floor of the house. The downside was that the back of the house became really cold in the winter – ice in the corners of the room cold. One amusing aspect of this type of heating was watching ladies in their dresses poof up like Hershey kisses when the furnace was on. At this point in the family event, my mind was charting my flight path for the evening.

With the creation of the caroling group, I had instituted a personal Christmas Eve tradition. I began delivering my Christmas cards to my friends dressed as Santa Claus. I enjoyed the moment of realization when the kids in the cars around me figured out that it was Santa on the road with them on Christmas Eve. There had been many warm, smiling moments. My grandmother had sewn the costume just for me without the benefit of a pattern. Working with me, she had a customer who was almost as big a perfectionist as herself. The suit had the usual trousers and overcoat, but it also included a vest, for that North Pole sporty, indoor look.

The gifts were being sorted out and my grandmother was making sure that each individual piece of wrapping paper was being carefully removed for future use. The preferred method of removal was judiciously cutting the tape with my grandfather's knife. After the holidays, she would actually iron the wrapping paper for use the following year. It's funny how I could recall seeing the same paper patterns year after year, appearing on progressively smaller packages.

Although I had an original drawing waiting for them to open, the most marvelous thing about my grandparents is that the nature of my gift to them didn't matter. I could've made them an ink stamp out of an old potato and they would've loved it, and I loved them for that.

After the gifts were opened and we listened to a couple of Christmas carols "played" on my mother's old upright piano, it was time for me to excuse myself and adjourn to the bathroom to begin my Santa transformation. About a half-hour later, I emerged, to the immense joy of my grandmother.

My mother just quipped, "You'd better enjoy your time being thin, because you're going to end up fat, just like your father, and then you won't need any Santa padding."

I tried to smile, but I'm sure that I just grimaced at her cheerful holiday comment.

A couple of pictures were taken by Grandpa Eugene, then I hugged everyone open to being hugged (my grandmother and my grandfather) and I was off on my mission.

This year, I started on my rounds with more trepidation than I had experienced the year before.

I was concerned about how my gifts would be received. I hoped for the best, arranged my cards in order of delivery, and backed out of the driveway, crunching on the hard-packed snow.

Traffic on Christmas Eve was never very heavy. Families were all bundled up in their best clothes and off to some friend or relative's house. The kids were often dozing in the back seat and they didn't usually notice me unless we were both stopped at a stoplight. Then things would get interesting and energetic. Their faces would light up and they would start waving wildly.

I always enjoyed that part.

And so, lost in thought, I puttered up and down the side streets to my various destinations. Most of my cards and presents were delivered to empty houses, like Mo's. At the houses where people were home, the reactions were usually the same. I would pull up and park at the curb, jump out, and run up to the door. After ringing the doorbell, I would usually hear something like, "I wonder who that could be?" and a face would appear at the window of the door. This was usually followed by an enthusiastic, "Oh my Gosh, it's Santa. Come on in Santa!" I would then be ushered into a family gathering of varying size, and all the folks would be very glad to see Santa. For the most part, the little kids wouldn't know what to make of the situation, because all of their relatives were accounted for and there in the room with them! Who could this stranger be? Could it be the *real* Santa? The parents would usually announce to the wee ones that they had asked Santa to stop by, even though they were often as surprised as the kids to have me there. There would be a lot of "Ho, ho, hoing," and a lot of hand shaking. After a few loud and raucous moments, I would get my friend alone and give them their Christmas card and present. They would thank me for the card and for coming by, and then they would tear open the present.

The girls were much better at masking their reactions than the boys were. The small collection of trinkets and figurines that I had received as presents over the years were somehow not seen in the same light by their new owners. The artistic doodles were received with a bit more appreciation. Now, having been in the Drama Club and having lived in two alcoholic households, I had long ago learned to sense a person's mood by their body language. This is a survival technique in certain families. My dear friends seemed to take immediate notice of the lack of fresh packaging. I sensed that without the original boxes, most of my presents were viewed as little more than my cleaning out of my closet.

I quickly said my good-byes at each home and hurried on to the next, all the while hoping that I had been mistaken and that I was just being overly sensitive.

Somehow the night seemed colder and the squeals of the children in the nearby cars seemed much farther away.

I continued on my way and, much to my dismay, the pattern seemed to repeat itself. Everyone seemed happy to see my whiskered face, except that by the end of the evening I was beginning to wonder if they had any real feelings for the face underneath.

I reserved going to Mike's house for last. Several of the carolers were family or very close family friends and would be at his large family gathering. I pulled down his street and parked as close as I could to his house. Before getting out of the T-bird, I gathered up the few cards and presents that were left. For a fleeting moment, I was struck by the fact that there was nothing left upon the seat. I was giving the last of my Christmas away. The visit to Mike's gathering started much like all the others, only much more so. There were more people, more children, and much more excitement. My entrance, being for the most part expected because of the year before, drew a big crowd of little people. This was Santa's second annual visit. There were just a few minutes to spare before Santa had to get back to work. I handed Mike his card and present, and he became my very jovial tour guide. It was time to say hello to everybody in the house. The kids trailed behind, and everyone wanted to get a picture on Santa's knee. After the kids were done, the adults wanted to get pictures, too.

Everyone was having a special moment, but I felt oddly detached.

After a little small talk, I ended up in the basement, where some of the food was being served. I was familiar with this basement. We often held our caroling practices there. Adjoining the central area at the foot of the stairs was Mike's brother's bedroom. I had always admired his bedroom furniture. In my little six foot wide room under the stairs I had half of a bunk bed to call my own. Charles, Mike's younger brother, enjoyed the pleasures of a family heirloom, an elaborately carved, black walnut, too-tall-for-the-basement-so-it-had-to-be-shortened, Victorian bedroom set.

I try not to give in to jealousy, but I had to admit that Mike's family had a couple of things that I wouldn't have minded having. Everyone there seemed to like being around each other. Their dad seemed very supportive of everything that they did, and of course, there was the family HO railroad set up at the other end of the basement.

I couldn't really imagine what it was like building it.

I couldn't really imagine working with one's dad on anything.

I had heard Charles and Mike talk about the track layout over the years and it always intrigued me that they were all contributing to it. I snuck a peak at the track. It was covered by a couple of sheets for it was not allowed to get dusty. I thought that my 4-4-0 would work great with the layout. I had high hopes. I had confidence that Mike would be able to see that my train wasn't just an old toy that I was looking to get rid of; it was something special. If he looked closely, surely he would notice that the paint was pristine. All in all, it had only chugged about 30' on my little circular track. Other than not being in the original box, it was still pretty much brand new.

Eventually, the party quieted down and the kids got used to Santa munching on a cookie in the corner. I always found it a challenge to try to eat through that bush of whiskers and beard that being Santa required, and there was no way that I could figure out to consume a cookie without consuming some beard hairs along with it. Yum!

I found Mike and said that I should get going. I reminded him about the present. He found it on the table near the front door and he opened it.

I watched his face very carefully.

He smiled, thanked me for the card and the present, and he led me to the door. It was a very pleasant exchange. If it weren't for the fact that he had looked puzzled for a moment and had dropped the box on the table with a little too much indifference, I never would've suspected…oh, yes I would've.

The best laid plans of mice and men often go astray.

As I looked back at my train lying on the table, I had an intense urge to step back in and grab it. I felt that it would probably not be used with infinite childish joy on the winding track in the basement, as I had imagined.

I felt very sad, but it is hardly good manners to grab a person that you have just given a present to by the shirt collar and explain to them that they have just received something of personal importance and not a piece of junk!

Mike thanked me again and wished me a Merry Christmas.

The closing door made the empty night seem unnaturally quiet. Inside, people were making merry, and Santa was feeling out of sorts. It was rather late, but I decided to mull things over for a while and I went for an extended drive.

I drove down the side street and onto Elvin Road. The evening was mine alone it seemed. The streets were almost completely empty. There weren't any cherub faces squashed up against car windows to ease my feelings of isolation. I imagined that most parents had already tucked their children into bed, and were waiting for the right moment to bring out the gifts and pack them under the tree. The stockings were being stuffed with candies and tiny toys. The children dreamt of piles of packages and of the myriad joys inside. In their simple lives their greatest worry was that they'd get too many articles of clothing and not enough "cool" stuff.

Everything was as it should be, except in my own heart.

Eventually, I found myself driving slowly down Lincoln Avenue by the lake.

The mansions lining the side of the lake were twinkling with more lights than I could possibly count. The preferred color seemed to be white. Occasionally, I would pass a house with an assortment of colors, but for the most part, the lights were white. They were laced through the bushes and up into the tall trees. They were strung upon the eaves and up the sides of the driveways. They outlined the windows and illuminated the porches.

They warmed up everything in sight - except my mood.

With the best of intentions I had set myself up for disappointment on the most important night of the year. I had planned and prepared to bring as much Christmas joy as I could to those in my life, and I now felt oddly empty.

The engine turning over and the crunching of the brittle snow were all that could be heard.

I thought about how much I had given of myself, and what high hopes I had had. I thought about how much the gifts had meant to me, and how now they were all gone. I thought about how the seat next to me was empty. I had received during my journey not one card or present, even though I had made my intentions to drop by again this year known to all.

I thought about how everyone had loved Santa's visit, but didn't seem all that interested in who was under the beard.

I thought and I thought and I thought, and as I was turning around to go home, it dawned on me.

God had given his best present to us all on Christmas morning, and almost no one had any clue as to the value of that gift.

It was then that I began to understand the enormity of God's Love.

And then I heard a quiet, "Well done, my son," from the Blue Lady, and a warm-hearted, "Merry Christmas, Little Nicki," from Zotia.

1975

CHAPTER SEVENTEEN
Releasing the Imprisoned

Most people got drunk or high, stayed up late, and passed out in a daze on New Year's Eve. Or, at least that was my impression.

Not being like most other people, I had another surreal vision instead.

I had stayed up as late as I could, watching the festivities on my little TV at the foot of my bed. I suppose that I could've watched Guy Lombardo and the big Times Square ball bring in the New Year on the big console TV in the upstairs living room if I didn't mind sitting in an emotional icebox between my mother and my stepfather, who had stopped speaking to each other for weeks now.

I couldn't quite decide which was more effective, their screaming insults at each other, or their efforts to club each other into submission with the infamous "silent treatment." The silent treatment was one of my mother's favorite tools, and it was quite effective when used on Steven or Danielle. Whenever they were abused with it, they somehow felt unloved, and so they would try to make amends. The silent treatment didn't really work on me because if my mother wasn't speaking to me, then she wasn't being sarcastic or demeaning, and so I had an upgrade in the quality of my life through her silence. The silent treatment was an energy-effective way of showing displeasure to people around her, but since it didn't work with me my mother was forced to be more energy wasteful when she wanted to ruin my day.

Handling me required active cruelty, as opposed to inactive cruelty.

The odd thing was, as much as she seemed to dislike me, with every breath I took I hoped that someday she would change her disposition and want to be my mother. Maybe stress made her mean, or the fact that I reminded her of my dad. The only thing that I'd actually done to her in an act of aggression is that I'd looked her straight in the eyes once, when she was scolding me. She'd instructed me to sweep the basement steps and then she had gone into the living room. A few moments later, she came back into the kitchen and yelled at me as I was going out the back door.

"I told you to sweep the basement steps, mister. Where do you think you're going?" she had demanded.

"I swept the steps," I said.

"Don't lie to me," she snapped back, moving towards me.

"I just got done doing what you told me to do," I pleaded.

"Then you couldn't have done a very good job." She marched over to the steps and inspected them. Finding no fault in the sweeping job that I'd done she became even angrier with me, and she glowered at me like she wanted to smack me for embarrassing her.

I looked her square in the eye, which I never normally did, but I found what she was doing to be unusually unfair.

"You think I'm a bad mother, don't you," she spat out between her clenched teeth. When she saw that I wasn't stupid enough to take the bait and respond, she stormed away. I couldn't tell if she resented her entire life, if she resented her entire family, if she resented ever having had children, or if she had resented my spoiling her birthday party by arriving three weeks early, but I was certain that whatever category her resentment called home, that I would be a member of that group. I had no idea how I had become a member of her core resentment group and I had no idea how to petition her to get out.

My mother, when perturbed, was anger, wrapped in resentment, and coated with sarcasm, not that I would ever utter such a sentence out loud, but knowing these things made being out of sight and arm's reach easier to accomplish. During my more sentimental moments, I wondered if she just needed a job, money of her own, and less stress in her life.

The problem with Nathan was that he didn't accept the anger in her nature and avoid her when it was out for a walk. He was brought up believing that a man's home was his castle, and that the man was the king of that castle.

I acted like I deserved being consigned to the dungeon and so I was often left alone and quietly tolerated, unless she was in a really bad mood and I had been foolish enough to cross her path.

Nathan believed that he made the family rules, since his paycheck kept the family alive and provided a roof over our heads.

Nathan didn't seem to realize that there are two ways of petting a porcupine, with the grain and against the grain. He insisted upon petting my mother vigorously against the grain, until something shook loose. He couldn't get it through his head that she was not some filly that he was going to break to wear his saddle. It was more likely that the filly that was my mother was going to stomp his head into the ground when no one was looking.

I think that there was a part of my mother that direly resented having been born a woman, but whenever that thought cropped into my head, I would push it out as quickly as possible, for what good could come from dwelling on that possibility?

If my mother had been born a man, then certainly either she or my Uncle Dominic would be dead by now, for one form of anger would certainly have killed the other form of anger – "accidentally."

And so, there they sat, at two ends of the living room, in absolute silence. The TV droned on about new resolutions and hopeful things for the future, and the two of them made every effort to make sure that the New Year was just as cold and detached and seething as the last year had been.

There was no hope of a hug and a kiss between them when midnight struck. In fact, it was more likely that Nathan would be snoring loudly in bed at the other end of the small house, just to avoid that moment, sleeping over his unopened Christmas presents that had been put back under their bed.

Wondering what gave the two of them such strength to fight on the way they did, I fell asleep.

I'm not sure that where I found myself next could really be considered a place at all. It was a space, a confining area, yet it didn't exactly have walls, like a prison cell or a dungeon would. It was large and dark, and filled with people and animals, oddly unmoving, but not really appearing to be dead. They looked more like elaborate rag dolls, strewn haphazardly together. If I stared at one of them long enough, I could detect a small amount of movement, like a slight turning of the head. Their eyes, animal and person alike, were glazed over, and they weren't aware in any way of each other.

"What IS this place?" I asked in my mind.

"This is a dark and secret place that is supposed to be protected against discovery or intrusion," the Blue Lady responded.

"What is it for? What happened to these people and animals? Are they dead?"

"They are worse off than merely dead. These innocents have had their lives taken from them so that they can serve as a sort of secret energy battery to the dark lord that binds them to this place."

"They're being spiritually fed upon?"

"Yes."

"Why are we here? Why do I need to know about this?" I asked.

"Your power of free will has the ability to free these souls."

"Free them? How did my free will even know of them? How did my free will bring me here?" I pleaded, confused.

"You did something long ago, back when you were fourteen years old, that almost no incarnated soul has ever done."

"What was that?"

"You prayed that Jehovah accept your free will and take control of every aspect of your life. Don't you remember?"

"I remember asking God to bring me back to Heaven, if possible, which He obviously didn't do."

"Since you have sincerely and completely surrendered your free will to His will, you have become a powerful extension of His Love in the physical world and in the spiritual world, and tonight, he asks that you consider releasing these prisoners back into His care."

"How would I do that?"

"Merely call upon Him and his emissary, Archangel Michael, and all will be done as requested."

"I call upon the great I AM of the Holy Bible, Jehovah by name, and I humbly ask that He send Archangel Michael to this place to release and redeem these souls that have been imprisoned in the darkness, far from his Light and Love. In Jesus' name I pray, Amen. Will that be sufficient?" I asked.

"That will be more than adequate."

"Do I have a connection to these souls? Do I know them?"

"They know of you, and your direct connection and authority comes not through personally knowing them, but rather through personally knowing their jailer. Without these souls energies kept in reserve, their jailer will be much less powerful in the struggle to come."

"There's going to be a struggle?"

A light began to shine all around us, and the prisoners began to stir as the fogginess faded from their eyes.

"There will be a struggle."

"Am I going to be involved with this struggle to come?"

"My boy, you've been involved with this struggle for untold millennia, but it is almost at its end."

"Untold millennia?"

"Go back to resting. You're going to need all of your strength in the times ahead."

"For how much time ahead will I be struggling with this unspecified jailer?"

"The merest blink of Jehovah's eye."

"That's poetic, but not helpful."

"How could making you worry by answering your questions be considered helpful?"

CHAPTER EIGHTEEN
Love and Madness

Who is it who can completely explain love?

Those who have never surrendered to it have no clue as to its nature, and those who have been embraced by it often have no clue as to how to describe it.

It is a sublime and desirable form of insanity.

If a person can succinctly describe the how and the why of their attraction for someone then it is probably not true love. Anyone who can completely answer the question, "Why are you with them?" does not know true love, for true love demands answers like, "I don't know. I can't get them out of my mind, or my heart, and when I'm away from them for too long, my soul begins to ache."

Of all of God's mysteries, explaining true love is perhaps the most difficult.

There are many related categories to true love that are easily defined, like infatuation, covetousness, and lust, but true love remains difficult to understand by everyone who has not yet been touched by it, and difficult to explain to anyone who has been touched by it.

It is a madness that begins with a thought.

My madness began with an image, an image to two brown eyes looking directly into my own.

Most people would probably find this strange, but like my stepfather, I'd discovered that most people found my direct gaze disconcerting. My mother used to refer to it as my "Beethoven stare," and at an early age I learned to look at other people's mouths or chins when talking to them. There were even times when I looked up into the other person's eyes and I stopped their speaking and derailed their train of thought. Such seemed to be the intense nature of my look, which many didn't seem to enjoy experiencing.

Chalking it up to yet another supernatural superpower designed to set me apart from the rest of humanity, I adapted.

My adaptation caused some to feel that I was weak-willed or afraid because of my not looking them in the eye, like my uncle, but I felt that appearing a little timid would probably be the path of least resistance for me and avoid a lot of confrontations.

In the long run, it really didn't, but such was my initial thinking on the matter.

The pair of brown eyes that had worked their way into my subconscious belonged to Marci.

After the Thanksgiving Day parade, on our ride back to school on the bus, I'd looked her in the eye on several occasions, just to see what her reaction would be. If I scrambled her brain or made her uncomfortable with my gaze, then there probably wasn't any reason to try and develop a more personal relationship with her. She'd been dropping hints like hand grenades for quite a while that she thought that I was cute, and the message had been received through several tried and traditional high school channels, like through friend-girl gossip, and through intentional friend-boy hints deftly delivered. The only real difference in the two delivery systems being that the friend-girls always wanted some bit of gossip to take back to the gaggle, some hint that something bigger was brewing, unseen. The friend-boys always delivered their intrigue with matter-of-fact honesty and then moved on to some other topic, as if the delivery of the gossip had been their only concern. And when they would be interrogated later by some member of the initiating gaggle, as was the tradition, they'd be able to say proudly, "I told him what you wanted me to," and then be done with the process. The gagglers, however, would be disappointed that no additional information or commitment had been acquired.

Hooking people up like sorting scrambled puzzle pieces was just one of the social sports of being in high school, and the more unlikely the couple, or prolonged the process of hooking them up, the more satisfying the end product, even if it didn't last.

No one took pride in hooking up the fickle, the trampy, or the asocial.

They were left to the whims of fate.

But anyone who had never been in a serious romantic situation before, who washed their hair more than once a week, who didn't smell badly, and who was associated with some recognized subgroup within the school, like being in the band, or the choir, or the Drama Club, was considered viable raw material for the mating game. There had been a handful of previous occasions where one gaggle or another had decided that I needed a turn at the mating game, but I hadn't responded to the various overtures and the interest had died out each time, without any loss of tears upon anyone's part, I might add, and I was proud of my record.

This time, however, my logic was dissipating and I was beginning to get a taste of what love might be all about. My natural caution and timidity seemed to be evaporating at a frightening rate, and all I could think of was that, "Maybe she..."

All through Christmas break I had reflected back upon Marci's unbroken gaze, and eventually, the rest of her face joined the picture. And there, located precisely where it should be, right under her cure little nose, was Marci's smile. I found the combination of her unbroken gaze and her unwavering smile intoxicating. We hadn't talked about anything particularly earth-shattering back on the bus in November. As far as I could recall, we just laughed and gossiped about other people, which was always a safe topic, but I found that by the time school was ready to resume in January, Marci's infection within me had grown to enormous proportions, and I wasn't sure what to do about the situation, for nothing logical seemed appropriate.

Only something monumentally insane would do, and that thought both scared and thrilled me at the same time.

My moment of temporary insanity struck on the first day back from Christmas break, during lunch. While everyone else in the choir room was getting caught up in the whirlwind that was the musical auditions set to begin at the end of the week, I found myself up in Mr. Chase's office. I wasn't exactly sure why I was hanging out making small talk with him about the musical. There was a part of me that wanted to talk to him about what dating was like, because I had no father figure to talk to about the topic. I had talked with Grandpa Eugene once about how he had come to the attention of Grandma Menafay. That story had centered around his having a job, some sharp clothes, and a brand new Ford to impress her with.

I didn't have a job, my clothes were adequate but nondescript, and my car was hardly new, although it was unique and stylish, so his story didn't prove to be very helpful.

I didn't know how my mom and dad got together, but since their union had proven to be such a disaster I didn't feel that my life lacked anything by not knowing. My mother having hooked up with Nathan in the back of some local bar, surrounded by the ghosts of yacht lies and her surreal girlish giggling, sort of made me want to take a shower, so that was no help. As for Grandma Zotia and Grandpa Nelek, I just assumed that he'd fought his way into her home, clobbered her over the head with some sort of club, and then whisked her off to America before he could be caught by her outraged family, not that I was going to ask.

Mr. and Mrs. Chase seemed very much in love, the kind of love that one sees on TV or in the movies, and I was tempted to ask him about how they got together, if the moment ever presented itself. The privacy required for such a discussion seemed unlikely with the endless parade of people traipsing in and asking Mr. Chase questions about the upcoming auditions. He answered all of their inquiries in stride as he calmly worked away at his regimented lunch. Like little battalions laid out in formation for battle, his lunch elements were slowly being divided and conquered. I was always amazed at how many little courses there were in his typical lunch. Even Mr. Chase's food seemed to speak of love that I didn't fully understand. At home, dinner was more often than not something discovered within a throwaway aluminum tray in the oven, shining in grease in a hot plate on the counter (which did wonders for my adolescent acne), or floating in boiled scum at room temperature in a pot at around 6:00 p.m.

Sometimes we had real family sit-down meals, but these were either on holidays and involved company, or were as rare as holidays and involved my mother and stepfather being on amicable terms.

From time to time I made pizza for the family, but these meals required my being home with no chance of being caught unprepared like a defenseless rabbit out in the open in the kitchen, surrounded by half finished pizzas, by a drunken Nathan barging through the back door.

I had just about reconciled myself to the fact that I wasn't going to get a moment alone with Mr. Chase when Marci entered the office. I don't remember what she had come to ask him because when she gazed over at me, my mind went blank, like someone had just pulled the plug on the TV tube of my brain. She finished talking to Mr. Chase and was about to leave when she looked over at me and smiled that smile.

I reached down and removed my class ring. Without Marci being able to see what it was, I held it out to her behind Mr. Chase's back. With a confused look on her face, she moved towards me to take whatever it was that I was offering her. Having very large hands, she knew immediately what it was when I dropped it into her palm, for the ring was an impressive size. Her eyes went wide as she looked deep into my eyes.

I mouthed the words, "I love you," such that no one else could see, and then I got up to leave the office as the class change bell rang. I wished Mr. Chase a great day. I gave the shocked and seemingly frozen Marci a wink and I collected my books and went off to class.

Although it had been a risky and insane thing to do, the look on Marci's face indicated that, at least for the moment, the chances of my being embarrassed and rejected were very slim.

I had no idea when I would be seeing Marci again, or where my impulsiveness would lead, but it felt right not knowing. It felt like good things could grow from the insanity that I had just planted. Fifth hour flew by and I had no idea what the discussion was about. I was in my own world, and I liked it there.

Then, as I was leaving fifth hour, who should I find outside of the classroom door but Marci, waiting for me. Where she had come from and how she'd gotten there so quickly such that most of my class had still been leaving upon her arrival was a complete mystery. She didn't say a word, but reached out and placed into my hand a yellow envelope, and then she turned quickly and joined the hall salmon, all swimming on to their last class of the day.

I made my way to the auditorium, and after I had taken attendance and accomplished my other menial duties, I slumped down in the seats so that I could read Marci's note undisturbed. One thing was obvious, there was no ring in the envelope, and so I interpreted that as a very propitious sign.

Inside was a poem, written on beautiful, flowery stationary. For a moment I wondered how she could write a poem and transfer it in perfect penmanship to such beautiful stationary, all within the confines of a single class period. Her efforts impressed me in a way that made me smile.

> Love is a beautiful word.
> It expresses many feelings.
> I love you.
> My love for you is not cruel or harsh,
> It's caring and smiles and beauty.

You're stronger than I.
You're loving and kind.
You make me feel beautiful.
You respect me,
And for this I love you.
For you I'd do anything.
My feelings are hard to express;
I love you!
Love releases pain – it makes you free.
Love is a beauty in people.
Love is you...
Love is us.

I reread the note several times before the class period was over.

My entire world had changed in less than a day. Less than a day – in actuality, in less than one hour we had both declared our intense love for each other. I had said much less than she, not having had a poem prepared or on the tip of my tongue to share, but I had provided a ring in the bargain, and so I felt that our unanticipated romantic exchange had been on relatively equal terms, although I knew that I'd have to polish up on my poetry skills soon in order to be able to keep up.

The bell rang and I found myself the last one in the auditorium quite quickly. I heard someone running from the direction of the choir room doors, and then, there she was. When she saw me, she stopped running and seemed to be composing herself as she came forward. I sat in the front row of seats and flipped down the seat next to me for her to join me. She seemed torn by two conflicting thoughts that chased each other across her face, unbridled happiness and concern. She held out my ring to me.

"You're sure that you want me to have this?" she asked, timidly.

"I'm sure," I responded warmly, and when she shifted her hand, I could see that somehow, somewhere she'd found some yarn and had wrapped it around the ring until she could wear it, for it was far too large for her small fingers. I got the fleeting impression that she'd been wearing it for a while inside out, with just the yarn showing, and the ring part hidden in her palm. The yarn looked a little damp, like she'd been squeezing it tightly.

"And what you said in Mr. Chase's office?" she queried.

"I don't make a habit of saying things that I don't mean," I replied.

"I hoped you'd say that. For the last two hours it's all seemed like a dream. I thought about us before, of course, but you never showed any romantic inclination before."

"I wasn't insane before."

"And you're crazy now?"

"It would appear so, and I'm not pleading temporary insanity. This may be permanent. I may indeed be crazy about you," I whispered.

I had certainly kissed girls before, but never had there been such a feeling of connection, of rightness to the act. All of the kisses that I'd ever experienced before suddenly fell into a category that could only be labeled "Not true love." Marci didn't say anything more. She just put my ring back upon her hand, ring part to palm, like she wasn't sure how she should wear it. I opened her hand and turned the ring stone out, for all to see.

She smiled at me, grabbed my hand in hers, and we kissed.

How long the kiss lasted, I really couldn't say, but when we were done, we just leaned against each other and held hands in the empty auditorium.

After a while I said, "So, should we try out for the *Sound of Music*?" knowing full well that playing Maria had been her dream since the instant the musical had been announced.

"She looked up at me, smiled, squeezed my hand, and said, "Perhaps we should, Captain Von Trapp."

And then we pondered what wonders the rest of the week might bring to us.

The best laid plans of mice and men...

The auditions for the yearly musical were a huge deal. The musical itself was considered the biggest publicity event for the high school, involving even more departments than anything happening at the athletic end of the school. Since the laying of the foundations for the auditorium, the biggest one in the entire county, back in 1970, the spring musical had been the showpiece. The school involvement numbered literally into the hundreds, once one considered all of the students who tried out, ran tech, built sets, played in the orchestra, sewed costumes or were involved in the publicity for the show.

It was an event greatly anticipated, and many young actors and actresses prayed that their favorite show would be selected for their senior year. No one knew what the show would be until it was announced by Mr. Chase.

No one knew that I had a hand in selecting the show for that year.

In a rather bizarre turn of events, Mr. Chase had decided to do *Bye, Bye Birdie*, and he had pulled me aside early in the year to make sure that I would be interested in trying out for the musical. That is not to say that I would be guaranteed the leading role, but merely to make sure that after the show was selected that *someone* who had played major roles in school would be interested in trying out for the leading role. To select a show that no one was really interested in would be a calamity, considering the effort and expense that was going to be put into the production.

I told Mr. Chase that I wasn't really interested in playing a watered-down version of Elvis and being in *Bye, Bye*

Birdie, and that if he asked me for my opinion, I would rather vote for *The Sound of Music*. Our discussions continued, and I made a commitment to him to design the set pieces and to get some drops painted for the school that could be used forevermore, as opposed to having to rent them each year. Since a full-sized drop would be about 21' tall and 50' wide, it was quite a commitment on my part, and Mr. Chase showed a great deal of faith in me for agreeing to let a high school senior tackle such a project.

I was just happy to be out of the house on the weekends.

To make a long story short, no one was aware of how the show had been selected that year, or that I had anything to do with it, and when I found myself in a conversation about the musical, I just pretended that I didn't know anything. When I learned that it was Marci's dream show, then I began to dream along with her, of playing Captain Von Trapp to her Maria.

There were to be two days of general auditions and then call-backs set for Friday. The official cast would be posted the following Monday.

As predicted, everyone who had any experience in performing in the high school turned out to audition for the show, even elementary school children, who had aspirations of becoming members of the Von Trapp family singers. The local papers announced the auditions and the publicity train for the show pulled out of the station, only coming to a stop when the show closed, months later, in April, after Easter.

Everyone that I knew had a favorite part that they were hoping to secure, and everyone was buzzing about what lines were being used for auditions and what songs were to be sung for what part. When auditions began, everyone assembled in the auditorium, filled out an audition sheet, and was assigned a number. Then the group was broken down into three different sections.

Mr. Devries would be holding drama auditions on the stage, where most of the people auditioning waited until being called upon.

Mr. Chase held his musical auditions in the choir room, and a local choreographer, Mrs. Dell, held dancing auditions in the band room, which was located behind the stage itself.

Mrs. Dell was also a band parent and her son was scheduled to play in the pit orchestra.

Crystal, not wishing to take her singing voice out for another public walk, aspired to playing Maria's romantic rival, the Baroness, which would focus upon her dramatic strengths.

Mo and Juliet each wanted to be one of the featured nuns.

Kevin talked about going out for the Captain, but since his singing voice was completely unknown, the gossip was that his chances were slim. People who have never sung solos before were seldom given the leading role in a Silver Lake musical, for rather obvious reasons.

Doreen wanted the part of the nun who found Maria irritating and who was constantly trying to get her expelled from the nunnery. I just smiled when she shared that with me.

Tyler and Victor seemed excited about playing Nazis, which seemed a bit creepy. I could understand Tyler's desire to a degree because of his interest in WWII, but I think Victor was attracted to being one of the bad guys of the show.

Denny was trying out for the Captain and Max, but figured that he'd probably end up in the chorus somewhere.

The most bizarre character desire was by Hayley Cress. Going completely against type, she coveted the part of the Mother Superior. Although her singing voice was perhaps up to the task, anyone who knew her as a person was flabbergasted to think of how much her personal character would be at odds with the Mother Superior's character.

Even with the masses of people flooding into the room, there was still a very good chance that Marci, who was an excellent soprano soloist, and myself a baritone, would be top contenders for the lead roles.

Amidst many well wishes, both for our aspirations in earning major roles in the show and for our newly announced romance, Marci and I settled down to begin the long process of elimination, and then I caught sight of him walking across the stage towards the audition table.

His name was Chris and he'd played several supporting roles in the plays throughout the last three years. He was a taller fellow, with a moderately pleasing singing voice, but what concerned me about his being there was another piece of his personal history, which, up until that moment, had seemed immaterial.

Chris had been Marci's boyfriend last year.

I suddenly got an odd feeling in the pit of my stomach, like I was unwittingly lining up to be the brunt of some cosmic joke. I tried to shake the feeling.

"Is this going to go well?" I asked myself.

There was no reply, which I did not take to be a good sign.

"Earth to Blue Lady…"

Just then, to add insult to injury, Marci's little brother, Joey, plopped himself down next to Marci.

"Holding hands, I see. Mom won't want to hear about that," he chuckled.

"Go away, Joey. Go and sit with some of your friends in the little kids section and leave us alone," Marci whispered back.

"Can't do that, sis, mom gave me specific instructions to keep my eye on you and your new 'boyfriend,'" he cooed.

"Hello, Joey, nice to meet you. My name is Nicholas, the boyfriend. Hold your hand up for a second. Cool. See how much larger my hand is than yours? See how much bigger my arm is than yours? I think your sister asked you to sit with your friends. I'm normally a very peaceful fellow, but I can 'help' you find your friends, if you like. My guess is that they're sitting over there, with the other elementary school kids," I said, smiling pleasantly in his general direction.

Joey got up to leave, adding, "I'm still telling mom about the handholding."

"There was never any doubt about that, bug, now run along before you get squished," Marci quipped with an air of frustration.

"I'll keep a running list of my transgressions, if your mother thinks that's necessary. Would she prefer them in alphabetical order or in timeline order?" I asked Marci after Joey was out of earshot.

"Do you plan on committing many transgressions?" Marci laughed.

"Now see, that depends upon one's point of view. From your mother's point of view, even the most innocent gaze from across the room might be interpreted as a transgression, whereas I shall make it my personal duty to make sure that you never feel transgressed."

"Never?" she asked, with a dubious look in her eye.

"I don't believe in transgressing. You will never have to ask me to slow down or to stop in our relationship. I respect you far too much for that."

"Go on, I'm still listening. I'm not sure that I completely believe you because it sounds so odd for a boy to say, but I'm still listening," Marci urged.

"Although I've never shared this with another soul, particularly not another female soul, I don't believe that true love revolves around selfishness. Selfishness is lust, and lust is meaningless and self-destructive. It shall be my goal to make you completely at peace around me, not completely nervous and defensive, as your mother's worries would imply. Anyone can be a cad, but not everyone can be a gentleman, as

I shall endeavor to prove. I'm not like anyone you or your mother has ever met before."

"If you're telling me the truth, then you certainly aren't like anyone that I've ever met before," Marci said, looking me squarely in the eyes as if she had discovered a pearl inside of an oyster.

"After we've been together for a while, I hope you come to realize that I don't believe in lying or distorting the facts to serve my own purposes. Although I shall always try to be supportively tactful, I shall never lie to you, unless someone has a gun to your head and lying is the only way to save your life."

"You don't lie – ever?"

"I'm trying for 'ever,' but I recognize that I'm not perfect."

"So I've gotten myself a boyfriend who's not going to knowingly lie to me and who has promised never to make me feel nervous or defensive?"

"That about covers it. I'd give you a kiss on the lips right now, in front of all of these people, but that would make you nervous, so I won't."

"What if I asked you to?" Marci inquired.

"I'll do anything that is in your best interest, but kissing you publicly in front of all of these people and your little brother probably wouldn't qualify as being in your best interest," I responded.

"You have that level of self control?"

"I don't, but God does, so if I put Him in the driver's seat, I'm sure to get to where I'm supposed to be."

"You owe me a kiss, later."

"Will that be with or without compounded interest?"

"Definitely with interest," she said, squeezing my hand.

The audition process got under way and we had to go our separate ways. When I was acting, she was singing, and when she was acting, I was dancing. Finally, I had a chance to sing for Mr. Chase. Everything else being basically equal, I thought that the singing audition would probably weigh in heavier in casting Captain Von Trapp, and so I gave it my all. I sang "Edelweiss" with all of the compassion that I could muster. Everything seemed to go really well. I looked over after my audition and saw that Doreen was crying, which I took to be a high compliment.

At the end of the first day of auditions I felt very good about my chances, and Marci seemed a shoe-in for Maria.

The second day of auditions began much like the first. However, a disconcerting murmur began buzzing around the auditorium. Mr. Devries couldn't seem to find a Max. Max is supposed to be the charming, self-indulgent, comic relief friend of Captain Von Trapp, and for some inexplicable reason, Mr. Devries seemed extremely concerned that none of the guys auditioning for the show knew how to read the funny lines. I had purposefully avoided all public interest in Max. I didn't discuss the part or give any insights to my friends on how the lines should be read because I didn't want the part of Max to become some sort of whirlpool that I could get sucked into. Listening in on some of the director's passing comments to each other, it seemed that there were a couple of different ways of approaching the casting of Captain Von Trapp, but no viable solution to casting Max.

I felt like I could see the walls of a box begin to be erected around me, and I didn't like to speculate on where this would lead.

I made call-backs along with Marci and we reported back to audition on Friday. During call-backs, it was the tradition of the directors to mix and match people to read various roles, even roles that they weren't auditioning for, in order to see the range of the person's acting ability.

I could already see into my own future.

"They're going to ask me to read Max, aren't they," I said within my own head.

"Yes, they are," the Blue Lady replied.

"What if I refuse?"

"That would show them that you aren't interested in what's best for the show, but only in your own selfish desires," she stated.

"But why are they so fixated on Max? It seems all out of proportion. No one is going to leave after the performance and say, 'If only they'd had a funnier Max.' What if I don't read the lines correctly? What if I'm not funny, on purpose?"

"Would you be true to your own nature if you do that? Wouldn't that be a form of lying, knowing that you can do something well and then fooling others around you into thinking that you can't do it at all?"

"You knew that this was going to happen, didn't you?"

"Although you have the free will to change anything that you like about your life, there are certain things that will come to pass, if you remain true to your higher self," she whispered.

"But Marci will be Maria and I will only be..."

"True to your higher self, if that is what matters to you."

"You know that I don't have a choice in this."

"And that is exactly why I am here with you today. There are very few people who will choose what is painful and disappointing over what will bring them joy and satisfaction."

"You could've warned me sooner."

"And what would I have said? I let you believe that you and Marci would be playing beside each other as Captain Von Trapp and Maria as long as I possibly could."

"I could still choose to screw up my Max audition."

"Could you, really?"

"No."

Like reading God's handwriting on the back stage wall in slow motion, my ears heard my name and the words that I already dreaded and I went onstage to read the part of Max, opposite Chris, Marci's old beau, reading Captain Von Trapp, Crystal reading the Baroness, and Marci reading Maria. Before I uttered my first line, I already knew that the die was cast. I didn't try to make myself funny, but I placed the emphasis in all of the right places, showing that I at least understood what the funny lines were about, and that was all it took.

The cast was announced and I was spun around publicly in the cosmic irony of, "Dude, I didn't see that coming, I thought your audition was fabulous," and "I can't believe that you have to act opposite of her old boyfriend, and he acts like a piece of carved wood!"

Marci was almost as disappointed as I was, but I didn't have that much time to mourn the death of my romantic dream, for I had promised to create a set for the show and I was a man of my word.

I learned that being true to my higher self was always an admirable thing, but not always an enjoyable thing. In fact, it could be downright painful. As cosmic irony would have it, Joey was cast as one of the Von Trapp boys. Over time, Joey seemed to realize that tormenting me about finding a moment to hold hands with his sister was probably not a wise thing to do, especially since the casting of the show had separated Marci and me more than his taunts ever could've accomplished.

With every rehearsal, the shadow of Mama Lauren Eston seemed to grow more and more, intruding into our daily lives.

CHAPTER NINETEEN
Pastor Fenrick

Pastor Fenrick had started out as the spiritual leader of a small church located at the end of my street, Grace Baptist Church. Before discovering this sanctuary, my religious commitment had been erratic at best, boiling down to a few summers of coloring pages of Jesus, and applying stickers of glory at Lakeshire Presbyterian Church, when I was quite young. This led to attending summer Bible school and my eventually attending Assumption Baptist Church. Throughout my sophomore and most of my junior year, my high school choir director, Mr. Chase, had graciously allowed me to go to church with his family from time to time. After Easter of my junior year, I settled on Grace Baptist Church and made it my first real spiritual home.

My immediate family believed in many things, but sharing Sunday with God and Jesus was not on the list. It appeared that my first young experiences with church had been more of an opportunity for my mother to find some peace and personal time during the summer months, and had little or nothing to do with my brother or myself discovering religion. When asked by others, my mother would say that we were all Presbyterians, although to my recollection, she never set foot in a church unless it was for a wedding or a funeral. God and Jesus' involvement with my family was limited to an image on a received Christmas card, or as a tiny Woolworth nativity figure, still stamped with a price of 15 cents on baby Jesus' flat backside.

My family didn't visit God's house, and my efforts to bring Jesus home with me were not met with appreciation. To try to talk to my mother about Jesus would actually make her cry, and there was no point in mentioning him to my younger brother Steven, who found mocking pleasure in calling me "fish boy." As for Danielle, it's difficult to get the attention of someone who has to have their bedroom window screwed shut because they sneak out all night. They tend to have priorities that don't include spirituality or religion.

And as for my stepfather, well, there was something about me that he just wanted to slap out of existence, so I wasn't going to add pestering him about his eternal soul to the list of reasons why he didn't like me.

I began attending Grace by sitting quietly and inconspicuously in the back pews of the Sunday morning service. I didn't attend Sunday school because of a bad experience that I had on Easter Sunday at Assumption. In my eagerness to learn more about God and Jesus, I had recently read a book called *The Day Christ Died* by Jim Bishop. Through reading that book, I imagined what Jesus might've looked like on his way to the cross, and it was nothing like the assumptions made by my well-meaning but seemingly unimaginative instructor at Assumption. Perhaps God was making an inside joke when he allowed the church to name itself.

I saw in my mind's eye an abused, swollen and bloody shamble of a man, his head down and unrecognizable, stumbling without acknowledgement or fanfare towards his destiny to save humankind.

The Sunday school teacher presented a picture of a quietly suffering and majestic man-God weaving his way through crowds of confused and misled sheep-le, with just the slightest indication of blood and discomfort sprinkled on for dramatic effect. Instead of the writhing agony that made me wince when I thought of it, the classroom discussion seemed to focus more upon Jesus' power and destiny and heritage, making his ultimate ascension a minimal moment of discomfort, which Jesus ultimately brushes away with the words, "It is finished," amidst a chorus of angels singing sweetly.

I couldn't explain in words why I felt that the discussion was so inherently wrong and misleading, but to begin the process that lead to Golgotha, Jesus had been beaten bloody to within an inch of his life. How could he muster the strength to stumble nobly forward, with almost no blood on his body? It wasn't that I enjoyed thinking of Jesus as bloody and swollen, but how could the movies continually overlook these basic facts?

My face must've shown my internal discomfort because the instructor called upon me to share, seemingly to add my support of the image already presented, but I didn't comply.

I felt very alone in that room as I shared a vision of a person hardly worth a second look, being escorted to an ignominious death, just one more among thousands, at a time when people were generally inured to the suffering of others nailed to crosses or to the walls of the city of Jerusalem.

The class ended in an odd silence.

That was the last Sunday school class I ever attended at Assumption. I thanked Mr. Chase and his family for allowing me to worship with them up to that point, and then I indicated that I had found my own church, which was more local. I never shared with them the reason for the change because I didn't wish to seem unappreciative of the wisdom and experience of my elders. It seemed to me that if my instructor couldn't read the Bible and come to a logical conclusion about what he'd read, then what business did he have advising me about the mysterious unseen path to eternal salvation. If he couldn't get the information about what we do know right, then what were the odds that he'd get the information about what we don't know right?

My time of publicly communing with God at Grace Baptist started out being limited to the Sunday morning sermon, but I eventually joined the choir. I spent months listening to the word of God, while watching Pastor Fenrick's back from the choir stalls.

Pastor Fenrick was a tallish man, with hands like baseball gloves that would enthusiastically envelope any hand offered in greeting. He was probably close to forty, although knowing another person's age meant little to me at that time in my life. He had dark, carefully groomed, short hair, and he was usually seen wearing glasses and a large, inviting smile.

Of all of the men that I had ever known in my life, I would've rated Pastor Fenrick as one of the top three, which is why I silently adopted him as a sort of father-example figure.

This choice would come to be a source of great spiritual and emotional concern and confusion for me in January of 1975.

I approached Pastor Fenrick with the idea of starting a theatre group at the church. It was an idea that Pastor Fenrick received enthusiastically, and several discussions ensued about how to get such a group off of the ground. The main concern seemed to center around how I would juggle the multiple theatre groups that I was involved with, since I was already active with the Silver Lake Players and the recreation department's Young People's Theatre.

Pastor Fenrick liked the idea of starting out with one-man performances of major biblical characters, to generate interest for a theatre group, and a script for a one-man presentation about Paul the Apostle's life was acquired and studied.

Pastor Fenrick and I had a meeting concerning the script and when it could be presented. Everything looked to be on track to start the new theatre group, until I arrived at church that cold Sunday morning at the end of January and discovered that Pastor Fenrick, a person whom I considered to be my spiritual mentor, had inexplicably hanged himself in his church office.

That was when suicide went from being an abstract concept, to something so real and immense that it could never be ignored again.

No one who showed up to church that day had any idea what was waiting for them that Sunday after the Super

Bowl. Upon entering the church's foyer, it was clear from the crying of so many people that something seriously wrong had happened. We were gently ushered in as the service was supposed to start, and the choir director made the official announcement that Pastor Fenrick was dead and how he had accomplished his passing. His family, his wife, son and daughter, were in the first row of pews, absolutely beside themselves with grief.

The congregation didn't know what to do or think. The shepherd was dead, and in a manner which went against everything that the shepherd had told his flock for years. The church lost its grip on the foundation of its faith on that morning, and as a group, that grip would never be found again. There was no heart in the building anymore and this place of gathering and worship, a place designed to allow one to be closer to God, had been turned into a mockery of itself with a single, inexplicable act. Grief counselors addressed the crowd, but their words meant nothing. If Pastor Fenrick's words, which had seemed so strong and full of faith, had proven themselves, by his actions, to be made out of worthless air, then how could anyone else's words be taken seriously at that time?

After the mourning service, people began leaving, but rather than shaking the meaty hand of the man that we had all looked up to and admired, we shook hands with his surviving family, shattered and crushed by his actions.

When I walked slowly to my car, I instinctively knew that the congregation that I had proudly been a member of just hours before would never function as a congregation again.

In the weeks that followed, the building saw fewer and fewer familiar faces, until there was little sense in keeping up the charade, and the building was put up for sale. The congregation split up like a spiritual explosion in slow motion, and quietly dispersed itself to the four winds, merging with dozens of other churches, or deciding that churches built by men and populated by men were not to be trusted.

Grace Baptist Church was well on the road to becoming a memory that no one would speak of, and its once-admired pastor became an enigma of faith, as opposed to being remembered as a pillar of faith.

Little did I know then that my relationship with Pastor Fenrick was far from complete, and that Pastor Fenrick's spiritual journey was far from over.

He and I were destined to cross paths on another occasion.

The first time Pastor Fenrick dropped in on me was not too long after he died, and it was in the middle of a bitterly cold night. It was normal for my bedroom under the basement stairs to be cold because there weren't any heating ducts that lead to where I slept, but this turned out to be an almost unimaginably cold experience.

I woke from a fitful sleep to find that the temperature in my room had dramatically dropped. Something at the back of my mind warned me of the presence of a pair of unseen spiritual beings, and that thought chilled me to the bone. There was something distinctly evil in my bedroom with me, and neither Zotia nor the Blue Lady was offering me any more insights or comfort regarding the situation.

I found myself almost frozen, with fear or from the extreme chill, I wasn't sure. Inside my head, I was screaming for answers about what to do next. Who was here and what did they want with me? All I knew for sure when I woke up to a room that felt like the back of an old, neglected freezer, was that there was something in the room with me and it was *evil*. I couldn't see anything, and there was no sound whatsoever, but the feeling of dread was intense. Although I was aware that my pretending to be asleep would make little or no difference to the nasty thing stalking me around my bed, I wasn't sure of what to do next, other than to pray for some sort of intervention.

I lay there, still as a board, praying with all of my might that I be protected from whatever had found me.

"It's the spirit of Pastor Fenrick, along with the malevolent energy of the demon that had convinced Pastor Fenrick to take his own life," whispered the Blue Lady.

"A demon?!" I responded.

"Be at peace, my child. Fear is the opposite of the Christ energy, and by embracing fear you make it impossible to remember your true nature. We are here with you, and you have nothing to fear, not from this minion, and not even from his master who sent him."

"Why are they here?"

"Pastor Fenrick made a serious error in judgment. Then he allowed himself to become overwhelmed with despair, and believing the demon's whispers that no one, not even Jehovah, would forgive him, he took his own life. He was afraid to travel down the Tube of Light to Heaven to be rejoined with his loved ones."

"Why would he be afraid? He never seemed afraid of anything."

"When a soul passes on, they indeed see their life flash before their eyes, but the perspective they view is Jehovah's. Pastor Fenrick saw his life with all of its flaws and sins of self-idolatry, and he feared that Jehovah would destroy him for his evil deeds."

"I don't believe that. Jehovah doesn't judge and destroy."

"That is well-said, my son, but you have not embraced the philosophy of self-idolatry that is taught to every new soul from the moment that it is born into this world. Pastor Fenrick used his position to judge and condemn others, which is against the teachings of him who Pastor Fenrick professed to be his lord. Seeing how far he had fallen from what he could've been, Pastor Fenrick became a lost soul, tormented unceasingly by this demon that he fell prey to."

"But why has he brought the demon here, to me?"

"He has reasoned out that of all of the people that he has ever known only you can help him remove his tormentor."

"Me? How can I do such a thing?"

"Because of all of the energies that exist and find peace within Jehovah's Heaven, you have been created from the power of innocence, and you are a brother to the Christ energy. No matter how hard the darkness has tried to pollute you, turn you to their purposes, or accomplish your spiritual destruction, you remain strong in your faith and in your Love. You have succeeded innumerable times against intimidating odds, whereas Pastor Fenrick succumbed to but the simplest of enticements."

"What is that smell?"

"That is the essence of all the things that you are not."

"I feel like it's breathing on my face."

"It is considering whether it would be more fun to torture you than his captive plaything."

"How do I get rid of it?"

"Since it has not attacked you directly and created a karmic imbalance with you, you need to repeat after me, 'Ego sum lux lucis."

"Ego sum lux lucis."

"Ego sum sarcalogos."

"Ego sum sarcalogos."

"Ego sum ego sum."

"Hold on, Zotia, this is going to get bumpy. Do not become drawn into the vortex," the Blue Lady added.

"Vortex? Did you say vortex?"

"Finish what you have begun."

"Ego sum ego sum."

The feeling began on the top of the right side of my head and it rushed down my body at incredible speed. It surged up and down my spine, and then it seemed to burst out of my chest with the power of a thousand fire hoses. It lasted only the briefest of milliseconds, but to me, it seemed like minutes. As I slowly opened my eyes, it appeared that light was dissipating from every corner of my bedroom, like a photographic flash of immense intensity had just been set off, and the remnants of its outburst were slowly handing my world back to the darkness.

"What did I say?" I asked, meekly.

"You said that you were the Light, and the Christ, and the I AM, and a portal was opened directly to The Presence of Jehovah," the Blue Lady said.

"The demon?"

"It never knew what hit it."

"It's destroyed?"

"Certainly not. Jehovah doesn't destroy. The demon in question has simply been relocated to a place beyond the reach of even its master."

"Will it die there?"

"It has the ability to bring its own existence to an end, but it may consider reason and be reborn into the Light."

"And Pastor Fenrick?"

"He still has some lessons to learn. He is free from his demon burden, but he needs to wander the world as a lost soul for a time. When he has fully realized all that he took for granted, and all the gifts that he misused in his lifetime, then he will be brought back to Heaven by Michael the Archangel, to continue his journey of spiritual ascension."

"How did Pastor Fenrick figure out that I would be able to help him with his problem when even I had no clue?"

"I put the thought of coming here into his head."

"Why would you do that?"

"To teach you a little bit more about your nature so that you may defend yourself when your assignment is at an end."

"That sounds quite cryptic."

"It was all just another bizarre dream, now go back to sleep."

"But I have more questions about...zzzzzzz."

CHAPTER TWENTY
Bizarre New Classes

Classes changed to my last semester in high school, and although I'll freely admit that I'd experienced some peculiar classes and teachers during my previous thirteen years in school, none of them really rose to the level of surreal perfection experienced in my last set. Some of the strangeness was amusing, some of it was alarming, and some of it was downright dangerous.

The amusing bizarreness was experienced on the first day of Photography class, with Mr. Harris. The rumor around school was that Mr. Harris prided himself on being a cool, hip, buddy-pal kind of teacher, in general, and an intensely cool, hip, buddy-pal kind of teacher if you were a girl and needed additional instruction on the finer points of photography in the darkroom. That he was young and had a sort of reputation for being open to hooking up with high school girls wasn't that rare of a condition in our huge school. One might think that such a thing would be weeded out and the offending faculty member fired, but such was not the case. Various people theorized that this type of behavior wasn't actively exposed because of the principal and one of the math teachers.

Whether true or not, the rumor was that Principal Shubinski, a supposedly happily-married man of many years, was having a long-term affair with a young math teacher by the name of Miss Nickels. The joke was that she was "Nickel" and diming him to death without his wife's knowledge. The only hard evidence that anyone could find to support such a claim was in the auditorium's ticket booth. During the school day, the auditorium lobby is a very large, unused space. The front and side doors to the facility are locked, and the bathrooms, which are available for the students taking classes in the auditorium to use, are on the opposite end from the ticket booth.

It was not simply the fact that the ticket booth existed as a solitary and private place that generated the gossip. It was the fact that the principal had ordered that the ticket booth be made "secure" from the inside, supposedly to keep the cash taken in at the ticket window safe. The booth consisted of an entry storage room with a circuit breaker box, a fairly good-sized coat room, and a small ticket room at the end. All of the doors and openings to the lobby had been secured by adding 2x4 battens, steel supports, and locks from the inside. In and of itself, even these measures wouldn't generate school gossip, but then one of the couch/beds from the office nurse's station was ordered moved into the ticket booth area.

It was this move that caused such immense speculation by staff and students alike, for no one could come up with a plausible explanation for why it was needed there. Although no one was ever "caught" sneaking down to the ticket booth, there had been a number of suspicious sightings in the area.

These rendezvous' were not limited to the principal and emissaries from the math department. The back corner of the school, behind the auditorium itself, was a maze of storerooms, dressing rooms, and practice rooms. The older band students were all aware of a certain practice room where no music was practiced. How this private area had been discovered is that a trusted band student, who had been given keys to get something from a storeroom, had used the opportunity to open the door that no one had ever seen opened. After his discovery of the room with the mattress, the posters and the candles, the news spread by word of mouth and the gossip game of the band became trying to figure out who the "special visitor" was. It was obviously a band parent, for no one had ever been seen hanging about who didn't have some sort of official relationship to the band, but who it was, exactly, remained a mystery.

There was frequent gossip about some of the teachers who sponsored traveling clubs like the ski club, or the world travel club. The school boys were generally ignorant of the personal preferences of the more aggressive male teachers, but the upper class girls were amazingly well informed. It appeared that the teachers got away with this arrangement through the combination of plausible deniability and adolescent infatuation. Only appreciative young ladies were invited into this exclusive arrangement, where they were secretly wined and dined and treated like princesses. There was little chance that they would come to a point where they'd want to expose the teacher that was taking advantage of the situation, because then the girl would be publicly labeled a slut, and would be shunned by the general population. A few young, attractive male teachers had perfected the art of hooking up with younger, attractive female courtesans-in-training, and the secret society flourished in the shadows.

Having a friend who was tuned into all of the gossip in the school, like Mo, made for some very enlightening conversations.

Back to Mr. Harris; he had a secret reputation for being a lady's man and his access to the dark room was the setting of several lurid tales of lust and intrigue. Whether the tales were true or not wasn't clear, but what did become clear on the first official day of class was that he wouldn't be "sparking" with any of the girls who were in class that day.

One of the fashion peculiarities from the seventies was having male shirts with somewhat puffier sleeves, executed in unusual colors. For the first day of class, Mr. Harris had unfortunately selected a stylish, pinkish lavender long-sleeved shirt, combined with a dark blue sweater vest and dark blue pants.

We all entered his class for the first time, the starting bell rang, and he proceeded to take attendance while sitting at his desk. Everything was going normally until he got up and walked to the blackboard.

An odd silence fell over the room.

Mr. Harris, recognizing the unusual amount of attention he was receiving, seemed to think that there was something about his presentation or his manner that was making this rare moment, for a roomful of quiet, attentive high school students is a rare thing indeed, even on the first day. He chatted on, making little jokes from time to time. The jokes weren't really getting the reaction that he'd anticipated, so he started getting a little confused by the classroom dynamic. Little guarded comments like, "Oh, my gosh," and "Can you believe it?" could be heard in the back of the room.

Finally, he blurted out, "OK, what's going on?"

A girl from the side of the room raised her hand and said, "Mr. Harris, can I go to the bathroom? I bit through my pen," and it was obvious by the ink on her lips that she had.

Thinking that her ink lips were the cause of the snickering, he let her go and tried to pick up where he'd left off.

When the snickering continued and grew in intensity, Mr. Harris stopped again and asked the class with increased irritation, "What are you all snickering at?"

One of the particularly cool kids in the back by the name of Lance said, "Mr. Harris, look down."

It was then that Mr. Harris realized that he'd come back from the bathroom with the tail of his shirt, which was a stylish pinkish lavender color, fully extending out of his open fly. The effect of his shirt tail, the dark blue pants and the dark blue sweater vest was quite striking.

He looked quickly up at the class, turned away, and then zipped up his fly.

When he turned back to face the class, his face was an unnatural color of embarrassment, as if his head were mere seconds away from exploding from the blood pressure.

He may have had a reputation for being a lady's man before that day, but no girl who had seen his aggressively exposed shirt tail would ever be able to see him as anything but the biggest joke that the school had seen in a long time.

He would have to romantically fish in another pond, preferably a deaf pond, for that class was certainly closed to him, unless he had a need to be giggled at in the dark.

The new class with the most alarming bizarreness was without a doubt World History. It was 'taught' by Mr. Moroni, who was a character in himself. To begin with, he was a very large man, quite tall and massive, with unusually short-cropped hair. It was the kind of haircut someone who likes to fight would have, so that there was nothing to grab. He had an odd preference for wearing white socks and sandals, even in the wintertime, and there was some gossip about his having taught at a prison before coming to Silver Lake High School. He drove a Volkswagen Beetle from the back seat, having had the front seat removed. He liked to bring in weapons like swords and daggers and such to add depth to his lessons. This kept the class enrapt because none of us were sure whether he'd use them on someone in a fit of rage one day.

As a teacher, I would say that his style was somewhat akin to being taught by Adolf Hitler's younger, bigger brother, and he had absolutely no tolerance for what he considered foolishness. Most teachers ignored the more problematic students who liked to gravitate to the back of the classroom, as long as they weren't a distraction, but most teachers were not Mr. Moroni. Mr. Moroni seemed to relish having the most diehard attitude problems under his "care," and he made sure that they knew how much they meant to him, almost daily.

One of his favorite things to do was to take an eraser and load it up with chalk from the edging of the blackboard while lecturing. He never dropped a syllable or missed a beat after he had decided to hunt some unsuspecting victim in the back of the room. Then, without warning, he'd let fly with his attention-getter, awakening someone from their stupor in a cloud of chalk dust. On the rare occasion when he missed, he ordered the offending student to bring him the eraser, and then they would go back to their seat and see the loading-up process repeated for their benefit.

He never missed twice.

From time to time there would be talk from some humiliated mouth-breather that they were going to get even and do something to Mr. Moroni's car. Invariably, someone else would mention Mr. Moroni being nearly crazy on a good day and the plans to escalate hostilities would quickly evaporate.

Mr. Moroni's desire to have everyone paying attention extended beyond the moment in question, and it was not uncommon for him to walk among the seats and bop someone on the back of the head for not having been attentive previously.

After a couple of weeks, all of the students in my class had been taught to schedule their personal foolishness for another class period, except for one. The boy's real name was something long and Italian, but Mr. Moroni had publicly renamed him "Dufus." The nickname had started out as "DeUfus," but over time was shortened to just Dufus. There were rumors that he was related to the local Sicilian mob, and that his family was part owner the local funeral parlor at the opposite end of my grandparent's block.

Dufus was a walking stereotype, which seemed to egg Mr. Moroni on to greater heights in order to "save his future and help him become a valued member of society." His hair was a mass of disorder, like his brains had exploded inside and then been frozen in their outward trajectories, he wore hippy-esque raggedy clothes with big, clunking boots, and his wallet was securely chained to his belt, as if it held the secrets of life itself within. He usually smelled of many unpleasant things and he seemed to have his own personal smell force field. He made strange noises when he was awake, and he made even stranger noises when he was asleep, and Mr. Moroni was determined to change his classroom behavior.

First, there were the chalk dust showers, followed by the long and drawn-out class lectures on how not to waste a young life by making poor choices. After these attempts to change his behavior proving unsuccessful, Dufus was physically relocated to the front of the room, and then came his "launching."

None of us saw it coming, because we saw only Dufus' back, since he'd been moved up front. He now sat right next to Mr. Moroni's desk. We didn't see Dufus nodding off, and since Mr. Moroni was a master at never shifting his voice to warn his victims, it wasn't until Mr. Moroni kicked out with his long leg and put Dufus and his desk into the air that the rest of us realized that he'd committed the ultimate sin. Dufus had disrespected Mr. Moroni within his reach, which had never been done before and would certainly never be done again.

Dufus and his desk slammed into the floor with him staring straight up at the ceiling, like he was an astronaut preparing to be launched into space.

The class was absolutely silent for a pregnant moment, and then Mr. Moroni spoke.

"Mr. DeCavalente, please sit up properly in your desk and pay attention.

There wasn't any giggling from the class, for everyone there was thinking the same thing. Were these two people, the irresistible force and the immovable object, going to take their conflict to a new level, or would they reach a truce? Even Mr. Moroni seemed to sense that if taken to the next level things would get out of hand.

The next day, Dufus reported to class and managed to stay awake, and somewhere during that class period, Mr. Moroni stopped referring to him as Dufus.

Although World History was dramatic and suspenseful each day, my class with downright dangerous bizarreness was my woodshop class. I never really understood why the system took so many lower-achieving and generally disinterested students, those who had trouble mastering a pencil and a calculator, and put them together in a room full of cutting, whirling, spinning, and chopping machines.

The school had a large vocational education wing that included an auto shop, a print shop, an electronics lab, a wood shop, and a metal shop. I had considered signing up for metal shop until I heard the story of some bone-headed idiot who had decided to spit into a crucible of molten aluminum, just to see what would happen. It wasn't hard for me to imagine the spit colliding with the 1,000 degree Centigrade metal and then exploding from the expanding steam, showering blobs of hot aluminum in every direction. I hadn't known anyone who had been in the class when it happened, so I knew that there could've been a degree of exaggeration to the story. It might only have been molten pewter, or tin, or pot metal, but whatever it had been, it had sprayed hot something on everyone around, and I wasn't interested in getting burnt by a temporarily insane mouth-breather.

Mr. Ripmeister was the teaching equivalent of a schizophrenic Baloo the bear. Most of the time, he came across as relatively carefree and upbeat, but if he was having a bad day, or if he was pestered with stupid questions while he was working on one of his pet projects, or if someone challenged his authority, he became a very in-your-face-until-you-back-down type of person. Most of the time, everything was fine because we used hand tools and sandpaper blocks, which greatly reduced the chances of serious injury, but eventually, we worked our way up to the high-powered, constantly sharpened, dangerous stuff.

One of the most intriguing aspects of the class was a hole in the upper window at the back of the room, right over the grinding wheels. The hole was oval in shape and the school legend was that a grinding wheel going at full speed had come off of the arbor and ground its way through the glass on its way out of the room. I stared at the oval hole several times, and although I wasn't buying the idea that a grinding wheel was moving so fast that it ground its way through glass without cracking or shattering it, I couldn't figure out how someone cut the oval shape, and for what purpose. It remained an enigma.

The class consisted of all boys, except for one girl, and no one really socialized with her because on the first day of class Mr. Ripmeister asked why each student had signed up for woodshop and she'd replied that she wanted to learn how to build a coffin. If it weren't for that comment, which unfortunately for her, no one was ever going to forget, she seemed quite normal in all other respects. She was dubbed "Vampira" and everyone gave her plenty of room to work all by herself.

The class was dangerous by virtue of the fact that when working with machinery, one really needs to be aware of what can potentially happen if one isn't careful. For instance, if one takes a large piece of wood and tries to sand it smooth on the six foot long belt sander without being very careful about where they put their fingers to hold it, not only do they sand off the end of a fingernail or the top surface of a knuckle, but the board that they then drop gets launched by the sander in the general direction of other students, who are standing by waiting their turn.

One woodshop disaster that lived on in legend from several years past was the story of a long-haired stoner of a student who wasn't particularly alert when operating a large drill press. The story ends with his ripped off scalp and his grossly abused face meeting up in the local emergency room to be reunited with innumerable stitches. Supposedly, all turned out well, and the incident did much to push him towards a life change. That was one tough form of drug abuse therapy!

Perhaps it was because I was blessed with an excellent imagination that I felt moved to immediately spring into action to stop a fellow student from sharpening their lathe tool on the belt sander, sending sparks out into the room *and up the flue to the dust collection system!* The fellow seemed to have no idea that a hot spark could start a fire or even cause an immediate explosion if the sawdust particles were fine enough.

How I knew that, I had no idea.

And speaking of the lathes, there is nothing quite like when a newbie woodworker turns their lathe up to maximum speed to turn a baseball bat blank and it comes loose because they forgot to lock down the tail stock. A three-foot long piece of ash spinning frantically, and whipping end over end head-high across the room is an exciting thing to see, as long as its not hurtling towards you.

Then there was the day when Mr. Ripmeister was demonstrating a technique on the table saw and he was distracted momentarily by the smell of smoldering wood coming from underneath the saw from a large pile of walnut sawdust. That moment of being unfocused cost him the very end of his thumb. After he wrapped his thumb and dug out the smoldering sawdust, he went to the hospital, and we spent the rest of that week sitting at the work benches sanding precut pieces of pine and doweling to make coffee mug stands.

Mr. Ripmeister's thumb eventually healed, but if one looked closely, it was obvious that a little something was missing.

Actually, I got the impression that a little something was missing from several of the students in that class.

CHAPTER TWENTY-ONE
1903

I had always known that my grandparent's property was haunted. It took me a while to figure out that nobody else was aware of that fact.

The house began its life as the first one-room schoolhouse purposefully built in Erin Township, way back in 1870. It had originally been located at the southeast corner of Decadia and Lincoln, in Silver Lake, and it was designated as Erin #5, the fifth schoolhouse in the township of Erin. Erin #5, was moved a half mile north up Lincoln in 1898, when the southern residents separated from Erin #5 district, and began their own school. This house then became Silver Lake Public School's first schoolhouse. It was initially called Erin Township Schoolhouse #5, then Lake Township Schoolhouse #2, and eventually just Silver Lake Public School.

The schoolhouse was decommissioned in 1923, sold, and then moved one block south to where it presently resides at the end of Morton Street.

My grandparents, Eugene and Menafay MacDonald, purchased the house in 1943. My grandparents put the master bedroom and sun porch addition on the back of the house.

In a worldly way, my relationship with Erin #5 could be traced back to my birth, when my grandparents owned the house, and my mother and father lived in the upstairs apartment.

In a truer sense, my relationship with Erin #5 began around the turn of the 20th century, over 100 years earlier.

I had, over the years, received flashbacks to many past lives. These visitations usually involved reliving some terribly painful death, but my "memory" of turn-of-the-century Erin #5 was more peaceful than the norm. I remembered walking south to school, down the main thoroughfare that served as both the unpaved main street, and the place where the Shoreline trolley tracks linking the area to Detroit, were located. The impression included a swampy, shrub-filled area, with relatively few large trees, simple people, and simple farms. The only visible link to cutting edge technology and real civilization was the ribbon of steel tracks that cut straight through the village and off through the woodsy re-growth of trees from Michigan's previous lumber harvesting. The tracks lead both to the north, and down to the south, skirting the edges of the very large farms that were located along the west shores of Silver Lake.

In that lifetime, I only lived to the age of eight, and then I died of TB, so stepping back into that consciousness didn't really allow for great depth of impression or thought. I did remember acquiring the ability to see lost souls, just before I died. I was able to talk with these spirits, and I convinced several of them to travel back with me through the tube of Light, when it came time for me to return to Heaven.

One of these souls would eventually be reborn into my current life as my younger brother, Steven. When I initially met his angry soul, fuming, ranting, and raving in 1903, he was just a spiritual animaloid, that is, one incarnation up from an animal, generally unable to process complex emotions and personal interactions, and often getting caught up in violence and anger as the solution to all problems confusing. He was like the soul of an angry bull that had just graduated to being a human being. He wasn't very good at being a human being, yet.

As my eight-year-old previous self, I remembered listening to the seemingly endless diatribes of a lost soul who enjoyed railing against a family who had rudely moved into the house that he had unexpectedly left behind after he died. The man had been immensely pleased with what he had built, and he was incensed that the invaders who had followed in his footsteps had dared to change and add on to the wonder that he had constructed with his bare hands. This soul had also been returned to my present life, and when we met again, I was his student at Silver Lake High School. The frustrated lost soul who had returned to Heaven with me had been reincarnated as Lewis Ripmeister, and he was the school's woodshop and printing teacher.

Lewis was still filled with immense personal pride in his woodworking abilities. He served on the staff of the musical and assisted in building the props and set pieces that were needed for the production. Sometimes, when he would go into a rant about the meaning of quality craftsmanship, it would jog my previous memories of our distant experiences together, and bring a fleeting smile to my face.

The more people change, the more they remain the same.

In 1903, the last year that I was alive to attend Erin #5, the day would always begin with a long walk to the school. Rain, shine, snow, or sleet, chances were that I would have to walk. If it were a particularly cold, rainy day, perhaps I would be allowed to take a horse or pony to school, although that would mean that my ride would have to stand out in the bad weather all day, and horses were far too valuable for such duty. If the weather was so bad that I needed a ride, then there was a good chance that my father was going to decide that I wasn't going to school that day.

My schoolmates would play in the yard until the schoolmistress rang the school's tower bell at 9:00a.m. The boys and girls would then line up. We each had a separate entrance. Erin #5 had two front doors that led into the vestibule. We would be ushered in, the girls entering first, then the boys, where we would all hang our coats on pegs and put our lunches on shelves.

Students were arranged by sex and by age, with the younger students located near the front. In the winter months, the prized desks would naturally be those that were the closest to the stove, the school's only source of warmth, which was centrally located in the classroom. The stovepipe exited the room through the back wall, over the blackboard, which was literally that, wall boards painted black with a chalky black paint.

On a typical day, Miss Macomb would cross to the desk and ring the tardy bell, which was a hand bell. We all then stood for the opening exercises, which would include "The Pledge of Allegiance," and sometimes we took turns reciting "The Lord's Prayer." We would then be seated, and the school day would officially begin.

Our textbooks were the *McGuffey Readers*. Miss Macomb would begin the day's lessons with the youngest students, and work her way up through the grades. The sessions with the teacher were referred to as recitation sessions. The grade being worked with would be called to the front recitation benches and tested orally. The hand bell signaled the beginning of the next session.

When we were asked a question, it was required of us to stand in the aisle next to our desk and respond. Respect was shown through the use of "Miss," or "Mister." "Mrs." wouldn't be used because we had no married teachers. Popular philosophy felt that a married teacher would not devote the proper amount of time to her students, because of distractions of life caused by a husband and children.

While one class was reciting, the other students would be busy studying, memorizing, and writing in copy books.

There would be two recess periods, in addition to the lunch break, during the day, one mid-morning, and one mid-afternoon. Weather permitting, we would be allowed to play in the schoolyard. The ringing of Erin #5's tower bell would mark the return to lessons.

If the weather decided to be agreeable, lunch would be eaten outside, and a short recess would follow. If Mother Nature decided to be disagreeable, lunch would be eaten inside at our desks. Lunch would be transported in a wooden bucket or pail, and would include some combination of corn meal cakes, corn bread or muffins, butter or cheese, fruits or vegetables, such as carrots, apples or pears, and beef jerky, or some other preserved meat.

The afternoon session was structured much like the morning. Miss Macomb might add some variety by reading to the class, perhaps part of a long story. Spontaneous spell-downs, singing sessions, and physical exercises were also used to spice things up at the end of the school day.

Having been moved twice, Erin #5 was possibly the most highly traveled house in the State of Michigan, assuming that all of the other well-traveled houses had been moved only once in their lifetimes, and that they lived, predominantly, in Greenfield Village.

CHAPTER TWENTY-TWO
Stitches

There are some moments in life that seem to assemble themselves in slow motion, and if you take the time, you can see all of the minuscule pieces falling into place. Unfortunately, every time that this awareness has come upon me, I've only had seconds in order to realize that something unpleasant, something inescapable, something dripping of déjà vu, was just about to burst forth.

Such was the case on that fateful Saturday in late March.

Being a Saturday with Nathan already home, it appeared that all of the classic warning signs of a family calamity in the making had been avoided. It wasn't a Friday and he wasn't out drinking. My mother had made goulash in the hot pan on the kitchen counter, and we were just settling down to dinner. The three of us, Danielle, Steven and myself, were sitting down to dinner in the kitchen at the table. Nathan was in the living room and hadn't responded when my mother indicated that the goulash was done, and so it was assumed that he wasn't hungry or he'd eat after the three of us were done. As for my mother, she often preferred to eat what we called box chicken warmed up in the oven after everyone else was done with their dinner.

I'm not sure how it started, but it whipped itself into a violent fury at incredible speed. The TV was on in the living room so it was not immediately apparent that my mother had said something to Nathan. Normally, one would think that attempts to reestablish communication would be a good thing, but that was not the case here. My mother had received a telephone call a couple of weeks earlier that a minor relative of Nathan's had died, and she'd decided that the information wasn't important enough to break the wall of silence that they'd so carefully built between them. For whatever reason, she had decided to tell Nathan of the death in the family at that time. Not being a man with very effective emotional control, Nathan had become enraged immediately, obviously shocking my mother who usually didn't make such serious mistakes when playing these interaction games. Although the relative was almost unknown to Nathan, the fact that he hadn't been able to make up his own mind about whether he wished to attend the funeral and see the rest of his family had made him temporarily insane. Screaming insults, he had risen from his easy chair, crossed the living room, and split my mother's chin open with a vicious blow within just a couple of seconds.

Realizing that Nathan was completely out of her control, she ran around him and out through the front door. She fled to the neighbor's house, there to seek temporary sanctuary, dribbling blood along the way.

Before I had time to process what I'd just heard, Nathan came barging into the kitchen, grabbing the hot skillet of goulash and threatening to throw it. Steven, having been sitting closest to the doorway to the living room, was unencumbered and able to leap from his chair and run out the back door just before Nathan came into the room. Steven ran into the garage and grabbed a small sledgehammer. Then he stood in the driveway, waiting to see if he would have to defend himself against his rampaging stepfather.

Danielle was sitting nearer to the back door. She didn't make a move to run because there had never been a time when Nathan had actually threatened her with physical harm. He had subjected her to humiliating and emotionally scarring moments, like trying to teach her to dance while he'd been drunk, but he'd never seriously threatened her.

Unfortunately for me, I was sitting at the back of the kitchen table, blocked on both sides by the side chair and the half wall along the basement stairs, and the chair that Steven had been sitting it that he'd shoved into my way on his way out of the room.

Nathan stared at me with hatred in his eyes from six feet away. He raised his fist in the general direction of my head.

"If I hear one word out of you, you're going to the hospital along with your mother!" he yelled.

He stepped forward as if he planned on bashing me upside my head with the hot skillet, but then he thought better of it and threw the skillet across the room in the general direction of the back door. It rebounded off of the ceiling just as the chord plugged into the wall got taught, spraying hot goulash everywhere. The skillet then crashed to the floor, seriously denting the linoleum.

Placing his face on the same plane as mine, he hissed, "Clean up this mess, right now, your lordship" and then he stormed out of the room, back into the living room.

Danielle was in a state of shock, and Steven wisely decided to stay out in the yard for the time being. The neighbors were beginning to trickle out of their houses. I could hear the neighbors to the east of us asking Steven what was going on.

Not wishing to be the next victim in the hit parade, I began to clean up the dinner mess. Danielle eventually recovered enough to go to her room and close the door, not that her door would prove to be much of an obstacle if Nathan lost his temper again. As I cleaned, I glanced surreptitiously from time to time out into the living room, where Nathan sat calmly in his easy chair at the far corner of the room, composing himself.

When I had the goulash about half cleaned up, there was a powerful knock on the front door and I looked out to see two policemen standing there. Nathan opened the door to them and they began to talk. I couldn't make out exactly what they were saying because they were on the porch and Nathan's body blocked them from where I was, but the discussion seemed to center around how sorry he was that he'd lost his temper at finding out that a dear loved one had died. He admitted that he'd been wrong in striking my mother, and he understood that my mother was fully empowered to have him thrown into jail for the assault if she chose to press charges. He assured the officers that he was completely in control and that there wouldn't be any more trouble.

The policemen went next door to discuss the situation with my mother, who was standing in the neighbor's driveway, holding a damp towel up to her bleeding chin. It was agreed that my mother would go to the hospital to get stitches and that she wouldn't press charges, as long as Nathan agreed to behave.

I knew that my mother would've preferred to have Nathan strapped to a barbeque and slow-roasted until dead, but the police didn't know her and so they accepted her "sincere" recollections of how the fight started and her desire to get things back to "normal."

The police returned to inform Nathan of his possible future if he didn't behave himself, and then they drove off.

I knew that Nathan would pay for what he'd done to my mother that day. I wasn't sure of the how and the when of the payback, but I was sure that no one would find her fingerprints at the scene of whatever it was going to be.

My mother came in the back door as I was finishing up and got her keys to drive herself to the hospital. She said nothing to me as she walked by. It wasn't often that she didn't get the last word but she hadn't today. The day had ended with her in a tenuous position of control over Nathan. It would be a long time before her chin would completely heal, but the scar would be there as a reminder of the events of the day for the rest of her life.

The kitchen ceiling and the linoleum floor were also going to bear the marks of Nathan's anger for a long time to come.

As she left, the expression on my mother's face seemed to say, "Never again," and I interpreted that to mean that she was never again going to let someone do such a thing to her and get away with it just because he was the breadwinner in the family. I definitely got a sense that she was going to somehow find a job and squeeze Nathan out of our family picture, forever.

Better him than me, I thought. At least he has a job.

I could hear Vicky whimpering at the foot of the basement stairs.

CHAPTER TWENTY-THREE
Schwooping

Having a lost soul enter my body in a desperate attempt to use my soul light to return to Heaven is a very disconcerting feeling. I never saw these souls, at least not clearly, but I certainly knew that they were there, quite often because of their smell. The Blue Lady called the process "desperation ascension," but I came to call it "Schwooping."

Lost souls had always seemed to seek me out, for reasons that were beyond my imagination. Being taken to a hospital, or to a funeral home, or to someone's old house, always made me a bit uneasy. Almost without exception, at some point, I would feel like I had been entered like a doorway and used in some way, by things that I couldn't see.

The Blue Lady eventually explained that lost souls who had become brave enough, were using my soul's connection to the Light to end their time of self-imposed exile on Earth, and return to Heaven. She also had to elaborate to me about what a lost soul was, since I barely had a clue.

It seems that when a person dies, a tube of Light or a bridge appears to them and this vision becomes a pathway back to Heaven. Before the recently deceased person can step up and move on, they get to see their life flash before their eyes. Tradition supports this suggestion, but what tradition doesn't get clear is that the flashback is from Jehovah's point of view, not the person's biased recollections. The soul in question gets to see every selfish thought and action and it comes to realize how their life has been, for the most part, an extended exercise in self-idolatry. If the soul has love within, then that love energy limits the amount of fear that they experience in relationship to traveling back to Heaven, and they step up, innately knowing that their transgressions against Jehovah and others will be forgiven. Those without love in their soul are overwhelmed with fear and believe that a righteous God will judge them harshly for how they've lived.

These souls are afraid to step into the Light and so they become lost.

They wander the world of the living, unseen, observing the people and the places where they used to frequent. One of the ways that they can get back to Heaven is to return with someone who loves them, when they eventually pass away. However, without loving relatives to piggyback on, the only two ways back to Heaven are through contrition, whereby Michael the Archangel is sent to retrieve the soul in question, or by using another shiny soul as a gateway.

I wasn't sure how many other people had this "gift," but it made for some disconcerting moments. The most dramatic of these would be like when I was sleeping in an unfamiliar place, like visiting a friend at Michigan State, or in a motel by the Mackinaw Bridge, where I would be shocked awake by someone plopping into my chest, like someone doing a belly-flop off of a high diving board and using my soul as the water.

Schwooping frequently occurred along routes that I regularly traveled, like down I-94 or I-696. Strange smells, combined with the feeling of being physically entered, marked the events.

One particularly dramatic schwooping event involved a lost soul who had been a mechanic in life. He must've been standing in the middle of I-94 east for quite a while, waiting for me to pass by, on the day he decided to return home. Who knows how long he had been standing in the area, watching the endless stream of embodied souls speed by, pondering his life, and how he wished he could travel on and be reunited with his family.

The Blue Lady communicated to me that any souls connected to the Christ energy, or connected to God, show up as brightly lit beacons in the half-lit semidarkness that is the world of the lost soul. Daylight and nighttime bear little difference in their limbo state, and they can see, or choose not to see, equally well under either condition.

There had been one particularly memorable moment at Silver Lake High School, when, in the press of the student masses in the hallway during passing time, a single student that I'd never seen before swam upstream against a sea of bodies, staring fixated at my torso, as he slowly drew closer. The student only stopped advancing when his face was literally inches from the center of my chest, staring and blinking at something that no one else could see. A bit uncomfortable by the intense and rather odd attention, I made a joke to him about his staring about to make me blush.

I knew what the psychic boy had seen, even if he didn't. He had seen my soul Light, which was something usually seen only by the dead, while they were in a limbo state of between-ness.

How many souls had wandered near to the freeways that I frequented, and had been attracted to my soul Light like a moth to a flame, I couldn't begin to guess. However, I did have some sense of how the mechanic had seen me pass by, at one point or another, and had decided to leap into the passing Light coming from my T-bird, in the hope of escaping his self-imposed banishment.

At the moment of unseen impact, the passenger compartment was filled with the intense smell of axle grease, gasoline, motor oil, and solvents, accompanied by the usual feeling of something forcibly pressing inside of me. Most schwooping events were mild by comparison, many amounting to slightly more than a passing sensation. They weren't usually accompanied by so many distinct smells, although being unexpectedly schwooped by a chain smoker was always an unpleasant, gagging experience.

Sometimes, the Blue Lady would tell me to drive to places that I didn't usually frequent, with the purpose of sweeping up the lost souls there. I was taught that there were several ways to return to Heaven and that Jehovah never forgot about any of his children, not even the most evil and spiritually lost of them.

CHAPTER TWENTY-FOUR
Unexpected Departures

One of the most difficult lessons that I ever learned from the Blue Lady was about the true nature of sin and transgression.

"What do you think sin is, Nicholas?" the Blue Lady inquired.

"Well, the Bible gives us a list of sins to avoid," I said.

"True enough, but do you think that a person who has never committed any of those sins is naturally a shiny soul and aligned with Jehovah?"

"Now that you put it that way, I'm not so sure. There have been a lot of people that I've met who seem to be above committing the sins of the Ten Commandments, but who give me a wary feeling when I'm around them, like there's something not quite right about them that I can't exactly put my finger on."

"Violating one of the Ten Commandments, whether you are caught and exposed or not, is like dropping a heavy black cannonball of evil into your own soul. Most people try to have more spiritual sense than to do that, but their souls are buried in darkness from Jehovah's point of view anyway."

"Why is that?"

"It all comes from selfishness. From the first moment that a soul screams for food or attention as a tiny babe, it begins to learn the dark art of meeting its own needs. As a soul matures, the intention is that it will grow out of making its own needs the center of its spiritual universe and focus upon other things, like helping other souls. This denying of the self reduces the influence of the ego and makes a person more like God."

"So selfishness is sin?"

"Yes, and transgression is the selfish sin that impacts another soul's life."

"If breaking one of the Ten Commandments is like immediately receiving a cannonball of pollution into your soul, then what is a sin of selfishness like, because I see people around me being selfish in their desires, their actions, and their thinking every minute of every day?"

"An individual sin of selfishness is like a grain of black sand, which seems trivial, almost insignificant, except when one considers how many grains of black sand can be collected within one short day. How many selfish desires go unidentified as something more benign? Buying someone dinner and bringing them flowers in the hope that they will sleep with you is nothing more than barely concealed lust, which makes every seemingly sweet compliment and moment of attentive charm nothing more than a drawn-out lie of intention. Very few people strive to fill their souls with Light by doing things for others without any type of ulterior motivation. The sin of selfishness has become so prevalent that it is now regarded as expected, even acceptable behavior. 'What's in it for me' is not a question ever asked of anyone else in Heaven, and yet it has become the mainstay of interaction down here on Earth. It is assumed that no one can be trusted, is that not so?"

"Yes, it's true. As a person who tries not to lie, I've frequently been disrespected by those around me who lie almost incessantly, and who cannot imagine that anyone can be committed to being different from them."

"There is only one power that can change that which has been tainted with darkness to the Light, and that is Love. A soul that values and serves only its own needs is no closer to Jehovah than Lucifer's soul is. And a soul that values and serves only the needs of those that support it is in the same dire circumstance. The love of family is better than the love of tyranny, but it is nothing compared to the love of all. Those who can only value the few live in darkness, whereas those who try to value the many live in the Light of Heaven. There are far too many of the first type of soul trying to change or eliminate the second type of soul, because shiny, caring souls remind self-idolatrous souls of everything that they are not."

"I see."

"And you know by personal experience. You have been assigned a task where you have been surrounded by angry, dark souls, and how many of them seem to despise you on sight, or interpret everything that you say and do in mean-spirited, negative terms, attempting to convince others that you are no better than they are?"

"That does seem to sum up most of the dynamic of my immediate family."

"Your family worships many forms of selfishness. How long has it been since you've heard from your father?"

"Well, you'd know more precisely than I, but it hasn't been since Grandma Zotia's funeral."

"Do you know where he is now?"

"I assume that he's up north with his family, welding seat belt links closed for GM."

"He lost the house up north. The family has relocated to Port Huron, where they are struggling to make ends meet."

"So he lives in Port Huron now?"

"No, his family is desperately trying to live in Port Huron. After he lost everything, your father left his family and went to Hawaii with a close friend."

"He left his family behind?"

"He did, he left a wife and five children without any means of support."

"Why would he do that?"

"He did it because his soul is so buried in black sand that he can justify almost anything that he does to himself, anything short of violating the Ten Commandments, that is. That makes him no different from 90% of the incarnated souls that walk the Earth right now. He places his needs as being the most important concerns in his life, making him a serious sinner, and then he acts in ways that degrade the quality of other lives that depend upon him, and that makes him a serious transgressor. These are the building blocks of self-idolatry, which then leads on to the embracing of evil. It is a simple process of learning to value others less and less over time."

"Is he going to come back to his family soon?"

"He tells his family that he is going to find work and eventually bring them to Hawaii to live with him."

"Is that the truth?"

"He knows that he is lying even as he shares the dream to distract his wife. He enjoys being out on his own, only worrying about himself. He is a typical soul, and it doesn't matter how many times he shows up in church and prays to Jehovah, since his prayers are crudely veiled requests for selfish gains, his prayers have no wings and fall to the dust from which they are made."

"Is there hope for him?"

"Yes, but not in this lifetime, for he will need to experience need and loss in intense ways in order to learn to value outside of himself."

"My Christian friends refuse to talk about the possibility of reincarnation. They are adamant that we all have only one lifetime, for better or for worse."

"Their assumptions would mean that premature babies who never speak the Christ energy's given name are doomed to hell. Their assumption is childish, offensive, and goes against the very nature of Jehovah Himself. What these souls have taken into themselves as truth makes it impossible for spiritual beings like me to have any positive interaction with them in their lives."

"Believing is seeing, it would seem."

"The innocent can always see the workings of God, even if they don't know exactly what they're witnessing."

"And what of the world's polluted souls?"

"They secretly believe that Jehovah is there to accomplish their bidding. I was just listening to a pastor tell his congregation that if they paid above and beyond Jehovah's required tithe of 10% of their gross income to the church, that Jehovah would then be *biblically required* to pay them back interest on the excess by one hundred fold."

"Who taught him to think that way?"

"His self-idolatry taught him a new way to sin and transgress against the souls in his care that way. The funds are pouring in and the pastor thinks that he's anointed and blessed."

"What does Jehovah think?"

"Jehovah thinks that he's learning to play for the wrong team while still pretending to wear His Son's jersey."

What makes a person truly evil, and how long does it take a person to travel from selfishness, through self-idolatry, and on to evil? It was a question that I pondered from time to time.

Was Hitler the same person at fifteen as he was at fifty?

If the answer was no, then the world would seem to be responsible for somehow turning him into a monster.

If the answer was yes, then he was destined to bring a dark cloud into the world, to accomplish what, it was hard to say, since it is difficult to find a shiny reason for the deaths of millions of people.

Many times, I had the feeling that I'd crossed paths with souls who were destined to bring their own type of dark cloud into the world. Sometimes, I'd meet the person and they'd seemed more or less normal, but then, after spending time with them, I'd notice that they weren't who I thought they were at all.

Such was the case with Shirley Kowalski and Lynette Frazho.

After the debacle of Homecoming, I did my best to stay out of the crosshairs of Shirley and Lynette, mostly out of a concern that I'd get caught up in a conversation with them that would shift to making fun of me for my uninvited romantic intrusion, and I'd have no way to accomplish a face-saving exit gracefully.

In my experience, cool kids could be counted on to be brutal. They thought of themselves as frank and honest, but my opinion was that anything said that is designed to hurt someone else's feeling doesn't qualify as frank or honest. Brutal remarks are the children of brutal minds, housed in brutal souls, and I wasn't interested in getting any closer to brutal people than I had to.

My math teacher, Mr. Scobas, should've been more careful avoiding brutal people.

Although Mo told me everything that she'd heard, it was very difficult to verify the details of the story because of the circumstances involved. All that was known for certain was that Mr. Scobas had never married, or seemed to make any lasting friendships beyond the daily interactions with his colleagues at school, and that he had lived with his mother for his whole life, right up to the end, when he had cared for her in her old age. At the beginning of the school year there was something in the school gossip about Mr. Scobas' mother dying, but he never spoke about it in class when I had him as a teacher. In fact, Mr. Scobas never spoke of his personal life or feelings at all. It wasn't that he was standoffish. It was just that he didn't reveal anything about his life outside of school. In retrospect, I realized that he was a master at having intense and lengthy discussions about nothing. I had talked with him several times, and it occurred to me that I knew nothing significant about him, except for the obvious, the way he looked, acted, and dressed.

He was a cotton candy man, a person appearing to have volume, but with no mass.

Another undisputable part of the story was the fact that Mr. Scobas had climbed into his bathtub and killed himself with a shotgun on Easter Sunday, for no known reason beyond missing his mother.

There were grief counselors for the students when the announcement was made after Easter break, and the entire student body was in a state of shock. No one knew what to think.

And then, about a week after the funeral, additional details about his life and death started to emerge. It appeared that after his mother's demise, Mr. Scobas had fallen into quite a funk, and during that time his life had somehow become entangled with the lives of two of his students. Although the gossip didn't have the names of the girls, supposedly because of confidentiality agreements, I knew that they were Shirley and Lynette. Snippets of conversations that they'd had during class that I'd overheard started to make sense.

They had originally decided to try to become friends with Mr. Scobas as a sort of twisted joke, like seeing if they were skillful enough to win over his trust because he didn't seem to trust anyone. They purposely tried to run into him whenever they could, like after school when he was going out to his car, or at the corner market, where he would go to get a few groceries. They would strike up a conversation with him and he, eventually, came to regard them as friendly.

Since their friendship was anything but sincere, and caring about Mr. Scobas' feelings was the least of their concerns, they continued to cultivate his empathy to see what they could get out of him. No one could possibly guess at everything that transpired between them, and when I asked the Blue Lady, she indicated that I didn't need to know all of the gory details, but rumor had it that at the time that he decided to end his life, he'd officially changed his will, leaving all of his money, all of his worldly possessions, and his house to the two girls. He had even decided to kill himself in the bathtub in order to make as little a mess as possible for them.

The school was all atwitter, wondering who the two heartless gold diggers were who had used him so coldly, but I already knew. The general reasoning was that if these two girls had indeed become his friends, then he wouldn't have felt the intense despair that had lead him to kill himself, because they would be in his life, helping to fill the enormous hole created by the death of his mother. If their motives had been sincere, then they would've functioned like foster children to him, reminding him of all of the good things in life.

The fact that he killed himself, combined with the fact that they benefited so grandly from his suicide, seemed to demonstrate a coldly calculating nature in the two girls.

The rumor was that they would legally remain anonymous until after their graduation and the estate had been settled, including the cleaning up and selling of Mr. Scobas' house. Then they'd take the money and go off to college on his dime, his cruelly acquired dime, and no one would ever be able to say for sure who they were.

God knew, the Blue Lady knew, and I knew who they were, and I was well aware that we didn't play for the same spiritual team.

CHAPTER TWENTY-FIVE
1931 & 1956

"Wake up, Nicholas."

The Blue Lady's voice was hardly more than a whisper in my ear.

"Nicholas, we have things to discuss. Wake up, my dear."

I opened my eyes and found myself resting on the grassy knoll of a hill, overlooking a beautiful vista with a shimmering lake.

"Wow, I can't remember ever waking up in a nice place before. Usually, you take me to dark and slimy places."

"Well, don't get too comfortable because we're not staying."

"Why not? I could get used to being here…"

"Which is exactly why we must move on, now get up. Let's go."

I was surprised to find the Blue Lady standing above me. I was used to her voice functioning much like a narrator, quietly explaining things in the back of my mind when I asked. It was quite infrequent that she appeared to me, fully manifested in one of my visions.

"Walk with me," she said, as she began sauntering down by the water's edge.

I followed her, right up to the edge of the water, stopping when she continued on, walking on the water's surface. She turned and looked back at me.

"Aren't you coming?"

"I can't walk on water."

Nicholas, this is a vision. You don't even have legs right now. Everything is an illusion. Assume that you can do what I do and follow along. What's the worst that can happen? You might get your imaginary shoes wet. What's the best that can happen? You might learn how to walk on water."

"I'm coming," I said, enthusiastically, rushing out onto the lake like it was nothing more than painted blacktop.

"In order to continue in your assignment, you need to be fully aware of the types of souls that you've been sent here to interact with."

"Types of souls? Isn't there only one type of soul?"

"In the broadest sense, yes, for all spiritual life originally sprang from the life essence of Jehovah, the All-Father."

"But in a specific sense?" I looked down at my feet, intrigued by how the shimmering waves seemed to flow around them. And then I noticed something that I found a bit disconcerting. I found that beyond the shimmering surface, I could see to great depths, and there, frolicking beneath my feet were enormous sea creatures, similar to, but unlike anything that I'd ever seen before.

"In a specific sense, during the course of their spiritual evolution, or by virtue of an unfortunate birth, souls have become 'different' along the way." The Blue Lady noticed that I was caught up in the sea creatures below my feet and she stopped walking. "Do you find them interesting?"

"If I weren't with you, I'd find them intimidating, perhaps even fearsome," I stammered, "Where are we, exactly? Are we in Heaven?"

"No, this isn't Heaven. If I took you back home to Heaven, you'd be overcome with such a sense of homesickness that I'd never be able to get you refocused on your assignment back on Earth."

"Where are we?"

"I could tell you that we were on some distant planet, or I could tell you that we were deep inside the cells of a scoop of pistachio ice cream. Would it make any difference?"

"I guess not, when you put it that way." I knelt down to get a better view below me. "Is this Earth during prehistoric times?"

The Blue Lady gestured with her hand and the sun skittered across the sky, bringing darkness. As the last ray of light was about to disappear over the horizon, a miraculous thing happened. All of the water that we were standing on began to glow, to emit its own light. Suddenly, everything beneath us was illuminated brightly and every creature stood out from the water with crystal clarity.

"This is not your home planet," the Blue Lady replied, "This is a special place that we of the Light like to come to in order to focus our peace."

"Are you saying that this is Heaven's version of a backyard Koi pond?" Just as I said that, a creature the size of a whale, yet with too many frills and fins and much too expressive a face, broke the surface of the water right next to my feet and glided by upon its side, giving me a long, thoughtful look. Although the idea seemed strange, I would've sworn that it smiled at me.

After a long pause, I waved at it.

It blew bubbles up at me and it gently splashed its tail just before it reentered the water. I was amazed at how many creatures seemed to be living in peaceful harmony under my feet. There was no sense of danger, and none of the fish were darting about, like they were trying to avoid being eaten by something bigger. It was more like an enormous, aquatic playground on a sunny spring day.

"Why can't I come to places like this more often?" I asked.

"Because you are too easily distracted," the Blue Lady said, helping me up to my feet. With another gesture of her hand, the water shimmered less and less until the creatures beneath us could only be seen if I stared intently. She took my arm and we wandered on, with no specific destination in sight, and the sunset now playing out its last moments on the horizon in slow motion.

"As I was saying, souls have become different along the way since the Beginning."

"Have they become different in a good way, or different in a bad way?" I asked.

"Would you need to have an assignment if they were different in a good way?"

"Probably not, so, what do I need to know about the souls that I have to interact with?"

"You need to be aware of what they are capable of, which is why we are here." She waved her hand and we were magically transported to a street in what appeared to be New York City, only to some point in the past. The skyscrapers weren't as colossal as I had imagined, and all of the cars seemed to be old fashioned, like from the twenties.

"When are we?"

"The year is 1931. The place is the island of Manhattan, and this is your new apartment building."

"Hey, you're just like the ghost of Christmas past, from *A Christmas Carol*."

"I differ from that ghost in that I have not brought you here in order for you to remember. I have brought you here in order for you to understand."

"I lived here?"

"You never really got a chance to live here."

"Why don't you just give me my memories back from this life? Wouldn't that save us some time?"

"I would never consider doing something so cruel."

The Blue Lady's statement caused me immediate concern. There was something familiar about the apartment building, and that faint trickle of familiarity was beginning to make the hairs on the back of my neck stand up.

"There you are," the Blue Lady said, indicating a man and a woman with two suitcases trying to get to the apartment building before the rain got any more intense.

"I'm the boy?"

"Yes. You are twenty-eight years old, and you were born into one of the ninety-five brothels of New York City in 1931."

"I agreed to that?"

"You did."

"At some point in time, I'm going to have to sit down and have a long talk with myself about all of these crazy things that I seem to have agreed to along the way. Why would anyone agree to be born into a brothel?"

"It was necessary."

"It was necessary to accomplish what? What could God have needed me to accomplish that would involve being born in such a manner?"

"There is literally no soul that lives that Jehovah has given up on, and often, He has to ask His most cherished children to bring His Light into the most terrible and darkest corners of existence, in an effort to save them from themselves."

"Did I volunteer, or did I agree, when asked?"

"Why?"

"Because I want to get a sense of how cosmically self-destructive I am by nature."

"In the beginning, you volunteered."

"And lately?"

"You have agreed to see the assignment out to the end, for which Jehovah is appreciative."

"So, what am I doing here?"

"You and your dance partner have just received confirmation that you'll be dancing in a Broadway show that will open soon, featuring the comedians Burns and Allen and the singer Eddie Cantor."

"That sounds like great news, considering the economic times. Who is that girl and why does my heart hurt when I look at her?"

"She is your soul mate. You and she are angelic twins, literally two sides of the same coin."

I began weeping uncontrollably. There was something about seeing that girl that caused my soul to shudder and my eyes to tear up. It was like remembering how to breathe after being dead for a long time. I dropped to my knees as the two dancers hugged joyfully and entered the lobby of the hotel. The Blue Lady allowed me to cry for a short time, and then she put her hand over my heart and the hurt, the emptiness, slowly receded.

"They're happy?"

"They are."

"They have no idea what is waiting for them inside?"

"No idea."

"And it's because God needs to send His Light…"

"And His Love."

"…into the darkness?"

"That is correct."

The Blue Lady helped me to stand and we were transported inside the hotel, to the couple's new room.

We watched them enter and unpack, carefully placing their few belongings in the even fewer pieces of furniture provided. The man went to put their suitcases away in a closet and noticed a crawl way board ajar, leading up into the attic. He got a chair and climbed up, curious about what was above their room. Much to his surprise, he discovered the attic area full of suitcases and personal belongings as if dozens of people had placed everything they had in the world in storage there. Nothing that he saw was of any obvious value, but at a time when many people had lost everything, any bit of something that one could hold on to became important. Not wishing to seem like he was contemplating taking anyone else's things, he got down and put their suitcases up on the shelf, blocking the crawl way door.

Just then, a note was slid under the door. It was an invitation to a dinner party, to be held in the newcomer's honor, in the manager's apartment. The couple appeared pleased at the aspect of attending a party, since they'd been so long without a job or any real social contact. They were both gypsies, which meant Broadway dancers without close family or ties. They lived from opening night to opening night, trying their best to make a living during a time when living had become a challenge for almost everyone.

"Welcome to my parlor, said the spider to the fly," the Blue Lady said, and with a gesture, we appeared in the manager's apartment.

The manager, who was a seemingly cheerful woman, welcomed the dancers in with a great fanfare of emotion, ushering them into the apartment quickly, and then checking out in the hallway to see if anyone had been out to see them entering. Immediately, the man commented on the artwork that was on the foyer's wall, opposite the entranceway. It appeared to be the torso of a female athlete, executed in some sort of plaster, without head or limbs. The manager made some brief comments about her fascination with modern art.

"There's something wrong about that torso," I blurted out.

"It is a torso, but it isn't art, unless you reside in the abyss," the Blue Lady replied.

The two guests were shuttled into the main room of the apartment, where several other people waited to meet them, standing around an elaborate feast which included a punch fountain. The dancers were initially overwhelmed with appreciation about the welcome, and commented on how they hadn't seen so elaborate a party spread in a long time, even when they were working steadily.

"The trap is now sprung, and the innocents are lead to the slaughter," the Blue Lady whispered.

I watched as the party-goers slowly and carefully surrounded the two guests. Whereas the smiles were wide and the welcoming handshakes prevalent in front of the two guests, evil winks and sidelong glances were exchanged behind the newcomer's backs as the group tightened formation. The dancers were asked to sample all of the dishes, which seemed unusually bountiful in meat, a very expensive item for the day. When asked how they could afford such a spread, the manager just laughed and said that it was provided though the generosity of a number of acquaintances, causing the rest of the people in the room to chuckle in an alarming fashion. After the manager felt that enough time had been wasted in mock entertaining, she collected up a chalice of red punch from the fountain and offered it to the girl.

She took the cup, thanked the host, and tasted the punch. Immediately, she drew her hand up to her lips and looked with wide eyes at the fountain. Then, realizing what she had just tasted and what the two of them had just been fed, she dropped the chalice and began to scream.

The party goers rushed the two innocents, laughing maniacally, and the image faded away.

"We were killed. We were more than just killed. We were spiritually poisoned with human meat, toyed with like sacrificial cows, and then…"

"Violated and murdered, which is why I wouldn't return your memories to you when you suggested it."

"And what is it that I needed to know by revisiting this scene of atrocities?"

"Dealing with the manager's soul is a part of your assignment, an assignment that is coming to a close."

"Are you saying that her soul can be salvaged? She's a sexual sadist and a cannibal, so how am I supposed to plant a seed of Light into a creature like that?!"

"You don't need to be concerned about the specifics right now, merely be your true self in that soul's presence and your task will be completed."

"That soul is currently in my life?!"

"It is."

"Can you tell me who it is?"

"When the time is right, you won't need to be told, you will know."

"But I don't know anyone who is a sexual sadist and a cannibal."

"That soul's transgressions against the children of the Light are numerous and unspeakable, and so being a sexual sadist and a cannibal are the merest of footnotes defining their spiritual nature. A viper dressed as a bunny still has its original fangs and disposition. Your task is to be aware that there are fangs that lurk unseen in your life, and to continue to pretend that you believe in the illusion of the bunny."

"Will you protect me from this soul and others like it?"

"I will teach you how to use your free will, which will be a much more powerful gift."

"What happened to this manager person? Was she ever caught and prosecuted?"

"There are crimes which are so heinous that most minds can't consider their possibility. She lead her small group of cannibals for another four years, and then, when it seemed that she and her atrocities were about to be revealed, the last remaining members of her group did to her what she had done to so many others before, and then they disappeared into the night mists, taking their evil somewhere else unsuspected."

"Are we done here? I feel dirty and that I need to take a shower."

"We have one more place to visit."

"Will my past self live through that encounter?"

"No."

"I'm seeing a very disconcerting pattern here," I quipped.

The setting dissolved into the great room of a magnificent palace, decorated with paintings, elaborate sculptures and precious marbles.

"This is nice. It's quite a step up from the apartment building that we just left."

"Appearances can be deceiving, for there is no more Light and Love here than there was where we just left," the Blue Lady explained.

"Is this another corner of unspeakable darkness?"

"Precisely, only more attractively decorated. You see before you three children. They are the offspring of a famous Austrian war hero and this is his ancestral home. It is 1956 and the master of the house has recently passed away. He survived two world wars but he could not survive the secret desires of his young wife, who poisoned him. The children are unaware that they too have come to the end of their lives."

"And I am?"

"You are the boy, the oldest of the three."

The children are all together, sadly writing some sort of marionette play, using puppets of American superheroes as their characters.

"The superhero puppets were purchased by the Baron during one of his many trips to the United States."

The mother rushes in and sends the children off to their rooms. She collects up the marionettes with disgust and hands them to an unsavory looking hulk of a man who has followed her into the great room. The two begin discussing secretively and she tells him to get rid of the toys.

"I suppose that this woman is also a part of my assignment?"

"She is not your primary concern. Avoiding her lies and intrigues will be necessary, though."

"Speaking of necessary, do I have to view whatever it is that she's about to do? I get the idea. Couldn't you just tell me what kind of a monster she is, as opposed to my having a seat up front and center to her crimes?"

"As you wish, the Baroness is quite the social climber, and when she figured out how to climb even higher over the dead body of her husband, cut all irritating family ties, and still get to take everything with her into her new life, she leapt at the chance. The Baron's mourning period is now coming to a close. She plans on having all of the valuables in the mansion secretly removed and replaced with trash. After the stage is properly set, her main henchman there will strangle all three of you children and burn the mansion to the ground. His instructions are to make it seem like you children had been playing with fire and caused the blaze. She will cry for a few days, collect up the sympathies and spare cash of family and friends, and then she'll disappear with her new lover and begin a new life, devoid of distracting concerns like children."

"Another series of unspeakable crimes, but at least no one will be eaten in the process."

"Be careful not to waste any sympathy on either of the two souls that you have observed. It is one thing to wish any and all souls well, and it is quite another to feel sympathy for them such that you open a spiritual conduit that connects them to you. If such a conduit can be established by them, they will do everything within their power to pollute your soul and make you just like them."

"Empathize but don't sympathize?"

"Precisely so," the Blue Lady stated, emphatically.

"Will you ever be taking me back to the Koi pond?"

"Perhaps, after your assignment is complete."

"And if I survive."

"If you don't survive, it's doubtful that the Koi pond will survive."

"Too much pressure, can we try to end on a hopeful note?"

"Certainly, all of the forces of Light and Love are counting on you to succeed, even though you've been given the third most difficult task ever assigned by Jehovah since the beginning of recorded time - no pressure."

"You call that hopeful?"

"I was going more for ironically humorous."

"Who taught you that?"

"Actually, you did."

"Oh."

CHAPTER TWENTY-SIX
Putting the "Woe" in Woe-mance

No matter how bad the day was turning out to be, there was nothing that could keep it gloomy when I passed Marci in the hallway and she smiled at me like I mattered, or she passed to me one of her many notes, always written on some pretty stationary, like it was meant to be saved for posterity.

And save all of her notes, I did.

On the odd occasion when things would get loud and tense upstairs, I'd lie in my bed and reread her notes. I kept them with several black and white pictures of her that I'd taken for my photography class. I tried to find a way to work her into all of my major school projects, whether it was a skit for drama class or something for art class. I stole moments from her life whenever I could during the school day because after school, during musical rehearsals, opposing forces like her little brother were becoming more and more adept at making our spending moments alone impossible. Over time, I found that her time was being managed more and more finitely by her mother, and there was always a family project created to eat up each weekend, except for the required rehearsals.

Mama Lauren and I came to distrust each other's motives concerning Marci, even though we had never really interacted. I was being treated like I was every untrustworthy punk thug with a charming smile that she'd ever heard of, and she was beginning to take on a horrible shadow-presence in my life, her shadow presence intent upon pulling Marci into her darkness so that I would never find her again.

This will probably be one of the few times you will see my handwriting, 'cause I almost always print. Although you may not realize it, I have a hard time expressing myself. In the back of my mind I know what I want to say, but it has a hard time getting from there to my mouth or my hand.

I know the Bible says love is not jealous, and – well – I'm guilty of jealousy. I'm not possessive, because love is definitely not possessive.

My mom was jealous of my father's work, because work was such a big part in my dad's life. I'm jealous because I know there are many girls who wish they were in my place, and that bothers me.

I love my mom very much, and I know she'd give the world to me.

My mom likes you very much. She's just a little leery of you.

She doesn't know you like I do, and when she tells me things, she's just trying to protect me, because she doesn't want to see me get hurt.

My mom doesn't want to see me go off to college, because she's afraid.

She's afraid to be alone.

As the performances drew closer, I felt Marci being slowly squeezed from my grasp.

I couldn't drive Marci home anymore, and under no circumstances should her mother see the two of us together. I couldn't sit close to her during the musical rehearsals because of her brother, who would report home and get Marci crabbed at. Each time I managed to sneak in a private kiss before Mama Lauren arrived to drive her home, I felt like I was a criminal, committing some unpardonable sin that I didn't fully understand.

The rehearsal tempo increased, as it always does, until it was the performance week of the show, which triggered a flurry of finishing set pieces, painting scenery, and multiple tech rehearsals. Having a supporting role, my spare time was mostly taken up with finishing up the set. Having the lead role, Marci's time was taken up with acting in almost every scene, and when she wasn't onstage, she was dressing for her next scene.

The darkness backstage during a performance can be a very romantic place. At least that was what I had believed when I saw other couples embrace and kiss behind the scenery. For me, if there was a scene where the director had me enter from the same side as Marci such that we could grab hands for a millisecond, that became the limits of our romance, for every other moment was scrutinized by someone unsympathetic.

Eventually, the set was done and the props were painted, and so I had little to do but wait in the darkness and listen to Marci's amplified voice as she slowly declared her public love for the character being played by her old boyfriend. Their spending time together I didn't fear, for he was nothing when compared to the storm brewing that was Mama Lauren.

In my spare time, which was most of my time now, I read and reread the longest note that Marci ever gave me. Each time I read it, it brushed away the clouds of doubt and despair that had been gathering on my emotional horizon, and filled me with hope that everything would somehow turn out for the best.

Nick,

"I'd do anything." Is how I feel. I love you, and no one can take that love away from me.

Songwriters can express so many feelings; I wish I was a songwriter. You've heard saying like "I get all choked up when I'm with him, I can't say anything." That's how I feel. I ramble on and on, but to tell you how I feel about you gets all stuck in my throat. To look into your eyes makes my words melt.

I love you, I love being with you – and what being with you brings. I'd like to have you hold me in your arms and keep me there for eternity.

I love you, I need you. I feel safe when I'm with you, and all of the troubles of the world drift away.

I've always said that love is childish, and I don't mean it in a bad way. I mean it makes you feel silly. You feel this way because you forget your troubles and remember that you have someone to care for you. You do things that you never thought you'd do, like run home in the middle of a snowstorm with your shoes off, sing in the rain, and play-act, nah-nah you can't catch me and other dumb little games.

Love is BEAUTIFUL.

You're beautiful.

God is beautiful.

Everything is beautiful when you're around.

I've discovered so many things that I missed, before you. Most of all, I've found what I need, what I want to do. All these things I've found because of you.

Love is fresher than springtime, brighter than sunlight, more romantic than the moon. Love is between all people, but special love is between a person and God.

A different kind of love is between two people.

You and me, my mom and dad, and many, many other couples across the universe know about this special love.

Our love is sharing.

Sharing in each other's sad, happy, and in between, sharing in silence, sharing in respect.

Love is inner and deep found.

I found it in you.

I've lived in love all of my life. Our household is full of love. No prejudice can fill my life. People are equal, no matter what color, what they've done, each person deserves an equal chance.

If we're prejudiced how can they ever learn about the love that we know? That is what bothers me most. That's why I go on mission work, to spread love. Lots of people have seen our love and our love has been spread, and we must continue to spread it.

Separation next year can only mean more love, more spreading, our growth.

It'll be hard and I will miss you, but we'll make it. Besides, a few years cannot surpass eternity. I believe that we can make the world a little better, but we need the experience of an education and the time to nurture our ideas, and then maybe we can accomplish even more.

If only this was my graduation from college, then I wouldn't feel so nervous about writing this. I don't like the idea of waiting. I'm independent but impatient. I don't like to wait.

I love you, and I want to be with you, now and forever, but we have to wait.

I've learned so much, just being with you. You've taught me things that I never would've known if I hadn't met you. I want to wish you the best of luck for your first year of college. It sounds strange, but I won't be there. I just felt like I'd need some luck so I gave it to you.

I love you. Love is us.

I love you.

I miss you already and you're right here. Ahhh!

All my love forever,
Marci

The first performance of the show was a matinee for the school that I found anticlimactic. My schoolmates were either rowdy, making them distracting, or they were almost comatose, which was disturbing.

I was even robbed of the dubious honor of being the show's only comic relief. What ended up being the funniest moment of the production was when Hayley Cress, as the Mother Superior, ran offstage emitting a string of unrepeatable obscenities because she had messed up the words in one of the verses of "Climb Ev'ry Mountain." She had forgotten about her attached lavalier microphone, as had Miss Heinkel up in the projection booth. There was nothing that I could say in character as Max that could ever generate a laugh on a par with the outburst of Mother Expletive Superior.

I had the only really funny lines in the play, so getting a chuckle, even from the near-comatose was somewhat satisfying, but certainly not as satisfying as playing the lead beside Marci would've been. Had I been given the lead, then I could've claimed that my holding her and staring into her eyes was just a part of the acting required, but instead, our eyes only met as she dashed offstage to her dressing room.

I had hoped for more, considering how much of my time and life-blood I had invested in working on the sets and the tech of the production. Even while in the darkness of the wings, I had to keep an eye out to avoid being seen by Marci's pesky brother, Joey, or Mama Lauren, who seemed to have mastered the art of covering her reaction of loathing to me with a smile so sharp that it caused me to shiver involuntarily.

What I had originally dreamt of as a great artistic moment in my life had devolved into something more akin to a daytime nightmare.

It was under these circumstances that I was publicly caught in the act of transgression.

Thinking that we were alone, just outside of her dressing room, I had snuck up behind Marci and had given her an immense bear hug, proudly proclaiming, "I don't care what anyone else thinks, I've still got a leading role (indicating Marci)," and at that exact moment, Mama Lauren had turned the corner and frozen my soul with her indescribable, arctic stare.

My soul thus damaged, I meekly went away and waited until the auditorium was empty. Then I sat in the darkness, alone with my thoughts, which weren't pretty.

All around me, I saw people experiencing the magic that was high school theatre, making memories that would last a lifetime, scribbling notes, exchanging flowers, snapping pictures, and trying to slow time down to savor the moments.

The final curtain call came.

I received mild applause and went to my side of the stage. Marci received her applause and went to the other side of the stage. The curtain call seemed to be a metaphor for the entire musical experience. Throughout the show, I had tried to be as upbeat as possible with all of my friends and my acting seemed convincing to most, but not all.

Mo asked me how I was doing frequently, having the sensitivity required to know that my smile was about as genuine as Bozo the clown's. A couple of times she sat with me to listen to my tale of woe, as a genuine friend would, and I thanked her sincerely for caring. She would always reply, "What are friends for?" which sometimes caused me to look around at my many other friends and wonder.

The show closed and there was a big pizza party onstage. I found myself longing for the more intimate celebrations associated with smaller casts, like the fall play. The fall play had no room to invite the parents of the players for pizza and pop. Stage moms weren't a part of the Drama Club experience. How I wish that they weren't a part of the musical experience.

The sets that had taken seemingly forever to design, build and paint were hurriedly dismantled, the drops were folded up and stored away, and I found myself volunteering to do anything and everything in order to prolong my time in the auditorium, hoping to catch a glimpse of Marci as she and her family cleaned out her dressing room, removing all of her gifts and flowers. My exit from the show required no more than a single trip to the car with a couple of costumes and a bag of make-up, which is why I volunteered to tear the sets apart and schlep the props up to the back storeroom of the auditorium, just to be around right up to the end of the dream.

From the bright lights and colors of the school musical, everything seemed to subtly shift into shades of brown, not that this was such a terrible thing, for brown ended up being the color of my tuxedo for the school prom.

There was about three weeks between the closing of the show and the prom, which was the third Saturday in May. I had asked Marci if she wanted to go during the early rehearsal period for *The Sound of Music* and she was quite excited by the prospect. I didn't get the impression that Mama Lauren was very thrilled, but it seemed that the prom was so big an event that denying Marci the opportunity to attend could only be interpreted as unmitigated meanness and so Marci was finally given permission.

I scrounged money from whatever source I could, as the costs for the prom seemed to continually mount. First, one had to purchase the tickets, then rent a tuxedo, buy a corsage or nosegay, find a nice car or rent a limo, and then have enough money left over to go to a decent restaurant for dinner. It was quite a production of planning in and of itself, but I ultimately enjoyed the process. Each day in choir those of us who were going to the prom, and those of us who were paying for going to the prom, would collect into our respective groups to compare notes or stories of woe. Whereas one group might be discussing the outrageous costs of having their parents pay to have their hair done properly, the other group might be discussing the outrageous costs of everything relating to going out with a girl. It was all shared in fun, for there had never been any confusion about chivalry being expensive.

When prom night finally arrived, I dressed in my brown tuxedo with velvet collar and ruffled shirt, borrowed the keys to my mother's brand new Continental, and drove off to Marci's, with strict instructions to have pictures taken by someone of the two of us with the camera I was given, and to stop by my grandparent's house to show Marci off. We would be going with Frank Johnson and Doreen Bommarito, and I secretly prayed, for Doreen's sake, that Miss Heinkel hadn't volunteered to chaperone the dance.

I got to Marci's and I was a little nervous as I waited on the front porch. Eventually, I was asked in by Mama Lauren. Marci came out of her room in a beautiful, flowing, off white gown with a delicate lace vest, embroidered on the back with roses in pinks, creams and white. Much to my surprise, the nosegay that I had bought for her was a perfect match for her embroidery, as if it had been made specifically from the design on her vest. We both laughed when we realized how perfect everything was. Mama Lauren insisted on a battery of pictures and then we were off.

Navigating the dark blue barge that was my mother's Continental was an interesting challenge, but the car did make us feel that much more special, like we were out playing adults for the evening. We held hands as we drove over to Grandma Menafay and Grandpa Eugene's house, where even more pictures were to be taken for the sake of posterity. Unlike Mama Lauren's comments, which I found to be rather cold, detached, and clinical, my grandparent's comments seemed almost as giddy as we were. Grandma Menafay was absolutely effusive in her admiration and praise of how we looked as a couple.

On our way to pick up Frank, who lived on the lake, we found a quiet spot to spend a couple of private moments before our party officially expanded to a foursome. There wasn't any delay at Frank's house, as he came bounding out the front door, tie in hand. We got to Doreen's house, where the process of our getting to the prom got a little bogged down for a time because of all of the family members who wanted to take pictures, reminisce about proms gone by, and generally socialize.

At last we arrived at the dance, the Hilltop Country Club hall being a few miles northwest of the school. I dropped the others off at the entrance and parked the car in the lot, just like a considerate chauffeur would do. It was strange to see so many people all dressed up in their elaborate hairdos and expensive outfits. The inside of the hall was dimly lit and we found ourselves a table. Someone had obviously spent most of the day hanging streamers and decorations to further enhance the magical quality of the evening.

The official school photographer had set up his equipment in a corner of the lobby area and the line was quite long to get a portrait done. After all of the pictures that had been taken by the various adults, and all of the expense of actually getting to the dance, I didn't suggest that we get in line for an official portrait because I was a little concerned that I didn't have the money required for the picture. I wasn't completely certain that I'd have enough money for dinner. We knew that food was going to be served at the prom, but we'd also been told by people who had attended the prom in years past that it was going to consist of lettuce salad, room temperature mostacholi, overcooked chicken, hard rolls and butter patties. From the set-up at the far end of the room, consisting of a handful of warmers, there didn't seem to be any reason to doubt that the meal was just going to be passable.

More importantly, getting permission to go out to dinner extended the curfew for the event another two hours, so I didn't have to get Marci home until 1 a.m. After conferring with Frank and Doreen and several other friends in the room, it quickly became clear that no one else that I could identify had a curfew. Only Marci was tied to a strict timeline, a timeline that I dared not violate unless I wished to face Mama Lauren's wrath, directly or indirectly.

The festivities picked up tempo and the band started to play, their performance showing obvious confusion relating to the merits of volume vs. the merits of musical accuracy, but no one seemed to mind. The dance turned into a slow cycle of getting the girls drinks, making small talk, dancing from time to time, depending on the song, and watching the wait staff assemble what would eventually be our dinner. The only real difference between the first hour of the event and the third hour of the event was the degree to which the general populace had undressed.

The more bodies that were added to the room, the warmer it got.

The more serving trays set up with little heaters, the warmer it got.

The faster the dancing, the warmer it got.

Whereas the girls were more limited in their ability to adapt to the increasing heat, the boys frequently discarded clothing with indifference, until the dance floor was filled with shoeless, corsage-less, vest-less girls, dancing opposite shoeless, tie-less, coat-less, ruffle-less, vest-less boys, damp with sweat. When the temperature reached a point where a handful of the cool kids were beginning to unbutton their shirts, someone in charge decided that, ready or not, everybody should be seated and the feeding non-frenzy should commence. With excruciating slowness, various tables were called and we all lined up for dinner. Although I had been raised on a quality of food that was easily on a par with cold noodles and dry chicken, I had enough sense to take very little of it in anticipation of our real meal to come. Our party went back to the table and tried to make small talk over the general din of the background music, which was only slightly quieter than the live band had been.

Marci and I were having a good time, but what I quickly realized was how much money and effort had been expended in order for us to have basically no private time together. We tried to carry on our own conversation in a manner that didn't attract attention from anyone else, but there always seemed to be someone from the choir or the Drama Club coming up to share some bit of gossip or another, or insisting that one or all of us come out on the dance floor and dance with them.

Frank and Doreen seemed to be getting along well, but I didn't have a sense that any special effort was required to achieve that state. As long as there was no trace of Miss Heinkel or mention of her name, Doreen was an easy person to please. She was known for her simple tastes. Rumor had it that for Christmas, Frank had merely gotten her a five pound container of Sanders fudge. A can opener and spoon later, she was happy as a clam, and stayed that way until the end of the Christmas season or the bottom of the can was reached, whichever came first.

Once the idea crossed my mind of what I couldn't share with Marci during the dance, the more obsessed I was with a need to share with her at the dance. Then I started calculating how much time dinner would take, how much time dropping off Frank and Doreen would take, and how many minutes would be left for Marci and I to have to ourselves before she needed to be deposited safely back on her front porch. In my mind's eye, I could already see Mama Lauren, arms sternly crossed, standing on the front porch as we pulled up, making sure that under no circumstances would our goodnight kiss go uninterrupted.

As the time crept by, the ghost of Mama Lauren continued to grow in my imagination. And still, after being at the prom for hours, I'd had no opportunity to talk with Marci beyond small talk. We held hands under the table a couple of times, until we were both too sweaty to feel comfortable about it, and then we nudged and poked each other affectionately from time to time, but all in all, there was no real magic made between us. I wondered what memories we could've made with six hours, a car, a pizza, and a quiet park, as compared to six hours together caught up in an expensive herding ritual of passage called the prom.

The difference was obvious.

I had received permission to take Marci to the prom precisely because there would be no opportunity for privacy. There was no way that I was ever going to get permission from Mama Lauren to spend six hours in the park with Marci and a pizza.

That would be too dangerous.

We were to be officially released from our sauna at 11 o'clock, but the rule was, once you left the building, you were not allowed back in, so I tried to convince Frank and Doreen to leave and go to dinner earlier than we'd originally planned. For reasons that I couldn't fathom, they both wanted to stay until the last possible moment, sopping up the "magic" of the prom experience much like wiping a dinner plate clean with a hard roll. I could tell from Marci's expression that her thoughts had been running in the same direction as mine, as the steamy minutes slowly ticked by.

At last, the appointed hour arrived and we all grabbed our things and headed to the car. The evening air was cool and crisp and a refreshing respite from the stifling atmosphere of the hall. There was still a chance that Marci and I could salvage a few private moments at the end of our adventure.

The restaurant was called the Firehouse and it was considered a moderately-priced eatery. The fare leaned more towards steaks and fish, but there were also items like hamburgers and fries, but for inflated prices, no doubt because of the 'atmosphere.' Of the four of us, I was probably the most inexperienced diner. My family never dined out. I had eaten at restaurants with my friends after rehearsals, but all of those experiences were on the cheap because acquiring money, at least for me, was always somewhat of a challenge. One reason was because my mother had decided early on in my life that I wasn't worthy of an allowance. At the time that she'd made the announcement to the three of us, we'd never even broached the subject, and so it was obviously a peremptory strike to make sure that we never did. Her 'reasoning' was that we couldn't be relied on to keep up with chores and so she was just avoiding fighting with us about them. In retrospect, I believe that the true situation was that Nathan put her on an allowance to handle the family bills and buy the food, which was why we ate the cheapest form of everything that could be legally bought, from whitish hamburger to slimy hot dogs. And once we had run out of something, unless it was something that she personally required like milk, bread, or cigarettes, we were out of luck until the next shopping day, which none of us were allowed to attend. As for immediately required items, I was allowed to shop for her in those instances, although buying her cigarettes embarrassed me and gave me the creeps.

I enjoyed dropping by my grandparent's house because there I was always fed real food, often freshly made, the food having never once touched an aluminum TV dinner tray.

We settled into our table at the restaurant and I immediately began calculating which dinner option I would choose, based upon which dinner option Marci chose. If I was her, and I was experiencing a classy restaurant for the first time and not paying, I'd probably mentally flirt with ordering the surf and turf. She was more than welcome to order the most expensive thing on the menu, if she liked, however, that would mean that I would be having a small dinner salad with a side order of free oyster crackers and a big glass of water. I suspected that Marci was not so much a fish out of water in this experience as I was, and so I believed that she would make a less expensive choice, although I was beginning to be a little curious about what a surf and turf dinner would be like.

Marci ordered quite reasonably, a petit filet, which I appreciated, and I matched her selection with a filet mignon, not that I knew what it was, other than beef. In our home, the beef choices were sale hamburger and bulk TV dinner Salisbury steaks, which seemed to lack any resemblance to any steak my grandparents had ever cooked. Frank and Doreen ordered like they'd been there before, which was entirely possible since Frank had a part time job working at a factory that made things for Chrysler cars, and was the high school student with the most disposable income that I knew.

Small talk and tick tocks filled up the moments.

Doreen had ordered some type of fried chicken dinner, which struck me as odd since we'd just left a fried chicken dinner back at the hall, and she was definitely displeased with its quality. While I was trying my best to talk us back out to the car, Frank got it into his head to have dessert and tried to placate Doreen with some Black Forest torte. She had some, but it didn't remove her irritation over her dinner. Frank, unexpectedly, became absolutely enamored of the torte and ended up having two additional pieces, and then he asked if there was any more that he could buy to take home. One would think that this would cause a shift of discussion to desserts in general and the torte specifically, but Doreen just continued to simmer, like Mount Vesuvius. Seeing the look of "Someone needs to hear of my displeasure" growing ever larger upon Doreen's face, I paid our bill and tried to get Marci out the door before something bad happened. Frank talked Doreen out of going three rounds with the manager, but she insisted that she was going to leave a tip at the table of two cents, to show her displeasure.

I was holding the restaurant door open for Marci, and Frank and Doreen were halfway to the exit when we all heard our waitress blurt out, "What's this?!" As I ushered Marci out, I caught a glimpse of Doreen stopping and the waitress moving towards her, holding up two pennies in her fingers.

"Sorry about that," I said to Marci, "I've been friends with them for quite a while and they can be quirky, but usually it's in an amusing way."

"The whole triple dessert thing might've been amusing if I didn't have a curfew," she said, sadly.

"It feels more like a deadline than a curfew," I replied.

"You're right."

"The fates seem to have conspired to make sure that we don't get any time to ourselves tonight, but I hope that you had a relatively good time anyway."

We got in the car and she cuddled up next to me and took my arm. "I'll remember this night always," she cooed. "Don't worry, things will get better. Eventually, my mother will accept our situation and we won't have so much pressure on us."

"From your mouth to God's ears," I suggested.

The back door opened and Doreen got into the car. Frank then closed her door and got in the other side. The two of them were silent. Angry words had obviously been exchanged, either with the waitress or with each other, and we all drove back to Silver Lake in silence.

After dropping off the two of them, I had mere minutes to get Marci home, and as I navigated through the dark and relatively empty streets, I couldn't help but feel a bit cheated by our companions' choices. They had experienced a prom of their own making, both in good moments and in bad, and we had experienced a prom of their making, which hadn't been so much fun.

When I pulled up to the front of Marci's house, my thoughts of walking her to her door and giving her a goodnight kiss quickly faded. The front door was open and Mama Lauren could be seen pacing about inside. When she heard our car, she came to the door and looked out. I gave Marci a quick peck before she jumped out of the car. Her look had said it all as she pulled away and shut the door.

"I'm sorry" was what her eyes had said to me, "It will be better next time but I have to go now, my love."

I drove around a little, wanting to clear my head of disappointment and resentment, after all, no one at my house cared if I came home that night, although there would be some concern about what had happened to my mother's car if I didn't show up.

The next week in school, Doreen and Frank went on and on about how much fun prom was, not having the slightest clue about how they had negatively impacted our evening. I thought about enlightening them but decided against it. They wouldn't get my point anyway, because they were only cognizant of them, it seemed.

Instead of things getting better, I became an undeclared persona non grata in Marci's life, that is, until her birthday, which was almost two weeks later.

There was never a statement of, "Don't call here anymore." It was just that Marci was eternally busy and couldn't come to the phone. It wasn't that Marci wasn't let out of the house. It was just that she was so busy and her schedule was so structured that she wasn't allowed to have any spare time to spend with me. It wasn't that I was hated like the devil himself, it was just that I had ceased to be real in Marci's life, and there was absolutely nothing that I could do about it.

Ignoring the chill that I knew would run up and down my spine while talking to her, I called and spoke privately with Marci's mother, expressing a desire to paint an oil portrait of her recently deceased husband for Marci's birthday. Mama Lauren showed unexpected and unreserved enthusiasm for the project, and we arranged for her to provide me with pictures for reference.

Being considered an artist is a funny thing. Over the years, people had given me their old art supplies, assuming that I'd know what to do with them. For the most part, old supplies accomplished little more than to make me realize that in order to be successful, I'd need a great deal of money that I didn't have in order to either complete the set of supplies that I had been given, or to upgrade to a quality of art supply actually worth having. Whoever thought that oil pastels would be a desirable art medium was a confused person, by my assessment.

Armed with a mishmash of odds and ends, I started in on the oil portrait. Reading reference books on the proper technique for creating an oil portrait, I realized that I didn't have the proper brushes, the proper thinners or mediums, or even a full selection of the proper colors. I had several tiny, skinny tubes of low quality, highly diluted, bargain basement beginner art set cast-offs, but I was as poor as a church mouse and so I did what I could. What I lacked in quality materials and experience, I made up for in heart and desire.

After laboring intensely for several days, I completed the portrait in time for it to be reasonably dry before the scheduled birthday gathering. I had used turpentine to thin the oil paints and had painted thinly so the surface of the portrait was dry to the touch. I was given permission to come to the house to present Marci with her birthday presents, an oil portrait of her father in an antique, gilded frame that my Grandpa Eugene had donated to the cause, and a crucifix that I had carved out of the ivory of an old piano key and a scrap of rosewood from a classic guitar that I was constructing. Grandma Menafay provided the finishing touch for the cross, a solid gold chain. I didn't feel all that comfortable carving Jesus dead on the cross as he is normally depicted on a crucifix, but I knew that Marci would cherish the gift. So I made it, focusing upon Marci's appreciation, and not upon my own feelings of discomfort. I don't like thinking about how Jesus was tortured.

When I arrived to give her my gifts, I wasn't allowed to be alone with Marci, even for a minute, and after Marci had opened her presents, I was politely asked to leave. The family now had an oil portrait of a person that they loved dearly, and they were in the last stages of officially discarding someone they didn't love at all, me.

I received one last loving note from Marci, that went on and on about how much I meant to her, ending with, "All my love forever", but I began to suspect that love would never be able to bloom in Mama Lauren's shadow.

The day after Marci's birthday, I was informed by note during choir class that she would call me.

I waited.

Eventually, the house phone rang, and Marci and I arranged to go on a bike ride together, although Marci's voice on the other end of the phone sounded detached and mechanical, like she's been reduced to a human recording.

When I arrived at the appointed time, Marci jumped on her bike and sped off. I struggled to catch up with her. When I got near, I noticed that she wasn't wearing my class ring anymore.

That realization made further discussion essentially irrelevant, but the sad shadow play had yet to have the ending performed. All that was left to do was to officially end that which had been killed by actions of others some time ago. Marci was no longer the person who had warmed my heart on so many previous occasions, and my entire world became as chilly as my little bed in the dark corner of the centipede-ridden basement once again.

The funny, somewhat naïve, generally nice fellow that I had been throughout high school began to emotionally withdraw, to the point of near self-implosion.

Marci's last note to me read:

I registered for my classes this morning and Wednesday we get back to the "old grind."

I feel awkward writing this letter and I suppose, if I was smart, I wouldn't write to you at all.

It's over – forever. I'll never have strong feelings for you again.

I "held" on to you because of my father's death, for your sympathy, and because you enjoyed talking to me instead of getting sexually involved. I've always hated guys who went out with me to hopefully have some sexual enjoyment, but I've realized there are people more understanding of me, less demanding, and allowing me to be free.

I realized I hurt you – try to overcome that hurt – don't hold on or you'll make me hate you and all the treasured conversations we ever had.

There are no links between us - it's over!

My heart shattered, God decided that it would be a good time to return to me the gift of hugeness, and my normal-sized body slowly started to grow larger, for no apparent reason whatsoever. Other than sadness, nothing else had changed. I didn't eat differently or exercise less. In fact, I exercised more, crisscrossing the city on my bike, trying desperately to ride faster than the accumulating weight that dragged down on my heart. I even took up jogging, getting up to three miles before quitting, because my clothes, instead of getting roomier, were getting too small. Marci dropped out of my social circles and out of my life, becoming merely the back of a head sitting in the front row of choir each day. She no longer spent time in the choir room and she didn't make small talk with anyone before or after choir class. I asked around, but no one seemed to know what was going on with her. Just before graduation, Tyler Nagy shared that he had talked to Marci, briefly. He shared about how Marci had decided to look into a career as a nutritionist, and that I must've been eating an extra 1,000 calories a day in order to put on the weight that I had in the weeks since we'd been together.

"Of all the messages that you could've made sure that I received, it had to be that one?" I asked God.

"You needed to learn that true love might bring pain with it, but it is never about hurting the other person needlessly. Marci was in love with the idea of being in love, and not really in love with you, my son."

"That makes it all so much better," I quipped, "I feel as gutted as my Dad's first deer."

I went home and removed the pile of black and white pictures and notes from under the head of my bed and placed them in the bottom of my chest of drawers.

Instead of warming, as it once had, Marci's smile now burned me in places that I couldn't quench.

CHAPTER TWENTY-SEVEN
Mission to the Abyss

Death and rot has a stench, and the place where that aroma was perfected is Lucifer's abyss. Because of Jehovah giving ultimate authority to the concept of free will over even His own presence, Lucifer was capable of creating a dimension where Jehovah had been pushed out. It is an ashen, half-lit place where the colors of the rainbow have no place and souls trapped there or born there have no peace.

There were three of us, flying in silent formation, just above what passed as ground. The three of us were unique in that we were the only three souls targeted by Lucifer who had not been taken over by his soul snot. Each of us had called out to Jehovah at the last instant, just before losing our ability for independent thought. Our desperate pleas had been answered and each one of us, in our turn, had been saved from becoming Lucifer's mind-numbed minion.

A third or Heaven, our friends and comrades since the beginning of all things, had not been so fortunate.

I had the further distinction of having been considered Lucifer, the ha-Satan's, best friend. Before any soul in Heaven had any idea of the meaning of the word evil, we all believed that everyone and everything was an extension of Jehovah, and therefore we had no caution or leeriness born from being exposed to deceit.

Lucifer had changed all of that.

Lucifer had taught all of Heaven the capabilities of Pride and the concept of evil. His position, before he tried to mind-control all of Jehovah's loyal servants, had been as ha-Satan, which functioned as a form of prosecuting attorney. His was the task of analyzing the work of Jehovah's servants and correcting errors in perception, judgment, or procedure. Although constructive criticism was the original purpose, Lucifer came to believe that since he was the only spiritual being created singularly by Jehovah, that he was more than capable of replacing his "master." Pride is its own form of mind-numbing soul snot, although Lucifer had no idea that he was suffering from spiritually poisoning himself. Back when everyone considered Lucifer to be admirable and trustworthy, I had been considered his best and closest friend. I was an innocent soul, and as such, I was friends with everyone. I was also best friends with the Christ energy, which was how I was able to survive the effects of the unexpected soul snot attack.

Of all of the souls that Lucifer hates, he hates mine most of all, for I would not acquiesce, bow down to him, and call him my god.

I was Lucifer's most hated enemy, and here I was with two other angels, hated almost as much as I and we were traveling into the center of Lucifer's abyss.

All three of us knew why we were there and all three of us had agreed to come when asked, but none of us fully understood why any being of Light would be sent on a mission into the heart of darkness. Our glances revealed amongst us that we had no idea if we had it within us to actually do what we had been charged to do and get out spiritually alive. If we were captured, our spiritual death and public spiritual torture were almost assured. We would be made an example of, with extreme prejudice and sadistic pleasure.

Although Jehovah had made us invisible to the residents of the abyss, we had to be acutely aware of where we were and what we were doing. We couldn't descend into the heart of Lucifer's dominion from directly above, the shortest route, for it was a certainty that Lucifer would sense our arrival, even if he could've see us, and then we would be lost. We had to travel to the center of his dominion from far outside, just skimming the surface. We couldn't risk touching even one toe to the surface, for pieces of Lucifer's soul snot lived like snakes, hidden in crevices and shadowy places, keeping everyone within his kingdom docile and compliant.

We couldn't risk flying at any serious altitude because we would be separating ourselves from the confusion of smells and sounds at ground level, increasing the likelihood that Lucifer would detect us. We were forced to glide silently and slowly, making the smallest ripple in the air as we could, all the while inching our way closer and closer to the center of the biggest spider web ever created by a creature aligned with death, decay, and destruction.

We were there to retrieve souls, souls brutally intercepted by the minions of the darkness while on their way back to rejoining their loved ones in Heaven. I was assigned to retrieve a family of five, a mother, a father and three daughters. I wasn't sure how many souls my companions were charged with retrieving, but it would hardly make a dent in the untold numbers of unjustly imprisoned souls being held there in the non-Light.

It made more sense that our being asked to do this was more a test to see if we were free of fear, free of the soul snot's energy, and not about how many souls we could salvage.

Fear is the opposite of faith.

If there was any fear within us, we never would've agreed to attempt such an assignment, but now that we were within the belly of the Beast, our thoughts turned to whether any soul could be where we were and expected to do what we were charged with and not experience a twinge of fear.

Fear would bring distrust.

Fear would cause mistakes.

Fear would be the end of our conscious lives, if we gave in to it.

We each flew on, focusing upon the power of faith.

If the abyss could be accused of having a theme, the only word that would be appropriate would be random. It was neither picturesque, nor pleasing to the eye. It had some of the visual aspects of a battlefield and some feeling of precious materials having been ripped from the ground. Huts and small constructions increased in frequency until we came within sight of an enormous wall, rising above the horizon. Whereas the Great Wall of China had been designed and built to keep non-Chinese out, this mammoth structure was designed to keep the trapped within, under the dominion of the ha-Satan, now turned god of a world of his own creation.

Every prince of darkness and every demon within were literal pieces of Lucifer's personal life energy. Just as Jehovah used tiny pieces of His life force to create His children's souls, because of his great spiritual strength, Lucifer also had the capability of subdividing himself. His ability was not nearly at the level of Jehovah, but he never spoke of that limitation to his "children."

We knew that the great wall had six gates, for six is the number of incompletion which Lucifer had taken unto himself. Lucifer had pledged to thwart Jehovah's plans to bring all of His creation to spiritual completion, as represented by the number seven. Lucifer's number, 666, represented his efforts to keep the spiritual evolution of humankind from completion, to keep the efforts of the heavenly host from completion, and to keep the Ultimate Plans of Jehovah Himself from completion.

Without causing even the tiniest disturbance in the air to mark our passing, we slowly glided through the great gates. It had been easy enough to gain entrance, but egress was certainly going to be a different story. Within the massive walls there was elaborate architecture, if constructs without symmetry, balance, or pleasing pattern can be said to be architecture. Here in the abyss, only two things mattered, size and the ability to generate pain. The demons of the abyss were plentiful, and they scampered about like ants in the shadow of the master's hall. Even the temples built to worship the princes of the abyss were dwarfed by Lucifer's central palace, erected to remind every creature with the ability to see just who the god of this place was. There were only two design elements that repeated themselves throughout this realm, the numbers 6 and 13. The number 6 represented the demon lord himself, and the number 13 represented the demon lord eternally fighting the unnamable other, who existed outside of this place, the 6 fighting to destroy the 7.

Everywhere there were statues dedicated to the 6 destroying the works of the 7, and upon each of these "sacred" statues was a thick coating of what could only be assumed to be dried blood. Here was a place where merely being subservient wasn't enough, where only the maniacally faithful survived, and the rest were weeded out and offered up in fire and blood.

The city smelled of anti-life, if such an odor can even be described.

The three of us dispersed, each one of us drawn to a different part of the city, each one of us being spiritually led to a different group of souls to retrieve.

We all hoped that our charges would be located far from the center of this trap, far from Lucifer's immediate gaze, but before our concerns tried to well up into full-blown fear, we prayed "Thy Will be done," and journeyed onward. Specific telepathy wasn't required under these unique circumstances, and we all three knew that we were of one mind, one perspective, and one hope.

Uzziel swerved to the left and was quickly gone behind the visual clutter. Fanuel banked to the right, and I found myself being drawn towards the center, straight towards Lucifer's greatest physical monument to himself.

"I should've known," I quipped to myself as I gained a bit of height and picked up speed. If anyone was going to be asked to fly into Lucifer's lap and tweak him on the nose, of course, it would have to be me. Chasing anyone else, he would just be in a murderous rage. Chasing me, he would become irrational with fury, which may well work to all of our advantages, I realized.

Deeper and deeper into the tangled metropolis I flew, carefully wending my way to the center, just above the heads of the downtrodden miscreants that labored there. Some labored for a purpose, if assembled chaos can be considered a purpose. Some labored merely to show obedience to whatever prince of darkness they owed their supplications to.

After what seemed an eternity of snail-like travel, I at last came around a corner and entered a huge square, directly in front of the entranceway to Lucifer's personal cathedral. The objects of my mission were here, somewhere amidst the intense throng. I would need to get a higher elevation to find them. Just as I began to rise, I looked above me and noticed that I had just entered the square between the outstretched legs of a fallen angel. Initially, I had thought that I'd passed through a statue, but upon closer inspection, it became clear that this enormous former ally was a Sandalphon angel, an angel of my order, although I couldn't tell who it was. Most angels have androgynous faces, appearing to be a pleasing synthesis of male and female, except for the archangel Gabriel, who prefers to appear as a female. Angels are immediately identified, even from great distances, by the heraldry of their wings, but here, where bright rainbow colors had been bleached to the shades of dust, it was impossible to decipher who this was, towering over me. I scanned the square and my suspicions proved to be accurate. Where Lucifer would set out one mind-numbed Sandalphon angel as decoration, he'd set out a group of six, just as a reminder of his allegedly limitless abilities. Instead of flowing robes, the Sandalphons had been redressed in garish and minimal attire reminiscent of slaves. Each one held in their hand a gigantic staff weapon, capable of smashing or cutting down a wide swath of minions, should such a display of force or displeasure be deemed necessary. Each angel stared forward, unblinking, without the slightest sign of life or independent thought.

The family unit that I was sent to retrieve was part of a large group of mind-numbed new arrivals, contained in a sort of ceremonial pen in the middle of the square. Removing them without being noticed would be nearly impossible, since there were hundreds, possibly thousands, packed shoulder-to-shoulder in the pen. What they would be subjected to once they left the containment pen I didn't want to ponder, and I hoped that my two companions had found their assignments in a less populated, less central, and less dangerous situation. I couldn't sweep down at an angle, sweep them up and dart away, because even though my grabbing them would render them invisible to searching eyes, I would have to bowl over several dozen other bodies in order to reach them in that manner and the path of my egress would be easy to discern.

I decided to drop down from directly above, grow large enough to easily grab all five members of the family, and then fly straight up, changing my direction as quickly as I could to evade the Sandalphon guards. Although impressive in size and mightily armed, I knew that they would react slowly, like huge animated corpses. They wouldn't pose a serious threat, nor would the throngs of normal-sized demons.

It was the master of the house being alarmed and intervening that concerned me, for what could I possibly do to escape if attacked by Lucifer himself? With a last quick prayer, I descended.

Making myself quite small, I landed behind the family group. None of them even suspected that I was there, and then, expanding quickly, I grabbed up the five of them and leapt up into the air. This shift caused several others who had been standing close by to be forcibly shoved backwards. Confusion and panic erupted and the Sandalphon guards shuddered to life. The five souls that I was gripping tightly to myself seemed to stir from their stupor also, squirming and screaming for assistance, their minds not their own. There was only one way to remove the soul snot that infected them, but I didn't dare try to do it here, out in the open. With the confusion in the square, I was certain that no one would be able to hear the screams coming from my direction, but it was a long way to get out of the square safely. There was a rumbling from somewhere, like something huge had just been set into motion by all the noise. I knew that it was Lucifer, and that I needed to do something crafty within the next few seconds or all would be lost. Whereas the others frantically searching for me wouldn't be able to figure out where I was over all of the noise and confusion, the master of darkness would not have much of a problem.

I decided to take the offensive.

The Sandalphon were converging and I flew up and toppled the one I had originally noticed with a blow to the chest with my feet. As it was falling backwards, I swooped around and shoved another Sandalphon from behind. Arms and weapons flailing, trying to keep their balance, they provided me with enough of a distraction to double-back and make for the gateway that I'd entered through. I dared not look behind me, but I heard a bellowing and the sounds of a great concussion, as if something were being shoved out of the way with lethal force. I glanced over my shoulder just in time to dodge the body of one of the Sandalphon angels as it collided with the entrance arch, smashing it to rubble. I managed to get through it just before the top of the archway collapsed, but it was a close call.

My charges were struggling to get free of my grip even more frantically, and I had to get somewhere relatively private in order to try to bring them back to their senses. Stealth was no longer a major concern, as long as I stayed below the level of the surrounding buildings, which would block me, at least temporarily, from Lucifer's view. He might not be able to see me, but if he knew where to focus his attentions, figuring out my exact location from the screams of my frantic passengers would be a simple task. I darted down streets and alleyways in a haphazard manner, trying my best to avoid wide, open spaces. The din from behind me continued to grow, as Lucifer seemed to have picked up my scent somehow. I darted into a rather narrow cul-de-sac, and although it was a poor choice for a place to be caught within, it would serve nicely in my attempt to revive the family. The only way to remove the soul snot that they were infected with was to blast it away with pure Light, something that didn't exist in the half-light of the abyss.

I closed my eyes, angled my body in an attempt to keep as much of my Light as possible from flashing straight up and revealing our location, and let loose. The Light emanating from my chest filled up the cul-de-sac and left my family of five startled and numb. The snot began to come out of their mouth, and their eyes showed some signs of returning life.

"You shouldn't have done that, whoever you are. You won't have much time left in your life to contemplate just how big a mistake that was!" bellowed a huge voice, just out of sight. Then the walls around us started to shake and collapse. I bent over to protect the family and saw that additional soul snot was squirming out of the cracks and crevices around the debris at the feet of my reviving family. Before I could intervene, I felt myself being swept aside, along with most of the cul-de-sac, crashing into the wall at the other side of the opening.

"Found you, you little bug. How dare you try to deprive me of my playthings? For that crime you shall be severely…" Lucifer stopped midsentence and sniffed the air, "Could it be? Would my old friend Ophan be foolish enough to accept a suicide assignment that placed him literally within my grasp? Oh, we're going to have a grand time getting reacquainted today!"

Soul snot and demons were swarming over the family that I had been unable to protect, and Lucifer was slowly standing up to full height, enraptured at my seemingly inescapable predicament. He couldn't see me, but there was little chance that I could do anything to escape him while in such close proximity. If he had any sense of my two companions previously, they didn't matter to him now. It was obvious by the look on his face that I was going to be the guest for dinner, in all of the sadistic ways that this statement could be understood.

I braced myself for one last gambit.

I was a Sandalphon angel, and as such, being able to achieve great height was my heritage, but what I wasn't sure of is if becoming larger would achieve anything positive. Spiritual beings are not limited by the constraints of physical size. They are limited by the intensity of their concentrated energy. Lucifer was here in his own element, surrounded by a world that he had created for himself, able to draw energy reserves from literally every life force that walked, crawled, and slithered around us.

I was out of my element and far from the pure Light. My becoming larger might have no more effect upon him than a kernel of popcorn exploding, or of being swatted with a large volume of cotton candy, which has no mass.

I prayed to Jehovah and acted.

Rising up and enlarging at incredible speed, I matched and exceeded Lucifer's size, striking him under the chin with a concussion that rocked the adjoining buildings and shocked me with its intensity. I never imagined that I could actually knock him down, and as he flailed backwards, screaming in surprise and pain, I thanked Jehovah for reaching out and empowering my fist beyond my own ability to defend myself.

"What's this?! The Ophan I know is not a man of war, and yet you strike me down like a seasoned warrior. There can be only one reason for such an uncharacteristic display. You seek to protect others! I shall find them quickly enough, and they and you will enjoy the benefits of my never-ending hospitality. I'm so glad that you dropped by," Lucifer said, wiping his bleeding lip and collecting himself up from the demolished building that he'd crushed. He was now relishing a knock-down, drag-out fight.

Instead of staying large, I shrunk down to my original size and withdrew from my belt what looked to be a small child's toy. It was fashioned like a gun with a trigger, but it was designed to propel small disks instead of bullets or other projectiles.

"I am Ophan, Prince of Thrones, an Angel of the Presence, whereas you are nothing but the Prince of Deceivers, and I collect together the prayers of the faithful, which do not lose their potency, no matter the circumstances under which they are applied."

I shot a disk into Lucifer's enormous, gaping maw. The disk made contact with his vile flesh, burst open, and released the power of the Presence. Lucifer screamed in panic and pain. I had two more disks and I shot one into each of his great, gaping eyes. He began convulsing and thrashing uncontrollably, causing incredible destruction to everything within his reach. Every living thing within earshot scrambled for its life.

I flew towards the great gate that I'd originally entered and Lucifer attempted to follow me, although he had great trouble controlling his actions. His skin, bubbled and scorched, moved like a thing alive, trying to remove itself from his bones. Using his abilities, he reached out and closed the great gateway in my path, however, I outsmarted him. Instead of trying to force my way through them, I merely made myself small enough to slip through their joints, making them an impediment to Lucifer in his efforts to get his hands on me.

As I sped off to freedom, I looked back and saw Lucifer tearing the great gates from their hinges and reducing them to splinters in his uncontrollable rage.

I had survived, but I knew that the conflict between us was far from over.

CHAPTER TWENTY-EIGHT
Graduation

The day that every senior looks forward to but can't really appreciate until it arrives finally came, graduation. There was much to do about the end of the year activities, like getting yearbooks signed, passing out senior pictures to best buddies and favorite teachers, and ordering caps and gowns.

As far as any senior learning anything lasting at the end of the school year, there was very little chance that any of that happened. The officially recognized term for it is called "senioritis" and it seemed to strike everyone, to one degree or another.

For me, the effects were quite mild.

I did find my mind wandering, usually down memory lane to all things that had recently come to naught, but I didn't allow it to have a dramatic impact upon my grades. I had a 3.96 grade point average, with no honors classes, which was quite respectable. I would've had a 4.0 but we had a physical education teacher at Silver Lake who seemed to take unnatural joy in busting 4.0s for people like myself, those who didn't play an officially recognized sport. I'm not exactly sure how he got away with his policy, but he made it clear the very first day that we arrived in his required gym class that unless we were on a school team, the highest grade that we could expect in the class was a "B+." Getting a "B+" in a single class in an entire high school career resulted in a 3.96 average. I suppose that I could've taken an honors class or two to offset my mouth-breathing instructor's personal philosophies, but I was too involved in the choir and the Drama Club to want to waste time on additional homework.

As the days slowly ticked down, I found myself reflecting on how dramatically different things were about to be. Although the graduating class was huge, around 680 people, I had at least a passing relationship with a great number of my classmates, and there were some who had been a constant and predictable part of my life since I moved into the district in first grade. For better or for worse, they had become the set dressing of my educational life, and soon they would be gone. We would no longer be jostling into each other every day in the undersized hallways of Silver Lake. Those classrooms and special areas that had become my unofficial home away from home, like the auditorium and the choir room, were about to become the emotional property of the next graduating class and I would be relegated to visitor soon. Looking into the faces of those around me and listening to their chatter, it dawned upon me that there were few who had taken the time to imagine what life past graduation was going to mean to their social life.

Just before graduation, we had our Baccalaureate ceremony, which was like a dry run for the official graduation ceremony. It was a time to reflect on the achievements of the class and to honor various students for their accomplishments. On stage were the orchestra, the teachers representing the various departments, and the administrators of the school district. We were all decked out in our blue and white gowns, blue for the men and white for the women, and we all tried to quietly and patiently endure the event, which was much too long to be held in an auditorium without air conditioning in Michigan in June. I received several certificates of honor for various things like being in the choir, and the madrigal group, and the Drama Club, and being at the top of my class, etc. After the event was over, it was obvious in retrospect that the only advantage to being a senior at the ceremony was the fact that we got to march in after everyone else was seated, and we got to march out before everyone else left, so we were slightly less sweaty and wilted than whatever parent of ours had been able to attend.

We spent a lot of time lining up for things during that week, which was why I was seldom able to spend any time with my close friends. We would just wave at each other as we passed because none of our surnames were that close to each other such that we could chat while we baked in the sun. It was an odd realization that we were all to be involved in huge ceremonies where each one of us, individually, was essentially alone. I was used to being in a group, surrounded by my friends. I was not used to being in a herd, geographically separated from my friends, although they were in the same general vicinity somewhere.

Our class was far too big to have the graduation ceremony in the auditorium. It held an impressive 1,600 people, but with our graduating class of 680, that would mean that each senior could be allowed only one guest, like it was for the Baccalaureate ceremony, which was deemed unacceptable. The official matriculation ceremony was scheduled for the football field, which was at the other end of the building, where the "B+"s were handed out like candy. I much preferred the auditorium end of the building, where the "A+"s were handed out like candy, but I didn't make the rules. Each of us was allowed to invite two guests, which would completely fill up the football field bleachers.

I gave my two tickets to my mother and let her decide who would be attending, rather than try to express my opinion on the matter. If she was happy, life was quiet and I would be happy. She selected Grandpa Eugene to attend with her.

On the day of graduation the city was in complete chaos. There were hundreds of decorated cars with pom poms and painted sayings driving up and down the streets, squealing their tires and beeping their horns. The slogans were typical, things like "Free at last" and "Escaping twelve years of hell." I thought that it was a sad situation that some seniors didn't understand that they'd been in school for thirteen years, including kindergarten, but such slips-ups of perception were relatively rare, and most of the slogans were spelled correctly. I hoped that those that weren't spelled correctly were intentional.

I made a few pom-poms and attached them to the upper chrome strip that ran down the length of the T-bird and ended at the back wings. I didn't paint anything on the glass or the painted surfaces of the car because I had heard horror stories of the sun etching poster paint into these surfaces, making ghost images that could never be removed. All I needed was to damage the T-bird through thoughtlessness and I would never hear the end of it, so I decided to be cautious instead of dramatic.

Driving past the football field that day, it was obvious that every custodian in the district had been called in to help set up platforms, chairs, and drag in additional bleachers from nearby schools. The underclass AV helpers were scampering about setting up speakers on poles and running microphone cables to the speaker's lectern.

I arrived in my cap and gown with plenty of time to spare, for it had dawned on me earlier in the day that the number of people expected to attend the ceremony would mean that the auditorium and all other school parking areas would be filled to absolute capacity, and every side street near the school would be filled up too. As I turned into the auditorium lot it became apparent that a few hundred other people had come to the same conclusion, and I found myself parking the T-bird in the farthest back corner. At least I had found a space on school property. There were going to be a great many people in the next hour or so who were not going to be so lucky.

I wandered into the auditorium in order to waste some time. The lights were on but it was deserted, and I sat on the edge of the apron and contemplated just how much this big barn of a space had come to mean to me over the last three years.

It was relatively cool there because the place was empty and the stage lights were off. Once filled with warm bodies pressed shoulder to shoulder with all of the stage lights on, it became a very muggy place. During

Baccalaureate several large fans had been set up to keep the air moving, but after a while it appeared that their effects had been mostly psychological because the place was simply too big to cool with six humming fans.

All of the classes, and the plays, and the choir performances, and the musicals that I'd been involved with here flitted through my head, along with Marci's ghost, the ghost of affections past. Her smiles and her assurances of eternal love proved to be too bitter a pill to swallow and I got up and left before I burst into tears. I thought about exiting into the main part of the school through the choir room, but realized that if I wanted to keep from crying, going that way wasn't going to help my emotional state. Running into Mr. Chase wasn't something that I wished to do at that moment, and so I went up the center isle to the auditorium lobby and exited out the front doors.

Like a churning vista of whitecaps on a blue sea, all I could see down the side of the school was a mass of blue and white graduation gowns. Everyone was struggling to find the person that they were supposed to stand next to in the grand line-up that was to precede our grand entrance onto the football field. In the distance, we could see the people filling up the stadium seats, armed with their various cameras and signs of congratulations for their graduating senior. The most popular students would be cheered, both from their family members and from their close friends in the graduating class, but most of us would receive our diploma quietly, because most of us were not popular students. Some of the popular students had brought entire cheering sections for themselves, which was evident from the many large groups who had elected to stand in the track area in front of the bleachers, or over on the far ends of the football field, where no chairs had been set up. Each senior had received two bleacher tickets, but just like in Shakespeare's day, the event had attracted a large number of groundlings, who jostled for position to be as close to the action as unofficial, unaccounted for guests could get.

Somewhere in the throng would be my mother and my grandfather. He worked as the head custodian at one of the junior high schools in the district, so I knew that he would've had the sense to arrive early to get a good seat. He knew what to expect, even if my mother didn't. And as for other people who hadn't known what to expect, from where we were lining up on the sidewalk it was easy to see the endless lines of cars trying to find somewhere to park up or down the various side streets. The police were there to try to assist with the traffic flow, but unless someone got mouthy, all they really did was shake their head and point further away from the football field, as if to indicate that there might be a spot down there – somewhere. It was not like the problem had any real solution, short of chopping the senior class into subsets and having multiple ceremonies, and nobody wanted that. We were the last big bubble of students to flow through the Silver Lake system. The graduating classes after us would all be appreciably smaller, as indicated by the number of students in each grade.

Our class was big, noisy, spirited, and determined to be remembered.

When everyone had filled the football field and all of the seniors had managed to find their place in line, the procedures began. As those around me focused upon the voices coming from the football field in front of us, I happened to notice the color of the sky to the west of us, and it didn't look good. I wasn't sure how fast the dark clouds that I saw were moving, but they seemed determined to arrive in time to take part in our graduation, and that couldn't be a good thing.

At the appropriate musical cue, our blue and white ribbon of bodies started shuffling towards the football field. Many, many reiterations later, the last of us finally arrived at the center of the field and found their assigned seat. The entire football field, grass, encircling track, and permanent bleachers extending two stories into the air, was packed with people.

The opening remarks from the assembled dignitaries included several references to the greatness and uniqueness of the graduating class of Silver Lake High School, the class of 1975. These incendiary remarks seemed designed to get the collective consciousness of seniors to yell and scream and carry on as loudly as possible, in a feeble attempt to burn off some of our extra nervous energy. To a certain degree it worked, because after a few minutes of manic behavior, a polite silence settled upon the crowd.

The principal of Silver Lake High School took the stage. Being the seasoned and unflappable educational professional that he was, having been administering in the district for about a century-and-a-half, he showed no signs of nervousness as he looked up at the sky. He had a face made for radio, although on the rare occasions when he chose to smile, his face would actually light up and become friendly. In its natural state, his countenance was somewhat medusa-like, often freezing students in their tracks.

I kept eyeing the bleacher seats, in a feeble effort to locate my mother and my grandfather, and the western sky, where the dark clouds continued to race our way. There wasn't any darkness underneath the cloud bank, which seemed to suggest that it wasn't raining, but that could just mean that it was holding its load until it was properly positioned.

Principal Shubinski continued reciting the high points of our time spent at Silver Lake, throwing in a, "Pay no attention to the clouds off to your left. We have it on excellent authority that they'll be blowing right over us," comment every few minutes.

Just as the clouds were directly overhead and everyone started to believe that they'd actually blow over…

KA-SPLASH!

Without so much as a warning sprinkle, the sky opened up and began deluging the field. Everything was immediate chaos, and Principal Shubinski made a quick announcement that the ceremony would be immediately moved into the auditorium at the other end of the building because of rain. Nothing more was said because of the danger of running the sound system in the down pouring rain, and everyone moved to get to the school as quickly as possible. Those of us without instruments or equipment to save, and who weren't trapped trying to get down the various ramps to the bleachers, made it to the east entrance of the school the quickest.

Everyone was drenched.

The graduation gowns were so wet that they clung to our clothing and all of the girls' white gowns revealed what they were wearing underneath. Some of them had made some peculiar choices.

I decided to stay near the school entrance and wait for my mother and grandfather to get there. I was already drenched, so getting a little wetter hardly seemed possible. All of the seniors ran for the school entrance, and most of the parent attendees ran for their cars. The custodial staff rushed out onto the field to throw plastic over the piles of diplomas and to try to get the AV equipment indoors as quickly as possible. Girls were squealing everywhere, not that senior girls needed a particular reason to squeal. The sea of dripping faces flowed by, and then I saw them.

At first, my grandfather seemed fine as he and my mother rushed towards the entrance, but then she put her hand around his shoulder, like she was going to help him to the school, and something changed in his expression. As they moved closer to me, it appeared as if my grandfather was looking weaker and more distressed with each step he took. I became so concerned that I rushed out to them and forced myself between my mother and him, to help him through the doorway. Just inside, he was panting and gasping for breath like I'd never seen before. His forehead showed deep worry wrinkles and the thought crossed my mind that he could have a heart attack on the spot. I kept holding on to him to support him, intentionally keeping my mother from touching him because something strange about her touching him had caused his weakened state, I was sure.

"Daddy, are you OK?" she asked, seeming concerned.

"I'll be fine in a second, just let me catch my breath," he replied.

We moved out of the throng and over to a side hall, where his breathing started to return to normal.

"Why don't you go and find yourself a seat down in the auditorium. At least one of us should see this boy graduate. I should probably go get the car and wait for you. I'm sure that you won't be long," Grandpa Eugene said.

"You're sure that you're all right?" my mother inquired.

"I'm feeling much better. I told you, I just needed to catch my breath. Nick can help me to my car. They won't be able to continue until the diplomas are brought in and that will take them a few minutes. I'll park in the auditorium parking lot and wait for you after the lot thins out some."

"OK, good-bye Daddy. I won't be long," she said, and then turned to follow the stream of people through the school to the auditorium.

"Are you sure you're OK, Grandpa?" I asked him.

"I'm feeling much better. I'll be fine. Just walk with me to the car to make sure that I don't stumble and fall, Nick."

"No problem," I said, concerned by both his sudden attack and his equally sudden recovery. I shook my head. Certainly what I thought I saw wasn't actually what I saw. It must've been a trick of my imagination.

"It was no trick, Nicky," I heard the voice of Grandma Zotia whisper.

I got my grandfather safely to his car and he watched me walk away, back in the direction of the auditorium. There didn't seem to be any cause for alarm, other than the thought that my mother had sucked my grandfather's energy from him like some kind of vampire bat!

When I got to the auditorium, there was no rhyme or reason to anything happening there. The custodians had managed to get the diplomas down to the stage, but the stacks were all out of order and no one was taking the time to put them back in order. The senior class was just sitting anywhere they found a chair, waiting to see if their name was the next name read to come up and get their diploma. The various dignitaries were sitting onstage, dripping into puddles. There were very few parents there, for most of them had made a beeline for their vehicles. Instead of an organized ceremony with official and unofficial flashes from cameras, it was murmuring, overlapping cacophony. The only thing organized about the proceedings was that the two people who were reading the diploma names were doing as good a job as they could not to step on each other's announcement.

The truly ironic moment of the evening turned out to be Miss Heinkel announcing Frank Johnson's name at the exact same moment that Mr. Chase announced Doreen Bommarito's name. Although it might seem magical to the casual observer that this couple received their diplomas at the very same time, which would've been impossible under normal circumstances, the look on Doreen's face showed that she was quite displeased that Frank should be receiving his diploma from the hand of Miss Heinkel. Frank appeared to be relatively unaware that Doreen's name had been called, until they both met center stage to come down the stairs and she hip-checked him. From that point on she had his complete attention.

I just shook my head. I had no idea how their twisted love story was going to turn out, but it was obvious that someone was not going to like the resolution. Frank was no longer a student, technically, which meant that he could date Miss Heinkel on the sly to avoid public opinion, but if he chose to break off his relationship with Doreen, Doreen was certain to break something. If Frank was lucky, she wouldn't break anything that he owned – biologically. If he was unlucky, oh well. People shouldn't play with fire if they're afraid of getting burnt.

Quite unexpectedly, I heard my name called and I moved towards the stage. I smiled, shook hands with Mr. Chase, received my diploma, and exited the stage down the center stairs, without any special fanfare of any kind. My mother was out in the chaos, somewhere, but I had no desire to try and find her. I went back to my seat to wait for the end of the ceremony, not knowing if they had planned on doing anything more than just getting as many diplomas into as many hands as possible. When there were just a handful of unclaimed diplomas left and the recipient's names had been called off several times, the crowd's attention was brought to a series of large trophies on stage.

Principal Shubinski tried his best to bring the auditorium to order and to give the passing out of the school trophies for service as much solemnity as he could, but it quickly became obvious that the class of 1975 was just about out of patience for graduation niceties.

The official school photographer, Mr. Werther, had managed to collect up his equipment from the field and reassemble himself in time to get pictures of most of the graduating class, and now he waited to photograph the recipients of the school's highest honors.

Much to my surprise and amazement, I received one of the service awards along with Crystal Marinelli. We got our picture taken together holding the plaque, and then I graciously allowed her to take it home to show it off to her family at her graduation party. As we descended the stairs together, I turned and gave her a hug. It was the last time that we would share the stage together as students attending

Silver Lake. I had no idea if we'd be together in plays in the future, but our high school careers were definitely over.

"Congratulations, Crystal, you deserve the award. I'm not exactly sure how my name got on it next to yours, but I'll accept the mistake as divine providence and be thankful."

"Always with the self-deprecating jokes, funnyman, you deserve the award as much as I do."

And then she did something that I didn't see coming. She bent forward, squeezed my arm and kissed me on the cheek.

"I'll see you at my party," she said.

"I wouldn't miss it," I replied, and for a fleeting moment I recalled the Crystal of old, the person that I'd met way back in tenth grade, and the crush that I'd had on her. Had she finally shrugged off the bad habits that Hayley had spent most of the school year teaching her? Maybe she...

The last of the awards were handed out, and with a closing, "Congratulations to the graduating class of 1975," the air was filled with soggy, misshapen, bent and demolished graduation caps. It was going to be a graduation long remembered, thanks to Mother Nature and her sense of humor.

"I suppose that you'll be going out to get something to eat with your friends," I heard from behind me. I turned and came face to face with my mother, who was obviously anxious to get away from the damp and jostling crowd.

"I'd like to, if that's OK," I said.

"Did you get your grandfather safely to his car?" she inquired.

"Yes, he seemed much better after he caught his breath. He probably hasn't run like that in years. He said he'd be waiting for you in the auditorium parking lot," I said.

"Don't stay out too late," she said, and then turned to exit up the center aisle.

"Oh, by the way, I graduated at the top of my class, and I got a service award that I'm sharing with Crystal," I mumbled to myself, knowing full well that she couldn't hear me. In my mother's world, it was enough that she had attended my graduation ceremony. Additional sentimentality was never expected, and physical contact almost never occurred. However, after seeing her almost hug the life right out of my grandfather, I was suddenly grateful for her general aloofness.

The next thing that I knew, I was pinned from behind by a pair of arms. Since the arms were wearing a white gown, it took me all of a millisecond to figure out that it was Mo.

"Congrats, Mr. Special-service-to-the-school kid. We're organizing a group to get something to eat at Big Boy. Are you coming?" she asked.

"I might be able to find a few minutes in my very busy social calendar to pencil you in," I replied.

"Well, don't spend too much time arranging your calendar and miss out on the event. We'll see you there." Mo gave me a quick hug and ran up the center aisle.

"Who all is going?" I asked, but she couldn't hear me over all of the noise, "Not that it matters because social beggars can't be choosers." Taking a last gaze at the place, I strode up the center aisle and headed for the parking lot.

The sun was just starting to go down as I approached my car, one of the few still left in the lot. As I got closer, I noticed that someone had played a little graduation joke on me. The driver's side of the T-bird had been splattered with several raw eggs. When I opened the door, I noticed the great care that the attacker had taken in impacting the eggs at the exact point where the front electric window aligns with the back electric window. Hitting the egg there forced the goo through the weather stripping and splattered the remains on the opposite side of the inside of the car.

There was no question of my going out to eat with my friends now. I had to get home quick and scrub the car before the egg damaged the paint and the ruined the interior. When I sat down in the driver's seat, which was happily devoid of egg guts, I noticed something on the hood, under the wipers. I got out and retrieved it. It was a note.

Maybe it was a note from Marci, fluttered through my head.

I opened it, hoping for something nice or uplifting.

Dear Nick,

I'm not sure why I should even try to be polite to you, since you've been acting like a d---.

You seem to be the only person on the planet who doesn't realize that Mo is in love with you, and I'm sick and tired of hearing what a great guy you are and how thoughtful and kind-hearted you are.

In my opinion, you are an ass because there's no way that you could be so naïve as to think that Mo is just your friend. You have known that I've liked her ever since the parade at Thanksgiving, and yet you keep playing your sick string-Mo-along game that you're so good at.

Well, buster, I just wanted you to know that you don't fool everybody with your fake façade and I think you're sick in the head. We might've been friends once, but no more.

Be a man and let Mo have her own life, you coward.

Your ex-friend and someone too smart to believe in all of your lies,

Denny

"Wow, Denny seems quite certain that I'm a long list of unpleasant things," I thought to myself. I sighed deeply and tossed the note over to the passenger seat, to sit in the shell bits and the egg goo.

"Don't take his anger or his words to heart. He is being used as a hand puppet," I heard the Blue Lady say.

"Used by whom?" I thought.

"Someone that you don't need to know about just yet," came her reply.

"Oh great, the endless tag-team of supernatural terror continues. Can you tell me if Denny was the one who pulverized the eggs on my car?"

"Does it really matter?"

"I guess not. No matter who did it, it's up to me to clean it up."

CHAPTER TWENTY-NINE
The Return of Sammael

I got home and quietly cleaned the T-bird from the egg assault. My mind was tied in knots and I wasn't sure what to think about much of what had happened that day.

The graduation ceremony had been exhausting with all of its barely organized chaos. I had gotten chilled to the bone, both by the rain and by seeing the look on Grandpa Eugene's face when my mother had touched him. He looked as if the very life force was being sucked out of him. I couldn't shake the spooky feeling.

"What happened between my mother and Grandpa Eugene?" I asked the usually silent observers in the back of my consciousness.

"Don't be in such a rush to find out that which can bring you no peace," was the Blue Lady's response.

I searched for something witty to say, but found that her cryptic remark had disabled all of my witty parts.

"All will be made clear to you, in time," the Blue Lady added.

"And will that clarity bring me peace?" I asked.

"Eventually," was the response, after a long pause.

"And how long is 'eventually' where you come from?"

"Sometime after right now, and short of at the end of eternity."

"Helpful, very helpful," I wisecracked.

"Would David have wanted to learn about Goliath before he was even old enough to throw a stone?"

"I'm guessing that the proper answer would be 'No'. So where am I in this process?"

"You're just about to learn how to use a slingshot."

"And that is a good thing?"

"I only teach about good things."

"And who's going to teach me about bad things?" I asked.

"Every bad person whose path you will ever cross will be more than happy to share with you what they know about bad things. I would've assumed that you'd have noticed that pattern by now."

"Actually, I had noticed. Is it just me, or have I somehow been surrounded by bad people?"

"You have no idea, my boy," added Grandma Zotia, quietly.

"This is where a comment like, 'It's just your imagination' would be appreciated from the nice lady who seems to know what's in store for me in my future," I humbly suggested.

"Dwell neither upon the perspectives and apprehensions of others, nor upon what you have seen your 'mother' do this day. There are other concerns far more important in play," the Blue Lady insisted.

"Such as?" I asked.

"Allow yourself to sleep, for you are keeping an important visitor waiting."

"What important visitor? You mean someone like the prophet Elijah, or Abraham Lincoln?"

"He doesn't even suspect?" I heard Grandma Zotia's voice say.

"To be focused, one must avoid distractions," the Blue Lady replied.

"Hello, I can hear you two in there. Need I remind you that both of you are currently residing within my head, which would mean, I assume, that I have some right to be included in the conversation. Is someone good coming to visit me?"

"Good? Not exactly," the Blue Lady responded, choosing her words carefully.

"Important?"

"More important than you can imagine. Now rest."

Just as I began to drift off, I thought I heard my Grandma Zotia say, "You're not going to warn him that it's the Angel of Dea...."

The vision, like all of my previous visions, came with complete sensory clarity, including the clarity to mentally note that I knew that I was asleep.

I found myself in my T-bird, driving in a pea-soup fog, down a two lane, unpaved road. Whether I was in a city or out in the woods somewhere wasn't clear, because there were no signs of any lights anywhere, neither street lights nor building lights, and everything was as quiet as a tomb, except for the crunching of gravel under the tires. I could see just enough of the road under my headlights to be able to creep forward and still have a sense that I was in the middle of the lane. It's not my habit to drive in the middle of a two-lane road, but under the strange circumstances, it seemed like the safest place to be. I had no idea what lay on either side of the road. There could've been lawns, or drainage ditches, of 500 acres of swamp land for all I could guess. It had a strange smell that I couldn't place, not exactly like an open ditch or a swamp, but something related to the smell of stagnancy.

I inched forward.

This wasn't a memory from anything I'd experienced, or even a variation of a memory.

Suddenly, right in front of me in the fog, there materialized the figure of a woman.

I brought the T-bird to a halt.

She stood there in my headlights, staring at me with a very curious expression. It was like she had been expecting me, and her smile seemed vaguely familiar, but different from any that I could recall. Who was this girl? I was overcome with conflicting emotions, that she was both glad to see me and that I should be concerned about seeing her again.

She slowly began to walk forward.

One foot was slowly placed in front of the other and she moved forward, never blinking or breaking her stare.

When I noticed that she had moved forward enough to actually walk through the bumper and hood, I grew quite concerned. She was supernatural, obviously, but friend or foe was yet to be determined.

She kept smiling as her face moved closer to mine, and just as it passed through the windshield glass right in front of me, I realized where I'd seen this woman before. This was Sammael, Lucifer's Angel of Death! I hadn't recognized her earlier because she was smiling in a friendly, positive fashion, like we were old pals, as opposed to our being the bitterest of enemies. Before I could muster the mental focus to shift the car into reverse and try to back away from this apparition, she entered me.

The last image that was burned into my vision was of her smiling face morphing into the death's head of a skull, just before disappearing.

I bolted upright in my tiny bed, covered with sweat.

"What just happened?" I asked myself and anyone else who felt like chiming in.

"Who was that?"

"You know who that was."

"You mean that really was Sammael? But I thought that we'd prayed her on to The Throne of Jehovah months ago."

"You did."

"Then how could she be here, tonight?" I insisted upon knowing.

"Spiritual beings are not like incarnated souls, Nicholas. An incarnated soul is fully contained in a single physical body. Spiritual beings are not limited in that way. The energy of Sammael that attacked you before was *most* of her, but not *all* of her."

"So, if she is now less than what she was, and I was allowed to pray her more powerful self on to The Throne, then why would she attack me here in my bed tonight?"

"Was it, indeed, an attack?"

"Well, her face did turn into a death's head skull just before it vanished before my eyes."

"She wanted there to be no doubt that you'd recognize her. It was her way of saying, 'Remember me? I'm Lucifer's Angel of Death.'"

"I don't understand."

"You don't understand because it goes against all of the spiritual knowledge that I've re-taught you thus far, which is why it is so important."

"But I thought that since she was Lucifer's only archangel that she'd discorporate herself rather than allow herself to be reborn into the Light through the Christ energy, or being forced to stand in The Presence for eternity."

"And that was a very logical assumption."

"She didn't discorporate herself?"

"No, she did not."

"Is she still standing in The Presence?"

"No, she is not."

"But that means that she allowed herself to be reborn through the Christ energy."

"Yes, that is what happened."

The significance of what we were discussing began to dawn upon my sleepy mind.

"Has that ever happened before?" I inquired.

"Never. That has never happened, not since the dawn of Jehovah time."

"Are you serious? Are you telling me in your own roundabout way that she defected? Sammael, Lucifer's only archangel, ranked number two in the hierarchy of the abyss, actually defected to the side of the Light?"

"Well, not exactly. She attacked you, as she was ordered to do by her master, then you were allowed to pray her to The Throne of Jehovah. That part was not accomplished with her consent. However, once she had stood in the Light for a time and pondered how Jehovah was not cruelly destroying her as she had been assured that He would, then she acquiesced to be reborn through the baptism of the Christ energy."

"And the remaining bits of her energy that I saw just now?"

"She called out to them, wherever they were hiding, to rejoin with her in the Light. The only pathway that she was certain of to get to the Light was literally through you. She is now whole, and all that she is has been reborn."

"She schwooped me?! But that means…"

"…that no spiritual being is beyond redemption, not even Lucifer's greatest creation."

"When word of this starts to spread in the abyss…what is that smell?"

Before I could think another word, I was shoved on my back in my tiny bunk bed by an incredible, invisible force, which was barely preceded by a stench that defied description, which was so thick that it was almost un-breathable.

"Do you know what you have done? I have now lost the use of my spiritual right arm because of you," I heard Lucifer's familiar voice whisper into my ear. "It was bad enough when she was lost to my service before, but something about you, your energy, your stinking, wretched innocence convinced her not to kill herself in your God's presence, and now she has called all that was left of her to the side of my enemy."

The pressure upon my entire body kept increasing geometrically. I opened my eyes, but there was nothing to see, and I found that my spiritual senses could make out Lucifer's form attempting to crush me far better than my physical senses could. I labored to breath as the amorphous, gelatinous mass squeezed harder, like I was being attacked and eaten by an enormous unseen amoeba. The bed creaked and I could hear the bed slats beginning to splinter as the weight increased.

"You have been an endless thorn in my side and I'm going to end your interfering and your life right here. And then, when I've squeezed the last drop of life from this pathetic body that your God has sentenced you to inhabit, I'm going to drag your screaming soul back to my domain, where I'm going to get very serious about repaying you for the pain and turmoil that you've caused me."

The metal rails supporting the thin wooden frame under the mattress began to distort and twist as the splintering of the support frame and slats continued. I could barely muster the energy to continue breathing, and struggle as I might, I couldn't get a handhold on him. Every time I thought that I got a grip on his slippery, unseen mass, he just shifted his goo through my fingers. The thought that this may actually come to be the moment of my death flittered through my mind.

"You could've come with me and been one of my greatest allies, a prince in my universe, second only to me, but no, you had to cry out for Him to interfere. And then, instead of accepting greatness from my hand, you accepted crumbs from His hand and became a what? A what? A prince? No, you preferred to be a slave. A servant of The Presence whose job it was to make paper airplanes out of the prayers of the feeble-minded and fly them up to decorate His ego-bloated crown!

"He's killing me!" I cried out in my head, "Blue Lady, help me!" I mentally screamed.

"I cannot interfere, for the power that is free will forbids me," I heard her say.

"Can't I use my free will to beg you to interfere?" I pleaded.

The rails on the bed gave way and the support frame splintered, lowering my body to the carpet under my bed.

Now, with the cement floor underneath me, Lucifer would be able to generate the force required to squish the life literally out of my body, although I had no idea how anyone would be able to explain my death in the morning. I would be remembered as that strange boy who managed to self-crush himself to pulp.

"I can't fight with Lucifer. You must fight him yourself," the Blue Lady stated.

"How is that even possible?" I yelled.

"Stop believing that you are only what you believe yourself to be. Open up to the true nature of your existence," the Blue Lady pleaded.

"But what if I can't?"

"Then all is lost," she whispered.

I tried to find some inner peace, even as the pressure upon my body attempted to rip my head from my neck. Nothing that I believed from a physical world sense could save me. What did that mean? How can one relearn everything about one's own existence within just a few seconds? I didn't have the physical strength to throw this mass of stinking, putrid evil off of me...or did I?

What if it wasn't about believing in the effectiveness of force, but rather understanding the true nature of power?

Jehovah and the Christ energy were power.

Lucifer was limited to his belief in the use of force, and perhaps that was his fatal flaw. How could I call upon the power of all that is good and right and life-affirming in the universe without asking in terms of physical strength?

"That's it, you're remembering! Keep going!" the Blue Lady urged.

"I am not simply a body."

"Yes!"

"I am not simply a mind."

"Yes!"

"I am not simply a life."

"Yes!"

"I am an extension of the Great I AM!"

My mind went white with Light and every part of me felt alive with the power of the infinite.

"I am the master of my own destiny, and I use my free will to align myself with all that is good and righteous that exists. I am a child of the Light, the Christ energy is my brother, and my strength lies within the cores of a billion suns, where no darkness can touch me."

I'm not certain what happened next, or how long I lay there, in the splintered remains of my bed. I'm not sure if there was an explosion, or an implosion. I'm not sure if there was a physical flash of Light or a blast of heat from calling upon the power of the sun. I'm not sure if there was a sound, or even if I had spoken my declaration out loud.

All that I knew was that I had called upon the power of Life and Light and it had answered.

"No matter what comes next, rest assured that Lucifer will never dare touch you directly again. That is not to say that you and he are done battling, but he will never face you directly again. He will call upon his forebears now, for you have gotten too strong for his tricks."

"His forebears?! He has older family?" I asked, weakly.

"The lineage of evil goes back in time a lot farther than the Bible that you have read explains, but don't think about such things for today. There will be plenty of time to contemplate such things tomorrow."

I then became aware of a stomping sound moving through the kitchen overhead and coming down the stairs. It wasn't the drunken shuffling of my stepfather, so only one other person could be making sounds so heavy-footed and angry, my mother. In what seemed like an instant, the lights flashed on in the main part of the basement, and then came the hall light, illuminating my tiny bedroom. She stood there, as angry as I have ever seen her, her hands on her hips and glowering down at me.

"WHAT THE HELL IS GOING ON DOWN HERE?' she demanded, her eyes slowly drilling holes through my forehead.

"I'm not sure. I was sleeping. My bed collapsed," I replied, meekly.

"Like I can't see that? I don't know what you were doing to cause it to break, but don't think that I'm going to run out and buy you another one just because you've managed to smash this one. You're the crafty one, so you can figure out how to glue it back together tomorrow, and if I hear one more peep that I can't explain from this basement, you're going to end up living somewhere else. I've got no patience for foolishness or fools in my house. If you want to stay here, you'd best watch your step, young man!"

Her anger seemed completely out of proportion with the situation, for it wasn't as if I'd smashed the car or burnt down the house. My bed had been old and rickety since the moment that I'd been given it, so it collapsing shouldn't have generated that much scolding, but there was more going on here, spiritually, than what met the eyes. And what made that obvious was the look in my mother's eyes. They were cold, like shark or snake eyes. It might've been a trick of the light...

"It's no trick of the light," the Blue Lady whispered.

"She hates me," I thought in my head.

"More than you will ever know," Grandma Zotia whispered, "Which is exactly why I'm here with you."

"Do you hear me, young man?"

"Yes, mom, I hear you."

"And what are you going to be doing tomorrow?" she asked, through gritted teeth.

"I'm going to be fixing this bed."

"That's right. Fix it or sleep on the floor, it's all the same to me. Not another peep from you, do you understand?" she warned, pointing her long finger at my face as if she would drive it through my skull if I gave her any attitude.

"I understand. I'm sorry that I woke you."

"You're right, you are sorry, a sorry example of a son, if you ask me," she mumbled under her breath. She turned quickly on her heels and stormed out, slapping off the lights and stomping up the stairs to accentuate the outrage that she was feeling from being woken from her sleep.

"She doesn't love me."

"Not only does she not love you, but she's never loved you, not from the moment that you were born, nor in the 52 lifetimes that you've already shared together."

"Shared together?"

"Well, maybe not 'shared together'. She's killed you or had you killed 40 times," the Blue Lady revealed.

"What?"

"This is the only lifetime where the two of you have been in close proximity where she hasn't accomplished your death," Grandma Zotia added.

"Are you kidding me? Isn't my 'assignment' that you mentioned earlier over, now that Lucifer and I have had our tussle?"

"Oh no, my dear, she's your real assignment. It is Jehovah's intention that every soul, no matter how polluted, angry, evil, or dark, should be exposed to His Light. That way, when the time of their spiritual judgment finally arrives, they can never say that He didn't care for them. You're been bringing your mother God's Light for centuries, and she's been torturing you and killing you for your efforts."

"I'm not finished, even after having Sammael defect and having Lucifer personally try to wring the life out of my body?!"

"Oh no, my dear, you've barely begun," the Blue Lady declared.

"Will you tell me your name?" I begged.

"You already know my name," she replied.

"Sophia?"

"And…?"

"But that's the part that confuses me. It goes against what I've been taught in church," I responded.

"Why do you let the foolishness of others deter you from standing strong in believing what you innately know to be true? Who am I?"

"You are the Comforter, Sophia, the essence of Wisdom, the female aspect of the Trinity, and the Holy Spirit."

"See, that wasn't so hard, was it?"

"But if I share with anyone who you are and what you've taught me, I'll be rejected by even my closest Christian friends."

"If your closest Christian friends judge you harshly for not believing what they believe in but have never experienced, then they can hardly be considered your true friends. Let those who have never met me continue to teach confusion to those who have no real desire to meet me. Confusion is their most lasting gift to each other. We have much to do and that work cannot be accomplished through ignorance."

"So my choices are either stand with my friends and embrace what they don't know, or stand with you and essentially stand alone?"

"Those who stand in the shadow of ignorance are alone. You stand in no shadow at all, and whoever stands in the Light is never alone."

"Good to know. Am I going to learn a lot about pain and loss on this little journey that you've mapped out for me?"

"You will learn about many things."

"Will I survive the learning?"

"If you do not, then there will dire consequences for many others."

"Do your answers always have to be cryptic?"

"Yep, pretty much."

"Can I call you Cryptica?"

"No."

"Sorry."

The End of the Beginning

Book 2
Ophan
Dark Puppets

Book 3
Ophan
Thomas Never Doubted

Book 4
Ophan
The End of the Trickster